Recalled

A Death Escorts Novel

By Cambria Hebert

Other books by Cambria Hebert

Before

Masquerade

Between

Charade

Bewitched

Tirade

For all of those who love and support me.

You know who you are.

Recalled

Chapter One

"Dying - ceasing to live; approaching death; expiring: a dying man."

Dex

I'm going to hell. I've known this since I was ten years old. The year I murdered someone. Knowing my fate made it a lot easier to determine how I was going to live my life and what kind of person I was going to be. Since I wasn't going to heaven, why bother living like it?

And so, my destiny was sealed long before most even think about it. I never worry about it because I don't really care. I figure since I'm already living like I belong there, it won't be much of an adjustment. I actually look forward to one aspect of hell: the heat. After almost eighteen years of living in the blistering cold, I'm still not used to it. I still don't like it. Honestly, I don't like much of anything.

Sliding into the shadows of a narrow alley, I positioned myself so I could look for the lucky person who'd help me get warm. After a few people passed—without realizing I was watching, debating what kind of mark they would be—I settled on my victim. I had yet to see her, but I knew without a doubt it was a *her*. The sound of high-heeled boots cracked down the pavement with an intonation I recognized well: exhaustion. With every slap of her boots, another lighter noise caught my attention—coins hitting together as she walked.

I sank back, keeping an ear on the approaching footsteps. It wouldn't be long before I would be warming myself with a hot cup of coffee and a slice of homemade pie. I smiled at the irony that the very place I planned to go was the very place she just left. It was almost too easy. Usually, I liked a challenge, the thrill of outsmarting an impossible target. I liked stealing from people who were too stupid to know what happened right under their noses.

Not tonight.

Tonight the cold seemed colder and my stomach emptier. As she drew near, I straightened, pulled my cap lower on my head, and walked right out onto the sidewalk. I didn't look at her; I pretended she wasn't even there.

She wasn't as smooth.

I felt her stare and I knew her eyes probably widened at my unexpected appearance. Her steps faltered, just barely. In fact, if I weren't paying attention to the clap of her feet, I wouldn't have noticed.

But I did.

I looked up, right at her. Her startled, wary expression was exactly as I expected. So I did the unexpected.

I smiled.

This time her steps noticeably faltered before they quickened. Unfortunately for her, the sidewalks were icy and she slipped. Fortunately for me, I was right there to catch her, sliding my free hand down into the front pocket of her apron.

"Easy there," I told her as my hand closed around a stack of bills. "It's a long way down."

Her eyes stretched wide as I steadied her on the pavement and stepped back, stuffing my hands into my jacket. I could taste the coffee already. She continued to stare without saying anything. It was weird, and I got what I wanted, so I walked away.

"Hey!"

I froze, pivoting slightly on my heel. She couldn't possibly know I just picked her pocket. It was over in less than five seconds. Not responding would only confirm her suspicions, if she had any, so I raised my eyebrows in silent inquiry.

"Thank you."

Thank you? When she got home later and realized all her tips from the night were gone, she would regret those words. Although, I did teach her a very important lesson so maybe the thanks were deserved. Maybe this would teach her not to go walking around alone in a dark, not-so-great neighborhood.

"Yeah." I answered, because she was doing that staring thing again and I just wanted to get rid of her.

Thankfully, she seemed to pick up on the fact I didn't want to chat and she turned, walking to stand just below the bus sign. The bus rounded the corner and barreled toward the stop.

I opened the door to the little diner, welcomed by a blast of heat. The aroma of baking pie beckoned me. Then, for some unknown reason, I looked back.

Everything slowed.

The bus driver recognized he was going too fast and slammed on the brakes. The heavy bus fishtailed on the sheet of black ice and slid forward, coming up over the curb, pulverizing a bench and sliding right at the waitress.

No!

I shoved her out of the way of sure and certain death. She landed roughly on her side a few feet away.

Our eyes met.

I paused instantly to wonder what the hell I was thinking. Just as quickly, the bus plowed into me, stealing my breath and crunching my bones. I landed in the middle of the street, a crumpled mess. Everything was silent when I finally opened my eyes. She was there, leaning over me, tears on her face. I always knew I would go to hell.

I just never knew it would be so soon.

Chapter Two

"Alive - possessing life. In existence; active."

Piper

He seemed to come out of nowhere, appearing out of the shadows in front of me. It was his sudden presence that made me pause, caught me off guard. He wore a black toboggan pulled low over his head, a black quilted coat, and scuffed-up jeans.

I kept walking, knowing he was probably just heading into the diner for a late-night meal. He had the look of someone who couldn't quite get warm and needed something to fill him up. Working in this part of town gave me a lot of experience in recognizing hungry, cold people. I hoped Julia would take pity on him and let him order before they closed up the kitchen.

Even though I knew he probably wasn't anyone to be afraid of, I couldn't look away as I walked. There was something about him that held my stare.

And then he smiled.

It was the kind of ornery smile that told me he probably wasn't as innocent as I thought. Distracted by his unexpected behavior, I slipped, my heels sliding right over a patch of ice. I braced myself against the hard sidewalk, but never hit it.

The stranger caught me around the waist, his touch triggering things inside me I hadn't experienced in a while. It was quick, almost fleeting, yet carried the impact of a blizzard.

And then he spoke.

"Easy there." He smiled again and I was dazzled. "It's a long way down."

His voice was gruff and it matched his exterior so well. It made me wonder about his interior—what was behind that smile.

And then his hands were gone, stuffed into his coat. My feet were steady on the ground, but everything inside me wobbled. I stood there, trying to shake away the image in my head and the side effects of his smile.

He walked away, toward the diner, when I heard myself call out. "Hey!"

It took a few long seconds, but he turned and I actually felt grateful it was so cold and windy. He wouldn't be able to tell that the pink in my cheeks was from my embarrassment, not the weather. When he lifted his eyebrows, I realized I needed to say something else.

"Thank you," I told him.

He didn't seem to want me to thank him. He didn't seem to want to talk at all.

"Yeah," he said with the slightest hint of irritation.

I was keeping him from the last few minutes the diner was open so I said nothing more, turning away, instead, toward the bus stop. I really hoped it came soon. It was freezing out here.

And then it was like someone pressed the fast-forward button, throwing everything around me into chaos.

Just as I wished, the bus appeared, but instead of stopping to open its doors for me, it began to slide, the heavy end fishtailing across the narrow road. I stood there watching it barrel toward me, threatening to run me down, but I couldn't move.

Then I shifted, pushed out of the way, and landed just feet from where I had been. I looked up to meet the eyes of the stranger who captivated me. And then I watched as the bus smacked into him, flinging his body like a ragdoll, bending him at angles people weren't supposed to achieve.

I jumped to my feet as the cacophony of the crash died away and everything seemed to be silent for one long second.

The man lay in the street, crumpled and unmoving. I ran to him and dropped to my knees beside his head.

His eyes were open and they stared up as I leaned over him.

"I'm going to get help. Hang in there." I looked toward the diner where Julia stared at me from the sidewalk. "Call 9-1-1!" I screamed and then turned my attention back to him.

He hadn't moved at all. He still stared at me. I had no idea if he was dead, but I knew—*I knew*—when help finally arrived, he would be.

"I'm so sorry." I choked, the words sounding strangled to my ears.

I wanted to touch him, but I was afraid it would only cause him pain. Something passed behind his eyes—I didn't know what—and then it faded away into nothing.

"Thank you," I whispered, leaning over him, praying to God he heard me. I hoped he knew he wasn't alone, that he wasn't going to slip away without anyone caring.

Noise and panic erupted around us. People began to emerge from the bus; the driver wailed with horror and pain. In the distance I heard the piercing wail of sirens and the wrecked bus moaned where it lay.

But even through the chaos I felt as if we were in a bubble, somehow separate from the disarray. Snowflakes swirled down from the midnight-colored sky, their path never straight, and they began to coat everything around us. The stranger's black knit hat began to turn white and small, perfectly shaped flakes caught in his lashes.

He didn't move.

He didn't breathe.

Tears slipped from my eyes and turned icy on their path down my cheeks. I didn't brush them away. He deserved these tears. I sat there weeping, sitting vigil over his still form as all the color leeched from his skin and the snow blanketed him in white.

The snow didn't stick to me. Because I was still warm. Because I was still alive.

Chapter Three

"Proposition - An offer of a private bargain. A plan suggested for acceptance; a proposal."

Dex

Something wasn't right. Being hit by a bus should cause excruciating pain. I should be floating between consciousness and unconsciousness in varying degrees of "why me?" and "give me some drugs!" But, surprisingly, I felt fine. I didn't feel my shattered bones. I didn't hurt so much I wished I were dead. Maybe it was because I was frozen, numb from lying here on the ice and in the snow. Maybe along with my many other injuries, I also had hypothermia.

Slowly, I opened my eyes. I expected to see her face, the girl I stole from. The girl that should be lying here instead of me.

She was gone.

Probably reached into my pocket and took her money back, then left me here to die.

Except… I wasn't lying in the street.

I moved to sit up, and when I did so without screaming with the pain I *should have* felt, I looked down.

And looked some more.

My body was gone.

Like, gone, *gone*.

Where my legs and torso used to be was nothing, nothing but a translucent purple mist outline of where my body should be.

Well, that just explained everything.

Not.

I looked up, concentrating on more than myself, to see where I was exactly. It appeared to be an office of some sorts. The room itself was huge and I felt like the rug I sat on (was I really sitting?) was an island floating in the center. It reminded me of the pictures I had seen of sand on a beach. Behind me was a massive leather couch with pillows in golds and oranges, a huge wooden coffee table with a bowl full of white stones in the center, and two end tables with lamps. In front of me was a giant, almost bare black desk. Another bowl of white stones sat off to the right and on the left there was a metal tray with a glass decanter filled with an amber-colored liquid and four empty glasses beside it. In the center of the desk was a neat stack of papers, but no pen. Behind the desk was a wall of floor-to-ceiling, cherry-colored paneled doors trimmed in black.

Before I could do or look at anything else, I noticed the chair behind the desk—black leather and about as wide as a football player's shoulders. It faced the doors, which I didn't really notice until it began to spin around. I watched as a man revolved into view.

He was dwarfed by the chair—or maybe he just wasn't very big—but his utter stillness was chilling. When the chair completely faced forward, it stopped moving and the man stared at me for several long seconds. I immediately began to take stock of him—wanting to know what I was facing. He had a long face with sharp features. His cheekbones were well defined and he had a very long, pointy nose. His thin lips pressed in a line and I knew his sharp eyes missed nothing. His hair was dark but peppered with grey and he slicked it back from his wide forehead, which only made his face seem that much more prominent. I didn't speak as he brought up his hands and steepled his very long, bony fingers beneath his chin.

I moved to stand, but, instead, the translucent mist seemed to waft out around me—giving me no shape at all. On instinct, I tried to grab at it, to pull it back in. I wanted a shape. I didn't want to float away. My sudden movements only caused the mist to spread farther and make me even less.

Am I a ghost?

If there were one way to become a ghost, getting hit by a bus would probably do it.

"You are not a ghost." The man spoke, still watching me with his bird-like eyes.

Could he read my mind?

"You are simply, shall we say, between forms at the moment."

He could say that, but it didn't mean I understood.

I glanced again at my less-than-solid form. I wasn't sure if I would be able to speak if I tried so I decided, for now, saying nothing was probably my best option.

"I'm sure you are wondering who I am," the man said, finally dropping his hands into his lap. "I'm a dealer, and I have a proposition for you."

A dealer? I spent a lot of time on the streets and I was more than positive drugs caused death… They didn't bring you back from it.

And I was certain I was dead.

The man looked at me like he thought I would leap with joy at this "proposition." When I said nothing, he continued to stare. Finally, I decided being silent wasn't my best option.

"I don't do drugs," I said, surprised when my voice came out clearly.

The man smiled. Unfortunately, it didn't make him look friendly. "I don't deal drugs. I deal life and death." As if on cue, behind him the doors sprang open. Most people kept clothes and shoes in their closets. Some people used them to hide their junk. But this… *this* wasn't normal.

This man kept bodies in his closet.

They weren't piled on one another. They weren't crammed in at odd angles. If they were, it might be less creepy. These bodies were organized. They were hanging— on hangers—and in rows like suits. I had a sudden, vivid image of this man opening his closet every morning and pondering which body to wear.

Each one was limp and surprisingly thin looking as it hung there. They weren't naked, but each was fully dressed and groomed with care.

The man pushed out of his chair and stood. He couldn't have been more than five foot seven and he was thin… almost bony. He went over to the closet and pushed through the hangers like he was searching for a particular shirt, stopping when he found what he was looking for. He pulled the body off the rack and turned, lifting it up so the feet didn't drag the ground. This body was clearly taller than him.

My body.

The one that just got crushed by a bus.

But it didn't look that way. It looked normal… aside from the fact it was on a hanger with the chin lying against the deflated chest. My hair was dark and messy, my skin smooth and unbruised. The only thing that wasn't normal (besides me examining my own body from across the room) was the clothing. I wore khaki pants, a button-up shirt, and dress socks. I don't think I ever owned a pair of khakis… or socks without holes in them.

"You were killed almost instantly when that bus hit you." The man began, still holding up my body. "The ambulance came, put you in a body bag, and drove you to the morgue. You had no identification and only twenty-four dollars in your pocket. I didn't think the morgue attendant would miss you much if your body disappeared."

"You stole my body out of a morgue?" *Then hung it in a closet…*

"What if I told you that you could have another chance at life?" he said, and as he spoke, he placed my body back into the closet.

For most people, a second chance at life was probably a great opportunity. But when he dangled the offer in front of me, I realized it wasn't that appealing for me.

When I was alive, my life sucked.

I was born into poverty to a too-young mother who didn't know what to do with a kid. She had a different boyfriend every month and none of them wanted me around. I spent a lot of time on the streets—cold, hungry, and angry. When I was eight, my mother decided to be a better parent and she got a job and moved us to a new apartment. The apartment was still in the crappy end of town, but it was her way of trying to give us a better life. She even went three months without a boyfriend. We still had next to nothing, but sometimes there was food.

Then she got a new boyfriend.

He was the worst yet. He moved in and Mom was all excited that we'd be a two-income household… but she was kidding herself. The guy spent all his money on liquor and then he'd come home drunk and beat her… then me.

One night, he was being especially vicious and I decided I had enough. Mom was unconscious on the floor and I grabbed a knife. At the age of ten, I became a killer.

When Mom came to, she called the cops and shocked me when she took the blame. The cops labeled it self-defense based on Mom's black eye, the lump on her head, and her broken rib. She didn't bring home any more boyfriends after that.

Still, things didn't get much better, and I took to the streets. Life taught me how to survive, but death taught me living wasn't all it was cracked up to be.

"I think I'll pass. You can just send me to hell now."

The man—I couldn't help but call him Mr. Burns because he looked like that guy with the crooked nose on *The Simpsons*—didn't seem shocked by my refusal. Maybe I wasn't the only person who preferred death. "What makes you think you would be sent to hell?"

"Well, this sure ain't the gates of heaven."

"So you would rather burn for an eternity in hell than accept my offer?"

"My life wasn't anything I'm anxious to get back to. I might as well get a head start on hell. At least it's warmer than Alaska."

The man tilted his chin down. "Yes, I imagine living on the streets and being a pickpocket wasn't that glamorous."

I wasn't shocked he knew stuff about me. I mean, if he had the ability to steal my body, somehow turn me into a ghost, and then hang my body *in his closet,* knowing I was a pickpocket wasn't really impressive.

"Hell isn't much better. You won't be cold, but you will be hungry, just not for food. Your soul would be slowly eaten away by the confines of hell. You'll begin to shrivel and twist until you're completely empty, and then there'll be nothing but the stretch of time and the endless sounds of tortured cries from those around you."

So… if what Mr. Burns said was true, then life and death suck equally.

"What if I told you your life—if returned to you—would be very different than before?"

"Different how?"

"You would have money, a home, a car… You would never be hungry."

"Go on," I said, warming to the idea.

"Opportunity would be abundant and you could create a whole new identity for yourself."

I looked down at my misty form. I was tempted, sure, but still something kept me from accepting right away. "What's the catch?"

There's always a catch.

"In exchange for your life, your new and improved life, you would work for me."

"Doing what?"

"You will be an Escort."

On the streets, another name for escort was prostitute. "I don't think I would look good in a dress and heels."

"You joke. You're funny," Mr. Burns said, smiling. "Not that kind of escort. This is more exclusive. More important."

"So what exactly will I be escorting?" I asked, more confused than before.

Mr. Burns's little beady eyes gleamed with excitement and he smirked, causing his cheekbones to jut outward. "Death. You will be a Death Escort."

Chapter Four

"Remember - To keep (someone) in mind as worthy of consideration or recognition."

Piper

I was watching the sun rise and feeling sorry for myself when the doorbell rang. I sighed. Why did the doorbell *always* ring when you didn't want company? I dashed the tears from my cheeks, knowing there was nothing I could do about my swollen eyes, and went to the door.

"Who is it?" I yelled right through the white, peeling door.

"I have a delivery for Piper McCall," replied a phony deep voice.

I rolled my eyes. "I didn't order anything."

"Open the damn door, Piper!" Frankie yelled, dropping the fake voice.

I unchained the lock, turned the deadbolt, and pulled open the door. Frankie barely paused to look at me as she bustled by with her armload, yet she saw everything. "If I looked like you I wouldn't want to open the door either."

"It's barely six a.m., Frank. What're you doing here?"

"Did you think I wouldn't come when you called to tell me about your brush with death!?"

"I thought maybe you'd wait and come at a decent hour," I grumbled, locking the door and following her into the tiny kitchen.

"The donut makers are up," she said, flipping the lid open on a box of a dozen donuts. "Therefore, the hour is decent!"

Fried dough, sugar, and icing wasn't a healthy way to start the day.

"Where's my coffee?" I said, cracking a smile because she motioned to the donuts like Vanna White.

She handed me a very large cup. "Here, it's the boring kind. Cream, no sugar."

I took a sip of my boring coffee as she untied her red trench coat and slipped it off her five-foot-four curvy frame. Frankie liked her curves and her sugar habit helped maintain them.

"So you almost got creamed by a bus, huh?" she said as she rummaged through my cabinets for napkins and a couple plates.

My stomach clenched at the mention of the bus. I set my coffee on the table and pulled out a chair. "Yes, I almost got hit by a bus, but didn't because someone else pushed me out of the way." I felt my eyes tear up again and I blinked them away, reaching for my coffee.

"It was real bad, huh?" Frankie said, sitting down and patting my hand.

"He died. He pushed me out of the way and the bus crushed him…" My voice fell away. "It was awful."

"He died?"

"Almost instantly."

We both sat there for long, silent moments. The kitchen filled with the comforting scents of donuts and coffee, but I felt awful that someone would still be breathing and alive if not for what he did *for me*.

"The thing is," I said, my voice low, "I don't know why he did it."

"Well, I'm glad he did. I'm glad you're still here."

"Thanks, Frankie," I said, but in the back of my head I wondered if I was the one who should've died.

Frankie reached into the donut box and pulled out a glazed, then looked at me. "So if I eat this am I going to get fat?"

I rolled my eyes. "Depends on how many you eat."

"I plan on eating at least three. So go on, check." She held out her hand, the one still holding the donut.

"You're ridiculous."

"What's the use of having a BFF that can see the future if you can't exploit it?"

"I can't see the future, just portions of it." I reminded her as she rolled her eyes. "Most people would want to know lottery numbers. You want to know if you're going to get fat."

"Don't need lottery numbers. That's what all these curves are for… to hook a rich doctor who I happen to bump into while visiting my super smart, future-seeing doctor friend at the hospital."

I laughed. "I won't be a doctor for many years yet, Frank."

"All the more reason I can't get fat. So go on. Look." She waved her hand at me again.

I shook my head and sighed. "I might not see anything. You know it doesn't always work."

"It'll work," Frankie said confidently.

I closed my eyes and took her hand in mine. I took a deep breath and reached down into the part of my brain that seemed to be able to access my visions—something I don't think it really should be able to do. I asked to be let in—never demanded—and it opened for me, flooding me with a rush of warmth in welcome. I thought of Frankie and her donut habit and asked gently for an image of her in four years. It came easily and I smiled. She still looked the same—kind of like Marilyn Monroe—short blond curls, big smile, and major curves. Instead of opening my eyes, I tucked the image back and eased out slowly, thanking that part of me for the information. Only then did I open my eyes.

Frankie watched me, donut poised against her lips.

"You still look hot in four years," I told her.

She bit into the donut and made a sound of appreciation. "So good," she said around another mouthful.

"Just remember the future isn't concrete. It can change so you might want to rethink that box of donuts."

"I'm not going to eat them *all*," she said, snagging another with icing and sprinkles. "You're going to help me."

I started to shake my head, but she pinned me with a stare. "You could've died! And never ate another donut again!"

"Oh the horror!" I gasped, but I did pick up a cinnamon twist. She had a point. What was the point of living if I didn't enjoy it?

"So when's the funeral?" Frankie asked as she polished off her second pastry.

"I don't know. He didn't have any ID on him and the hospital wouldn't tell me anything when I called."

"Maybe you should just let it go," she suggested.

I jerked like she slapped me.

Frankie sat her coffee down and pushed her blond curls from her face. "I don't mean to be insensitive. But there's nothing more you can do," she said gently.

Maybe not, but I could remember. It seemed not forgetting what this stranger did for me was the very least I could do.

Chapter Five

"Deal - An agreement, especially one that is mutually beneficial. A business transaction."

Dex

A Death Escort. An image of a stiff black polo with a little embroidered logo on the chest that stated exactly that popped in my mind. It was ridiculous. Death escorted people. People didn't escort Death. Still, I wanted to know. "How exactly does someone escort death?"

"By killing."

He made it sound so simple. I guess in a way it was. It hadn't been that hard to stab and kill my mother's boyfriend.

"So let me get this straight." I held up a finger to count off my reasoning, but the movement only loosened my shape and I was left with no fingers at all. "You want to give me back my life so I can kill people for you?"

"Not just anyone. You will be assigned a target. Once that target is Escorted to their death, then you will receive another. You will only have one target at a time. There will be times when you have no target at all… You will be free to enjoy your money and life."

So basically I'd be an assassin with paid vacations. I guess it was a good offer for a guy like me. Still, I hesitated.

Mr. Burns sat down in his massive desk chair and opened the desk drawer to his right. Silently he pulled out a shiny red credit card and laid it on the desk. Next he pulled out a stack of crisp one hundred dollar bills and finally a set of keys, which I assumed were for a car.

"This first job will be your test—your initiation. If you complete it successfully, you will then be an official Death Escort. The more jobs you complete, the more power and money you will receive."

"And if I turn down your offer?"

His hand disappeared beneath the surface of the desk and then returned. To my right, a swirling black hole opened up. Angry red flames came licking out of it, reaching for me. From inside the hole I could hear hollow wailing. I felt a slight tugging feeling and realized the hole was trying to suck me in and the mist that made up my body began drifting toward it.

"If you turn down my offer, you can begin eternity right now. You won't mind if I keep your body, will you?" He steepled his hands beneath his chin again and watched with open amusement as I thought about my choices.

I always knew hell would be where I ended up, and I accepted that, but why not have a little fun before? Eternity could wait. I glanced back at the shiny credit card and stack of bills. "I accept."

The black hole snapped shut and Mr. Burns clapped his hands in glee. "Wonderful! Let's get you a body."

The closet doors were still open, still displaying his collection, but instead of going directly to my body, he went to the other end and began going through the others.

"Mine's over there." I pointed to it, ignoring the fact my finger spread out like a puff of smoke.

"Your body won't do for this assignment," Mr. Burns said with his back to me.

"What do you mean?"

"You're Target may recognize you, and we can't have that. You're supposed to be dead."

I was still processing that when he exclaimed, "Ah-ha!" and pulled a body from the rack. "I knew it was here." He turned and held it out. "How about this one?"

I stared at the flat, limp body. It was dressed in navy khakis (what is it with this guy and khakis?), a red-and-white plaid button-up shirt, and a navy sweater vest. It had dark blond hair combed neatly to the side, and even though his head lay against the chest, I could see the arms of a pair of glasses around his ears.

It was a deflated dork.

This guy wanted me to get dressed in a dork costume.

"No," I said, thinking of the way I looked… er… used to look. I had dark hair that never got combed. I wore the same pair of jeans everyday with a T-shirt, a dark hoodie, and a black puffer coat I stole from some homeless guy on the street. And even if I needed glasses—which I didn't—I wouldn't have worn them.

"New life. New body. No choice," Mr. Burns said as he took the body off the hanger and came around the desk. The next thing I knew all the mist that was me was pulled into the body and it began to inflate, to fill up with life—my life—and become whole again. I held out my arms and watched my hands become plump and then I flexed my fingers, enjoying the fact that when I moved I didn't have to worry about disappearing into a cloud. I looked down at my feet and legs, trying to get used to the idea that I looked like someone else. I lifted one leg and then the other, smiling when the body obeyed, and any worry this body might be awkward or hard to control vanished. It felt good to have a form again.

"Ah, yes, it fits! I knew it would," Mr. Burns exclaimed.

I guess bodies weren't one size fits all. I'm glad this one did because I didn't think I was up for a round of musical bodies.

"So how do you feel?" he asked, taking in my new appearance.

I felt like me. I didn't feel like I was somewhere I didn't belong. I didn't feel like a stranger in my own body… but this really wasn't my body, so I guess I was a stranger to it. Then a thought speared me. *Where's the guy who used to own this body?*

"Where did you get this body? Where did you get all of them?" I asked.

"Various sources. Don't worry. This person doesn't need this body anymore."

That didn't make me feel better.

"Have a look at the new you," he said, sounding like the host of a makeover show on TV as he pointed to a full-length mirror on the other side of the room.

I went toward it, the feet obeying my mind, and looked into the mirror. It's quite a shock to look in a mirror and see a complete stranger. Especially when you still feel like yourself. I stared silently at the blond hair and the dimple in my chin. The skin was smooth like whoever had this body before had an easy life. They weren't forced to withstand the harsh Alaskan elements. I was tall, about the same six feet as before, but my shoulders were broader now, probably because this body wasn't starved half the time. I had a wide jawline, a strong nose, and green eyes that peered back at me from behind wire-rim glasses. Seriously, wire-rimmed.

I made a sound and shoved my hands through the perfectly combed hair. The dark-blond strands fell over my forehead and I pulled them up until they were almost standing straight up. I reached under the sweater vest and untucked the ends of the button-up, letting them hang from the sweater. Then I unbuttoned the collar and sleeves, rolling them up a few times to expose my forearms. It was the best I could do until I got some jeans, Converse sneakers, and could ditch the glasses.

When I turned from the mirror, Mr. Burns frowned. "Well, I guess as long as you do the job it doesn't matter what you look like."

Then he held out a wad of cash and I reached for it, shoving it in my pocket. "Here's your credit card. The bill will come to me. Don't spend more than twenty thousand a month."

"Twenty thousand," I said, practically choking on the number.

"Yes, well, I know it isn't much, but this is your first job. You aren't officially an Escort yet. Once it's official, your limit will increase."

He must've thought I was offended by the amount. I tried not to outwardly react—I wasn't offended; I was shocked. I'd never seen this much money in my entire almost eighteen years! Killing paid well.

I reached out and took the credit card, glancing down at the name. "I have a new name, too?"

"Of course."

I glanced at the name again and wanted to roll my eyes. Dexter Allen Roth. It might as well just said Dork of the Century. I glanced back at Mr. Burns. "Just call me Dex."

Mr. Burns inclined his head. "You can call me G.R."

So I got saddled with Dexter and he got a cool name like G.R.? I shoved the credit card in my pocket and grabbed up the keys. "Are these to my new car?"

"Yes. I will take you to it shortly. There is also the key to your new apartment. The GPS in your vehicle will take you to its location."

"Sweet." I palmed the keys and glanced back up, my eyes falling on my body—the one still hanging in the closet. I felt I was betraying it somehow. "What about my body?" I asked.

"Once you become an official Death Escort, you can have it back if you like. The one you wear now will go back in the closet."

"About that… You said I couldn't have my original body because the Target might recognize me. Who's the Target?"

"The night you died, you pushed someone out of the way of the bus that crushed you. A girl."

"Yeah, so?"

"She is your Target."

I felt the denial inside me, but just as quickly, it was gone. Why not her? The Target had to be someone, and at least this girl wasn't a friend.

"She won't know who I am," I said, seeing no reason for the new body and the new name. This girl saw me for all of five seconds before I was smashed by a bus. *But she really looked at you,* a voice inside me whispered. That wasn't something I would forget because few people in my life have ever looked at me and *really* saw me.

Still, it didn't mean anything. She probably knew I was stealing from her and was about to call me out.

"Don't think your death went unnoticed," Mr. Burns said. I know he told me his name, but in my head he would forever be Mr. Burns. "Remember, in the business of Escorting, no detail is too small."

"Right." I agreed.

"Once the Target is dead, you will call me." He reached into the still-open drawer and pulled out an iPhone and slid it across the table. "My number is programmed in. I will arrive and take things from there. You have two months to complete the task."

The task of killing someone.

Chapter Six

"Morgue - A place in which the bodies of persons found dead are kept until identified and claimed or until arrangements for burial have been made."

Piper

Hospitals always smelled like harsh cleaning supplies with a slight hint of stale air. I wondered if after a few years of working here you'd get used to the smell. Maybe someday I'd be able to find out. If I ever finished college, that is.

I wound down the long, white, surprisingly empty corridor. Although, I guess given where I headed, the empty hallway shouldn't be a surprise.

No one wanted to hang out by the morgue.

When I called the hospital this morning, no one would tell me anything. I wasn't really surprised, but I wasn't ready to give up, either. I had to know more about the man who died for me. I wanted to at least know his name.

I paused outside the wide swinging doors that led to the morgue before taking a deep breath and pushing through them. Just ahead and on the left was a small station with one nurse behind a Plexiglas wall with a small cut out circle for people to talk through.

It was quiet in here. There was also a sort of stillness in the air, like the dead bodies close by somehow stole some of the life right out of the air. I shivered and pulled the sweater I wore closer around me.

The nurse looked up from her desk and leaned close to the circle. "Can I help you?"

I nodded and stepped forward. "Yes, I was hoping you could tell me some information about a body that was brought in last night?"

"Name of the deceased?" she asked.

"I don't know his name; that's what I wanted to know."

The nurse looked closer at me. "Are you a family member or next of kin?"

I sighed. "No."

"I'm sorry we can't give out any information," she began to say, but I held up my hand and she paused.

"Look, I know the rules. I called this morning. But, please, that man… that man in there… he died for me. He pushed me out of the way of a bus and got hit instead. All I want is to know his name, to know something about the man that saved my life."

She thought about what I said for long moments, then held up a finger. "Wait here." And she disappeared from the office and went down the hall.

I stared at the chairs in the waiting room with distaste, refusing to sit down. I wondered how many people sat in them, waiting to identify a body or to collect the personal belongings of someone they would never see again.

I thought about the dead bodies lying a few doors down, draped in white sheets, closed up in little drawers, waiting for someone to claim them or put them to rest. This had to be one of the saddest places on earth.

I heard the nurse's soft-soled shoes coming back down the hall and I turned toward the door of the office. Instead of her, a man in a white lab coat appeared and headed toward me. "Miss? You're here about the body?"

"Yes. Please tell me his name."

"I'm sorry, but I can't."

I let out a frustrated sound. "Yes, you can!"

"No. I don't know his name. He had no ID on him when he was brought in."

"How can that be?" I asked, thinking maybe the reason the police officers at the scene wouldn't tell me was because they hadn't known either.

He shrugged slightly. "It happens sometimes."

"Didn't you use his fingerprints or dental records?" I asked, frustrated.

"Well, yes, normally we could, but it's not possible this time."

"Well, why not?" I demanded.

"Because the body's no longer here," he said, watching me closely.

"What do you mean it isn't here? Where did it go?" Last I checked, bodies didn't check themselves out of the morgue.

The man cleared his throat. "We aren't really sure."

"You aren't sure," I repeated, flat.

"The nurse said you were at the scene of the accident. I was hoping you could tell me a few things, like if he spoke to you, if anyone else was there…"

"No," I cried. "No, he didn't speak to me. He died almost immediately. And no one else was there except for the people on the bus. It was only after he died that people started showing up."

"You never met him before?"

"No. Never," I said, feeling completely let down. All I wanted was his name.

He nodded. "Well, thank you." He turned to walk away.

"Wait," I called. "What are you doing to get him back?"

"I can't discuss that with you."

"Has no one come to claim him at all?" I knew the accident wasn't that long ago, but wasn't someone wondering where he was?

He hesitated, then said, "No. Just you."

I realized then his body would probably never be found. No one would come looking for him, and no one would care. The hospital would just sweep this under the rug like it never even happened.

I felt my shoulders slump. He deserved better.

The man came back to stand next to me. "I'm sorry there isn't anything more I can tell you. I'm sure he's at peace where ever he is."

I nodded.

The man reached into his lab coat and pulled out his fisted hand. "I shouldn't do this, but I really don't think anyone else will come by." He cleared his throat. "Judging from the clothes he was wearing and the condition of the body, excluding his injuries, I'm pretty sure he was homeless. He had twenty-four dollars in his pocket and this."

He held out his hand and opened his fingers to reveal a small picture, no bigger than a business card. The edges were tattered and curled like it had been carried around for months in someone's pocket. The image was slightly faded—a beach with crystal-blue water and a sandy, warm beach. The sun was sinking behind the ocean and it cast a golden glow over everything in the picture.

I felt tears well in my eyes as I reached out and took the photo. I flipped it over and on the back there were two words:

Some Day

If the man in the lab coat was right, then this was a homeless man's hope. His wish for something better, something more. It was his sunshine in a world of ice and snow; his warmth in the cold. Maybe he hoped he would get there someday. But he never would.

My hand curled protectively around the picture. I looked up, prepared to fight the doctor, to refuse to give this back.

But he was gone.

I looked over at the little boxy nurse's station and she was gone too. I was completely alone, standing here in the silence, looking down at a dead man's dream.

And I never got to hear his name.

But at least I had something of his. I traced my finger over the words, wondering if he wrote them. Something caught my attention and I looked up. I really couldn't say what it was that startled me… not a sound. It was more of a feeling of suddenly not being completely alone.

I stuck my hand with the picture into my pocket and walked out into the hall, going back the way I came. It was still empty and silent here, the only sound being my shoes on the white linoleum floor. Then up ahead I saw a dark figure disappear around a corner. I glanced around, wondering where he came from.

When I walked by the hall he went down, I looked, but no one was there. A funny feeling crept its way up my neck and I quickened my steps. No one was there, but still I felt like someone was.

I ran my thumb over the heavy paper of the card inside my pocket and wondered again about the man who carried this. Where did his body go? And why would someone take it?

Chapter Seven

"Reward - payment made in return for a service rendered."

Dex

You know, I didn't so much mind the dorky body when I got a look at my new car. In all my life—well, my life before I died and took on a new body and identity—I never owned a car. In fact, I didn't have my driver's license. I learned to drive in stolen cars. But Dexter Allen Roth AKA Dex did have a driver's license and he was also the new owner of a 2013 Mercedes-Benz SL550 Roadster.

And man, was it sweet.

It was a steel-gray two-seater with black and red leather interior, a hard top convertible that operated with the push of a button. A glance at the dash told me it went at least one hundred and forty miles per hour, and I couldn't wait to put this baby to the test.

Mr. Burns handed me the keys and I snatched them, not bothering to thank him. This wasn't a gift; this was part of my paycheck.

"The GPS inside is programmed with your new address," he said. "Familiarize yourself with the place and then get to work."

He started to walk away, back toward his mansion, and a strong—very cold—wind whooshed as he turned back. "Well, you might want to get a coat first." He laughed, amused with himself. He was quite jolly for a death dealer.

I didn't stand there pondering my situation for long. I had a car to drive. I jumped in and started up the engine—it purred like a kitten, and I grinned. I didn't remember to turn on the GPS until I was out of the driveway and speeding down the ultra-exclusive looking neighborhood. I'd never been to this part of Fairbanks, Alaska, and I glanced around, waiting for someone to come running at my car, yelling, "Stop thief!" or "Intruder!" But no one came and the guard at the gated entrance actually tipped his hat as the Roadster roared by.

I relaxed back into the leather and switched on the heat. *I really should get a coat. A leather one.*

About twenty minutes later, I pulled up to another gated community, except this one didn't have sprawling lawns and mansions. It held three-story townhouses with stone fronts and arched windows. The guard at the gate signaled for me to stop, so I did and rolled down the window, wincing at the cold air that hit me in the face.

"Are you visiting someone?" the guard asked.

"No. I live here." I responded with confidence. Then my eyes slid over to the GPS to see the address of my new place. "I'm on Brandywine Court. Number Eighteen."

"Oh, right. The new resident. Welcome home." He handed me a gate pass and a parking pass and then waved me through. Just like that.

I rolled up my window and slid past the towering townhouses and bare sidewalks. It was almost dark, but there were so many streetlights I could see everything. It would be hard to be a thief in this neighborhood. I snorted. There were probably cameras hidden in the well-trimmed bushes.

I pulled up to number eighteen, which looked like the rest of the townhomes, except the windows were all dark. I eased into the driveway in front of the two-car garage and pressed the button on the remote control clipped to the visor. The garage door lifted smoothly and my headlights bounced around the empty garage. After closing the door behind me, I cut the engine. Trying to make my way to the door in the dark, I realized I should've left the headlights on.

After I found the door handle, I gave it a try and was glad when it opened easily. I could pick a lock in the dark, but I've never used a key. I walked into the bottom floor of the house and groped around for a light, switching it on.

Gleaming tiles greeted me in alternating white and black, to my right was a washer and dryer, and to the left there was a row of coat hooks and a bench. I kicked off the brown leather shoes that came with my body and they skidded beneath the bench.

I walked out of the laundry room and into a wide room with dark-brown walls, plush beige carpet, and a huge couch in the shape of a U laden with a hundred pillows. But I didn't give attention to much else because hanging on the wall was a massive TV. It was awesome.

When I finished drooling over the TV, I headed upstairs into another large living area with a fireplace, another TV, a couch, and various other pieces of furniture. The floors were dark wood and there were expensive-looking carpets everywhere. The kitchen was open to the living area and it was all stainless steel and black granite. There was a bathroom with more granite and wood, and then I went upstairs where I found three bedrooms and an office. They were all stuffed with furniture and beds piled with pillows. Each room had its own bathroom. The master bedroom was as big as the apartment I grew up in, with wide windows, soft carpet, and a bed the size of a small country. The bathroom was stocked with soap, towels, and every other item I might possibly need.

I zeroed in on the contact supplies on the counter. Finally! I could lose the dorky glasses. I grabbed up the solution and the box of contacts. I poked myself in the eye five times trying to get the stupid things in there.

"Damn!" I shouted and my voice echoed around the room. How was I supposed to put a contact in my eye when my vision was so blurry I couldn't even see myself in the mirror?

I decided maybe glasses might not be so bad. Clark Kent wore them. If Superman could look good in glasses, then I could too.

I left the bathroom and went downstairs to the kitchen. I was starving. It had been days since I'd eaten. The fridge contained the basics: milk, bread, eggs, and cheese. The pantry had some cereal and some coffee. I was about to inhale the entire box of Cheerios when the doorbell rang.

For a minute, I stood there frozen like I was caught doing something wrong. Like maybe this wasn't really my house and the police were here to arrest me for breaking and entering. Then the doorbell rang again.

If it was the cops, I would show them my key. Can't argue with a key, right?

There was a wide hallway beside the kitchen that led to the double front doors with ornate frosted glass on each side. Based on the shadows moving on the other side, someone was definitely standing there.

I opened the door a crack, curling my lip at the cold air snaking in. "What?" I practically growled.

"I'm here for the job."

I jerked back and with my movement the door opened farther. The man standing on my front porch was small, no more than five foot five. He was thin, but not skinny, and dressed in a dove-gray top hat and matching pea coat. He carried a cane with a gold knob at the top that looked more like a prop than something he actually needed. Next to him was a small black suitcase.

"What job?"

"The butler position."

"You have the wrong place. I'm not hiring a butler."

The man furrowed his brow. "Is this not eighteen Brandywine?"

"Yeah, but—" I stopped midsentence. I wasn't really hiring a butler, but that didn't mean I *couldn't*. Someone had to use that washer and dryer downstairs… Why not him?

I squinted my eyes at him. "Can you cook?"

"Of course. What self-respecting butler doesn't?"

"You're hired."

I opened the door wider so he could enter. He came in, the end of his cane tapping on the tiles, carrying his bag with his other hand. "Don't you want to see my resume first? Find out what kind of pay I require?"

"How much do butlers cost?" I asked.

"I charge five hundred dollars a week."

"You're hired." I glanced at the suitcase he held. "Are you moving in?"

"Most butlers are live-in."

I nodded. It wasn't like I didn't have the room. "You can have one of the bedrooms upstairs, not the master, of course." My eyes slid to his cane. "Can you get upstairs okay?"

"Of course."

I guess his cane *was* just for looks. I locked the front door behind him and he sat his suitcase on the floor and offered his hand. "My name's Cadbury Hobson. You can just call me Hobson."

I shook his hand. "Nice to meet ya, Hobbs. My name's Dex."

"Hobson," he corrected and I ignored. "Nice to meet you, sir."

"You can check out the house. I'm getting some cereal."

I left him to do whatever butlers do and I poured myself a giant bowl of cereal and shoveled it into my mouth while I watched the sports highlights on the massive TV. I didn't really pay much attention to what the people on the tube were saying because I was busy thinking about everything that happened to me. I got hit by a bus and died. I woke up a ghost. I met a man with a closet full of bodies and a ton of money. I was offered a job as an Escort—a Death Escort. And for accepting I got a new body, a new car, a new house, and a pocket full of money. It was all pretty awesome, minus the glasses and the whole killing part. But I wouldn't think about that now. Right now I was enjoying the fact I had somewhere warm to sleep and food in my stomach. Tomorrow would have to wait.

After I'd slurped the last of the milk from my fourth bowl of cereal, sometime during the football highlights, I fell asleep.

* * *

For a man, there's nothing better to wake up to than the smell of bacon and coffee. Okay, maybe there was something else, but bacon was a really close second.

I opened my eyes and for a moment I had to think about where I was. I was at *home*. On my couch, where I fell asleep in my khakis and sweater vest. I stretched and sat up, looking over my shoulder toward the kitchen where Hobbs was frying up some bacon.

I stumbled toward the island and pulled out a stool.

"Coffee." I groaned.

Moments later, a steaming cup of dark liquid appeared under my nose. I took a big sip, grimacing at the strong taste. I never was a huge fan of coffee, but I liked its warmth.

Hobbs noticed my face and reached for my mug. Out of habit, I snatched it back, wrapping both my hands around it protectively. He said nothing but went to the fridge and pulled out a bottle with a blue lid. He popped the top and poured some of the liquid into my cup, still in my death grip, and then plopped in a spoon. I looked at the drink suspiciously before giving it a stir, then taking a small sip.

I never thought much about heaven, but once I swallowed, I decided this is what it must be like.

I grabbed up the little bottle with a blue lid and studied at the label. *Salted Caramel Mocha Coffee Creamer.* I'd never had coffee creamer before, but I decided it was my new favorite food.

"We need more of this," I said, taking another huge gulp of my brew.

"I'll add it to the shopping list, sir," Hobbs said as he placed a plate of bacon, eggs, and toast in front of me. I dug in with gusto.

Hobbs lifted his eyebrow. "Your fork is not a shovel."

"I don't pay you to tell me how to eat."

Hobbs made a sniffing sound and turned away.

"We need more of this, too. You cook real good, Hobbs."

"Hobson. Thank you, sir."

He made a note on a piece of paper on the counter. "Anything else, sir?"

"Pizza, pancakes, donuts, and meat."

As I chewed I watched Hobbs write more on his paper, then I paused. "Aren't you gonna eat?"

Hobbs glanced at me. "Usually the help doesn't eat with the master of the home."

"Pull up a chair, Hobbs," I said, kicking out a stool next to me.

He hesitated, then filled a plate with food and sat beside me. I got up and poured some more coffee and creamer into my mug, waving him down when he started to rise. Having a butler was unnerving. Was I supposed to just sit here while he served me? I was used to doing everything for myself so that seemed a little weird. Not that I wouldn't let him cook, clean, and do my laundry, mind you.

Speaking of clothes… I needed some.

I finished my breakfast and left a pile of money on the counter for Hobbs's shopping, and I drove to the mall.

Buying clothes seemed like a better idea than trying to come up with ways to kill someone.

* * *

New clothes—*cooler* new clothes—in my closet. Check. New glasses without dorky frames. Check. New Converse tennis shoes to replace the ugly leather loafers. Check. A brand new laptop and accessories. Check. New stuff was awesome. Especially when I didn't have to steal to get it.

I never went to the mall to shop before. Turns out having money and not looking like a thug actually resulted in people being nice to you. It was a new feeling. I kind of liked it. I spent a lot of money (but stayed under the limit Mr. Burns gave me) and got a bunch of stuff I only ever dreamed about having.

While Hobbs put away all my clothes and stuff, I broke into a large supreme pizza and a six-pack of root beer while I watched a DVD I found in the TV cabinet. Sometime during my third movie and second box of donuts, I got a text on the iPhone Mr. Burns gave me. I picked it up off the coffee table, curious.

You had your fun. Time to get to work, Escort

Mr. Burns. Of course it would be from him. He was the only one that had this number. He sounded like he knew what I was doing. Was he spying on me? I glanced around the room, searching the shadows for prying eyes. Of course, I didn't see any. Then I realized if this guy was spying on me, his watchful eyes wouldn't be visible. For the first time since I got here, reality hit me. Hard.

This wasn't some vacation. I didn't win the lottery. I was a Death Escort. That meant I had a job to do.

Chapter Eight

"Memorial - Serving as a remembrance of a person or an event; commemorative."

Piper

I got off the bus earlier than I should have and then had to walk home in the cold. But the cold was preferable to being on the bus. Riding on it made me feel like a traitor, like I was somehow dishonoring the man who died by sitting in the very thing that crushed him. I could've taken a cab, but the fare all the way across town would've cost way too much. I could barely afford to live now, and if it weren't for Frankie's love of sharing donuts and the fact I got free meals at the diner, I'd probably starve. Even still, I had it better than some people, as the little card in my pocket so boldly reminded.

I couldn't get over the fact no one claimed him. No one cared he died. Everyone should have someone. I guess his someone would be me.

The wind began to blow and with it came another strange feeling—like the one that came over me at the hospital. I stopped and looked around, but nothing was there. I began walking again, changing my footsteps and heading toward a small flower shop on the corner. Inside, I bought a bunch of daisies. They were cheerful—a spot of sun in the gray winter—and the only thing in the place I could afford.

The lady wrapped them in sunny yellow paper and tied them up with a purple ribbon. As I carried them home, I guarded them against the wind and ignored the prickling at the base of my neck.

Once inside my tiny apartment, I threw the locks and let out a sigh of relief. I pulled out the card with the picture of the beach and tucked it into the frame of the mirror hanging near the front door. Then I placed the daisies in a vase and sat it on the chest of drawers beneath the mirror. It was small and simple, but it was my way of honoring the man who died. My way of acknowledging the heroic thing he did for me.

I don't know if what I did mattered, but it made me feel better so I suppose it was worth it.

I turned when a dark shadow passed by the tiny window, momentarily darkening the room. When I looked through the glass, there wasn't a cloud in the sky to disrupt the sun's rays.

So where did the darkness come from?

Chapter Nine

"Introduction - a presentation of one person to another or others."

Dex

The first step in killing someone is recon. Well, it seemed like a logical first step. I've decided it would be easier to kill the Target by learning her habits and routine. Then I could decide the best possible way for elimination. Once I decided the best way to kill her, I could make a plan and carry it out. Job done, and I could collect my actual body, get a pay raise, and live richly ever after.

I drove the Roadster until I was just down the street from the diner where I knew the Target worked. I slid into an open parking spot down the street and got out to walk the rest of the way, stuffing my hands into my heavy black leather jacket and tucking my chin into my chest. The sidewalks were covered in salt, but there were still a few patches of ice and I avoided them, realizing my Converse weren't the best for walking on slippery ground.

Maybe I should buy a pair of boots… Nah, I like my sneakers better.

As I got closer I tried to avoid looking at the spot where I died. But it was no use. My eyes went there automatically. The bench the bus took out was still missing. But other than that, everything else appeared unharmed.

It was as if the accident never even happened. As if I never died. Except it had… and I did.

I forced my eyes away from the area and toward the diner. The glass windows were lit up and the open sign on the door glowed red and blue. I didn't hesitate to pull open the door and choose a table in the back corner, sitting against the wall so I could see everyone in the place.

A waitress with a black waist apron and white shirt came over and gave me a menu as I ordered coffee. The place wasn't that crowded. There were a few tables with people and a few others sitting at the counter, but that was all. A cook worked behind the cook line and two waitresses were busy at the counter, pouring coffee and working the register.

I didn't see the Target. I was pretty sure I'd know her if I saw her. After all, she was the last face I saw before I died.

I was slightly irritated my recon plans weren't going that well, and I buried my face in the menu. I might as well eat. It would look odd if I got up and left without ordering.

A few moments later, a coffee cup slid onto the table near my elbow and a few packets of creamer were plopped down next to it. I was still deciding between the pancakes or the cheeseburger and I didn't bother to look up.

"Need a minute?" the waitress asked.

I glanced up to wave her away, but my gaze held when I saw who it was.

The girl.

The Target.

She must've come from the back. I certainly knew her when I saw her, but this was more than recognition. Every memory from the last few seconds of my life came flooding back to me.

The way the cold ground pressed into me. The way my body felt shattered and broken. The way it hurt to breathe, and then I just didn't. The way my eyes clung to the last sight I thought I would ever see…

Her face.

Her beautiful face.

Her hair was long and wavy—dark like coffee, but with lighter strands mixed in that reminded me of the swirling coffee cream I recently discovered. Her dark, catlike eyes were featured on her pale, oval-shaped face, and her slightly rounded cheeks blushed a pretty pink.

She shifted on her feet and tapped her pen on the pad of paper in her hand, and I realized I'd been silent too long.

"Yeah," I said, clearing my throat and looking down at the menu I didn't really see. "I'll have the BLT."

"You want fries?"

I nodded and she made a mark on her pad, turned, and walked away.

I picked up the coffee and took a sip. The bitter liquid burned my tongue, but it brought me out of the memories and lent some heat to my cold body. I watched out of the corner of my eye as she worked refilling coffee, wiping down tables, and delivering food. She smiled at most everyone, but it never reached her eyes. To me, that meant she was more guarded than most people realized. Odd, I didn't get that impression the night I robbed her.

I don't know how much time passed before she appeared with a plate of food and sat it down in front of me. I did a double take at the BLT… I thought I ordered a cheeseburger.

"Do you need anything else?"

"Coffee?" I asked as she looked right at me. I waited for some recognition in her eyes but none came.

She came back to the table with a pot of coffee and filled my cup to the rim, then walked away silently, filling other cups as she went. I pulled out my phone and pretended to be involved with it as I ate the food one handed. Really, I was trying to hear everything she said to get some glimpse into her life.

Turns out my guess she was more guarded than she let on was right. She kept things light and friendly, but professional, so I was only able to get a few small details about her. Like the fact she was allergic to peanuts. I'd hoped for more knowledge so it was entirely frustrating. How was a guy supposed to do recon with an uncooperative Target?

Long after my food was eaten along with two pieces of pie and a third cup of coffee, I was the last guy left in the diner and she was finishing up her shift. The tab was already paid and I pretended to nurse my coffee when really it had gone cold long ago.

She came toward my table with a rag in her hand and wiped down the tables beside me. I got up from my seat, figuring this was the worst night of recon ever. I drank bad coffee, ate a sandwich I didn't understand (salad and bacon on bread… really?) and learned exactly nothing.

I headed for the door when she stepped in front of me and slipped on some water that had spilled on the floor. I caught her around the waist as she fell.

We both seemed to pause in the moment, standing in the center of the empty room, looking like we'd been dancing and I dipped her.

"We keep meeting like this," I murmured, thinking of the night she slipped on ice and I caught her. Only this time I wasn't trying to steal her money.

Her eyes widened and her voice was breathless. "Do I know you?"

We both straightened and I stepped back. "Of course not. I… You just remind me of someone." I adjusted the glasses on my nose.

She stared at me like she was actually just seeing me for the first time all night. Then she seemed to shake herself and smile. "Thanks."

I nodded and went past her to push out the door into the freezing night. Outside on the sidewalk, I paused to catch my breath. What was I thinking? I couldn't say things like that. She'd think I was a freak and stay as far away as possible. That would make it hard to kill her. Unless I did the killing from afar.

Yeah, maybe that would be better than this recon stuff.

I walked a few paces from the diner. When I got home, I'd make a plan on how to kill her from a distance.

Behind me the bell on the door jingled, indicating it swung open again. I didn't bother looking back.

"Hey!" someone called.

I stopped and turned.

She was there, rushing toward me, pulling a dark-green coat around her. She had snow in her hair. I didn't realize it was snowing.

"Yeah?" I asked, wondering if she was really talking to me.

Now that she had my attention, she seemed to grow a little shy. I just stood there and waited as I watched the snowflakes take up residence on her head.

"Do you have a car?" she asked.

I nodded and motioned down the street toward the Roadster. "Right down there."

She glanced at the Roadster, then at me. "Is that thing any good in the snow?"

I shrugged. "Guess I'll find out."

"Oh, is it new?"

I nodded again.

"Can I have a ride home?"

My eyes snapped to her face. She wanted a ride? From some guy she didn't know? Maybe killing her wouldn't be that hard after all. Maybe she already had a death wish.

She seemed to know what I was thinking because she said, "I know, it's kind of weird of me to ask… but it's really cold and I don't feel like walking."

"Don't you usually take the bus?" I blurted, thinking back once again to the night I died. Inwardly, I kicked myself. I needed to stop saying things like that. You'd think for two people who knew each other for exactly two minutes, there wouldn't be any history for me to keep bringing up.

She glanced at the bus stop and then back at me. She didn't seem to think what I said was unusual and I was relieved.

"I don't really like the bus," she said quietly.

We both stood there awkwardly for long seconds before I remembered it was my turn to talk. I pulled the keys from my pocket.

"I'll give you a ride. Come on."

And before I knew it, we were climbing into the tiny space of the two-seater.

She glanced at me and smiled tentatively when I turned the heat on full blast and it was only then I realized I just told myself I was going to stay away from her. Far away.

So much for that idea, I thought as I pulled away from the curb.

* * *

I drove slowly because once she wondered if my Roadster might not be very good in the snow, I started to wonder that too. I hadn't had any problems up until this point so I just tried to enjoy the fact I was riding around in a car that cost more than a hundred grand. (I looked it up online). She didn't say anything on the ride, except to give me directions, and I didn't try to make small talk.

She didn't live that far from the diner and when I pulled up in front of her apartment building, I left the engine idling at the curb. She glanced out her window and upwards so I assumed her apartment wasn't on the ground floor.

"I almost died the other day," she said quietly, still gazing out her window.

My hand tightened over the gearshift when I realized she was talking about the day I got crushed by that bus. When I didn't say anything, she turned in the seat and looked at me through the dark.

"But I didn't because someone saved me."

I swallowed, my eyes locked on hers. "Wow," I said, not really sure how to respond. Why was she telling me this?

"Maybe you heard about the accident? It was in the newspaper." She continued to watch me. I couldn't read her expression clearly because the only light in the car came from the dash as the streetlight in front of her building was burned out. Judging from the part of town we were in, that lamp probably hadn't had a bulb change since the nineties.

But even in the practically nonexistent light, I could see the whites of her eyes, and they were focused directly at me.

"I don't read the paper," I replied. "What happened?"

Even though I knew what happened, even though part of me said not to even talk about it, I couldn't help but want to know how she remembered that night.

"I'd just gotten off my shift. It was late, like tonight…" Her voice faded and the whites of her eyes suddenly disappeared. She closed them, like the memory was painful.

Then her eyes reopened and she said, "I was walking home and there was this guy… He was on the sidewalk too. A bus came around the corner and slid on a sheet of black ice. I froze. I knew it was going to hit me, but I couldn't seem to move. But then he pushed me out of the way and the bus hit him instead."

"Wow," I echoed again, wishing this body came with a better vocabulary. My stomach cramped as I remembered the feeling of the bus plowing into me.

"He died right there in the snow. He didn't have any ID. I don't even know his name." Her eyelids closed again and she took a deep breath.

"Didn't the newspaper say who he was?" I asked curiously.

She shook her head. "I don't even think they knew. I called the hospital, but they wouldn't tell me anything."

"You called the hospital?" Why would she do that? Why would she care?

"I wanted to go to his funeral. To at least tell someone what he did, that he saved me—a complete stranger. I wanted to tell him thank you."

"You did," I replied, remembering. She said thank you that night. On the street when she leaned over me. The echo of her words whispered in the back of my mind.

"What did you say?" she asked, her voice losing a little bit of sorrow.

Dumbass. I mentally yelled at myself. Way to make the Target trust you. Say suspicious things so she would run every time she caught a glimpse of you.

I pushed my hand through my hair—surprised to feel it shaking—and took a breath. There was no way she could think what I said was suspicious. There was no possible way on this earth she could know I was the guy who got flattened by the bus. To her, I probably looked like some dude who babbled stuff because he wasn't really listening to what she was saying. I mean, this was probably the first time I ever listened to a girl talk.

"What I meant was you did say thank you. Right now. Where ever he is, maybe he heard you."

She sat there for a long second, then nodded slowly. "Yeah. I hope he heard."

She seemed like she really meant it.

My stomach cramped again and I felt a clammy sweat break out on my forehead. My knee started bouncing up and down, knocking the bottom of the steering wheel.

"Are you all right?" she asked, leaning a little closer.

I lifted my hand to adjust my glasses, and it was visibly shaking. I buried it in my lap and hoped she hadn't seen. "Yeah, I just didn't get that much sleep last night,"

My knee was still bouncing up and down and all of my insides felt jittery and bouncy. Maybe those three cups of coffee weren't a very good idea.

"You don't look too good," she said, reaching across the small interior of the Roadster to brush her hand across my forehead.

I jerked and grabbed her wrist, pulling her closer toward me.

My sudden movement startled her and she fell forward when I yanked her. Her hair fell over her shoulders and brushed against my hand. She wiggled, trying to pull away, and I realized I was squeezing her.

I let go and she moved back into her own seat, rubbing at her wrist.

"I have to go," she said, reaching for the door handle.

"Yeah. Sorry about that. You just took me by surprise." I swallowed back the rising bile. What was wrong with me all of a sudden?

She pushed open her door and cold air rushed inside. I didn't realize how hot it was in the enclosed space until the frigid air slapped me in the face.

"Thanks for the ride," she said, completely out of the car but leaning down to speak.

I nodded and she shut the door, stepping onto the sidewalk toward the stairs of her building.

I didn't hang around to watch her. I was still jittery and my heart hammered in my chest. I sped down the street, not thinking about the icy roads or my car. I didn't even look in the rearview mirror to see if she made it into her building.

It wasn't my job to keep her safe.

As the voice in my head so boldly reminded…

It was my job to kill her.

Chapter Ten

"Vision - the ability or an instance of great perception, esp of future developments."

Piper

I shut the door and leaned against it heavily, trying to calm the swirling emotions inside me. Of all things, that was the last thing I expected to happen to me today. Or any day for that matter.

He was just a regular guy—another customer in the diner, no one I would've normally paid any attention to.

Then he touched me.

The vision was so fast, so swift it would've knocked me on my butt if he didn't have a hold of me. Ironic, really, because the only reason I had the vision at all was because he was holding on to me. It was just like before, exactly the same. It was an abrupt vision—more of an image really—of a man with very dark hair and dark, serious eyes. Those eyes were in direct contrast to the smile he wore on his face. It was a beautiful smile, full of joy.

And that was all of it.

So simple and I wouldn't have thought twice about it if I had it any other time.

But there was nothing simple about this.

Because this vision belonged to someone else. To the man who died.

The fact that I had visions was something I understood as being different, an ability that not everyone (okay, no one) else had. I had my first visualization at the age of fifteen and I really didn't know what it was at the time. And then I saw it happen in real time about two weeks later. I didn't understand how it worked and it took me a while to realize I only had a vision when I touched someone. It took so long to figure out because it didn't happen every time… just sometimes. The visions were *always* about the person I touched and they were always a piece of something that was going to happen to them in the future.

Until now.

Right before he got hit by the bus, the man touched me—he caught me when I slipped. The vision came over me and the next thing I knew I was hitting the sidewalk. When my sight cleared, I saw him lying in the street, clinging to his last breath of life.

Yes, I was studying to be a doctor and I understood death. I accepted it as a part of life. But watching the life drain from a man who was too young to die, watching his eyes, unfocused with pain, trying to focus on something—anything—was heart-wrenching. I'd never felt that kind of loneliness before sitting there in the ice and the snow, knowing there was nothing I could do for him. Knowing his last moments on Earth were full of pain and probably confusion.

Why? Why did he push me—someone he didn't even know—out of the way like that? It was the most selfless thing anyone could ever do, and his heroic action was rewarded with death. Maybe that's why the heroes of the world were becoming few and far between.

I hadn't even thought of the vision until much later, when I was home and the numbness of what happened began to wear off. It was over a steaming mug of Lipton Ginger Twist tea that I saw his smiling face again and I was caught off guard. How could that possibly be his future when he was dead? Why was I seeing him smile with happiness?

Since then, the vision haunted me. I saw it in my dreams. I saw it when I was awake. It was never far from the surface of my mind. Sometimes I clung to it, pretended it was a memory so I could think of the man who gave his life for me as someone other than the broken body I saw upon the ice. I almost convinced myself that the vision had been my mind's way of protecting itself, a way to give me something to hold on to after he died. After all, it was much easier to accept his death when I thought of his smile rather than watching the life drain out of his eyes and seep into the cold street where he lay.

But then the vision came to me again. Not as something I remembered, not as something I thought about, but as a true vision prompted by touch. Except this time I was touching the wrong man.

How could that be? What did it mean?

I had no idea, but when he walked out of that diner tonight, I had to follow. I had to know more about him. What was his connection to that man on the street? Did he know him? Were they friends? I'd never seen him at the diner before, and I was certain I would've remembered him. Maybe he knew his friend died on that street. Maybe it was his way of remembering. Maybe he knew where the body was.

Except he acted like he didn't know about the accident. But the things he said… sometimes I thought he spoke about that night.

We keep meeting like this.

His words drifted like smoke through the back of my mind. I couldn't help but feel like he was referencing when I slipped and the man caught me. But how would he know? There was no one else on the street that night and the witnesses on the bus saw nothing. The bus driver had been so frantic to stop the bus, he remembered only his own panic.

But I remembered. I remembered everything and there was something strange about that man. There was something about him I didn't know, something I wanted to know.

And when I wanted something, I usually got it. I was a woman with a stubborn streak a mile long. It was only a matter of time before I figured out who he was and what this vision really meant.

* * *

I was standing beside the door waiting when I heard the knock. Bursting forward, I yanked it open. "Get in here!" I said as Frankie stepped inside.

"Gheesh, what's the rush?" she asked, but added a little speed to her step. "Did you almost die again?" she demanded, spinning to face me. Her curls were wild, most likely from the wind, and her cheeks were red.

"Frankie!" I gasped. "No, I didn't almost die again."

She pulled off her red coat and threw it on the end of the couch, then sat down in the middle. She was dressed in a pair of dark denim jeans, a fitted T-shirt, and a bright blue blazer over top. The chunky black necklace around her neck was the gift I'd given her for Christmas this past year.

"Why are you still wearing that uniform?" she asked, wrinkling her nose at my waitress outfit.

"Huh?" I asked, looking down. "I guess I forgot to change."

"You smell like the diner."

"Who cares?" I said. "I had another vision," I told her excitedly.

"That's like an almost everyday occurrence, Pipe. Why would you call me over here for that?"

"I had it before. The night I touched the guy who got hit by the bus,"

"So you're having visions now without having to touch people?" she asked, intrigued.

I shook my head. "No. I did touch someone. Someone else."

"Tell me more," she urged.

I explained about the guy in the diner, the things he said, about getting a ride home, and how the visions were exactly the same. When I finished I stopped my pacing and looked at Frankie who was still sitting on the couch.

"You asked a stranger for a ride home?" she asked, lifting her sculpted eyebrow.

"Yes. Who cares about that? Did you hear what I said about the vision?"

"Well, I care. I don't really want to have to ID your body at the morgue." She sniffed. But then she said, "So what do you think the vision means?"

"I don't know." I frowned. I couldn't figure it out. "I was hoping you could help me."

"I'll help you if you take off that stinky uniform," she said, standing up and pulling me along to my bedroom. I stood there while she opened up the door to the tiniest closet known to man and peered in. Her blond head reappeared moments later, and she said "Your wardrobe is pathetic."

I rolled my eyes. We had this conversation hundreds of times. "I'm a struggling college student. I don't have money for clothes."

"Girl, you gotta get your priorities straight. I know you want to be some hero doctor, but you gotta look the part. Dying people don't want to look at a fugly mess."

I laughed. But then I thought about the man on the street. I wondered if he was able to see me before he died. Suddenly, it did seem important to look pretty.

Frankie must've noticed the change in me because she sighed. "It's not that bad in here. We can find something."

"Frankie. Will you help me?" I said, plopping down on the end of my twin-size bed.

She appeared again, this time with a scarf around her neck and several articles of clothing draped over her arms. "Of course I will; you know that." She thrust a pair of jeans at me and a long-sleeved white T-shirt.

I stood up and stepped into the jeans, pulling them up under my waitress skirt. "Well, what I want you to do is kinda illegal."

"Oooh. Do tell," she sang as she dove back into my closet. I had no idea what she was doing because I had hardly any clothes.

"Well, he drives this really fancy car. It's a Mercedes Roadster." I began and I heard her gasp from somewhere in the closet.

"You're just now telling me this? Is he rich? Is he cute? Does he have a brother?" Her words tripped over each other.

"I have no idea about any of that stuff," I said. "Anyway, I was thinking—"

Frankie cut me off to say, "How can you know none of this? Have I taught you nothing?!"

"He wasn't the talkative type," I said, discarding my uniform completely and pulling on the T-shirt.

"He's a serial killer. I knew it. He drives that car to lure in poor women."

I laughed again. "Oh my God, Frank. You're so paranoid. Will you just listen already?"

She sniffed. "Fine. But if you die, I'm not crying at your funeral."

"You will too," I argued.

"Fine. I will. But only a little."

"Anyway," I said, trying to get back to the subject. "I was hoping you could, you know, look him up, see where he lives?"

"I knew working at the Motor Vehicle Administration would be good for something someday, other than making me feel dead inside."

She now had a hat on her head, three bracelets on her right wrist, and one glove on her left hand.

"What are you doing and where did you get that bracelet?"

She wagged her eyebrows. "I told you I could find something."

"I got his license plate number when he drove off earlier. I'll give it to you and you can look him up."

"I'll do it on Wednesday. My supervisor is off. She has an appointment to get the broom she flies on serviced."

"You're too much," I said, giggling.

"I know you love me," she said, stepping back from the closet. It was organized into outfits that all hung together with accessories and everything.

"How'd you do that?"

She smiled and draped the chunky knit scarf around my neck. "It's a calling," she said and sighed. "Come on, I'm taking you to a late-night movie. You've been working and thinking too much lately."

"Can we get popcorn?"

"Sure, I already have it stashed in my purse. Candy too. That usher won't dare try to search me after what happened last time." She wagged her eyebrows.

I grinned at the memory of the very embarrassed usher's face. "I've never seen any guy get so flustered in all my life."

"It takes a special kind of man to handle all of this," she said, motioning to herself. "He was out of his element."

Most men were out of their element when it came to Frankie. Most women, too. But she was the best friend I could ever hope for. I wondered about what kind of information she would find on Wednesday. I wondered what his name would be. Most of all, I wondered what I would do with the information when I got it.

Chapter Eleven

"Reconnaissance - the process of obtaining information about the position, activities, resources, etc., of an enemy or potential enemy."

Dex

My recon mission didn't really go the way I planned. I couldn't call it a complete failure because I found out where she lived, but I wouldn't call it a success either. I acted so weird she probably wanted nothing more to do with me, and then I started feeling sick. My being sick probably had nothing at all to do with her (and everything to do with that nasty BLT), but I couldn't really shake the knowledge that as soon as I put some miles between us, I started to feel better.

Maybe the idea of killing her in such close proximity made me nervous. I'd never been the nervous type before. I mean, living on the streets really wasn't a peaceful place, so me getting nervous to the point of feeling sick around one girl seemed dumb.

Still, I wanted to go back to my decision to not get close to her. To just kill her and be done with it.

So I bought a gun.

Not a big one, nothing that would draw too much attention, but enough that it would get the job done. I stared at it now, taking in the black metal and every detail from the trigger to the tip of the barrel. I never had a gun before. All my years on the streets, I avoided guns because the fact was if you carried one around, it usually got used against you. That or someone was always a quicker draw.

I used to carry a knife for the times violence was unavoidable. But I didn't want to get close enough to use a knife on this Target. Of course, I really wasn't all that excited to use the gun either, but hey, a man's gotta do what a man's gotta do.

She was a college student; that much I heard during my recon mission. Someone asked her about her classes and she gave a fairly generic answer. I had no idea what she studied. I really didn't care. I figured she probably took most of her classes by day, then worked early in the morning or at night. There was one college here in Fairbanks so finding her shouldn't be a problem.

I glanced at the clock. Not quite lunchtime. I took the gun and slid it into the waistband of my jeans. Then I pulled on my coat and shoes. I was going on a field trip.

Chapter Twelve

"Stalker - someone who prowls or sneaks about; usually with unlawful

intentions."

Piper

Morning classes seemed to drag by, like this entire week. I just wanted to get to Wednesday. I wanted to know what Frankie would find out about the guy from the diner. If she got his address, maybe I'd just go to his house and knock on his door. Part of me really wanted to. But part of me thought I was insane. I shouldn't care so much about this one guy.

But I did.

I couldn't get him out of my mind. Whenever I went to sleep, my dreams were filled with his face and then the dream would change and I'd be staring at the man who died. As much as the guy in the diner filled my thoughts, the one who died was there more. There was something about him that pulled at my insides—a part of me that wanted to know him. And now I never would.

"Girl, what's with that long face?"

I looked up to see Frankie coming toward me. She was hard to miss in that red coat, and today she was wearing a pair of black knee-high boots and a black and white scarf full of butterflies.

"Frankie. What are you doing here? I thought you were allergic to college." I teased.

"I'm breaking out in a rash as we speak. Hurry, let's go to the food court so I can get some sugar to counteract all the…"—she made a face—"*learning* that goes on here."

"That's where I was heading. I don't have another class for an hour."

"Yes. I know. BFF here, remember? I know your schedule," she said, exasperated.

I smiled. "Well, shouldn't you be at work?"

"I took a lunch break." She shrugged.

"Is everything okay?" I asked. She never came to see me at school.

"Of course," she said, then leaned in close. "I got the info you wanted early."

Excitement tingled along my fingers. "How did you manage that? I thought you had to wait until your supervisor wasn't there."

"I like a challenge." She smiled slyly.

I grinned and shifted the weight of the books in my arms. "Well, tell me!" I demanded.

"Girl you're going to collapse under those books. Come on. I parked right over there." She pointed to the parking lot. "You can put these in there until after we eat." She grabbed a couple books off my stack and headed toward the car. "You must really want to be a doctor, putting up with all these books."

"You know I want to help people,"

"I help people all the time. You should've seen this woman today that came in for her license renew. She was blind in one eye and only had half the vision in her other eye! I have no clue how she even got a license in the first place. I refused to renew it. You know how many lives I saved by keeping her off the road?"

I snickered as she unlocked the passenger door of her Jeep Wrangler and threw in my books. After I added the rest to the pile, she slammed the door and we began walking. A strange feeling crept its way up the back of my neck and I turned back, looking over my shoulder at the parking lot. I didn't see anything other than students heading to and from campus.

"What's wrong?" Frankie asked.

"Nothing. I just got this weird feeling,"

Frankie looked over her shoulder too and saw exactly what I saw: nothing.

"You need sugar," she said, pulling me along.

"So what did you find out?" I asked, trying to ignore the prickly feeling I couldn't seem to shake. It felt like someone was drilling a hole into my back with their watchful eyes.

"Crap!" I said suddenly, stopping midstride. "I think I dumped my money in your car with my books." I turned to face back toward the parking lot and I swear I saw a dark shape almost glide behind a nearby building. My eyes narrowed on the spot, waiting for more movement, but none came.

"Are you sure?" Frankie asked.

I shook my head and stuck my fingers into my coat pocket. The little pouch I used to carry my money was there. "Oh, never mind, it's here,"

We started walking again. "Frank," I whispered quickly. "Six o'clock and a little to my left. Is someone following us?"

Frankie laughed like I said something funny and threw her head back and to the side. I saw her eyes darting around. "I don't see anyone but a couple of students walking around."

I nodded. "I could've sworn I saw someone behind the building back there."

"You're jumpy today," Frankie said, sliding me a look.

"I do feel a little anxious." I thought it was because I wanted to know what Frankie would dig up about the man in the diner. Now I was wondering if that had been the real reason.

We picked up our pace toward the building that housed the food court. Students were coming in and out steadily. I glanced at my left toward a pile of snow left over from the plow and caught another dark shape duck down behind me. How had it gotten just ahead of me when only moments before it was behind?

I watched the spot, but nothing happened so I kept quiet. The building was just in front of us now with a long, clear sidewalk leading to the main doors. I pulled them open and we walked inside. The student center was three stories with us coming in on the middle landing. There was a wide open area with wide steps leading down to a bookstore and some leading upstairs toward the food court. Over to my right was a large, bright blue UAF tapestry with the college logo on it—a polar bear—that hung from long cables in the ceiling.

Behind it, I saw another dark movement.

Someone was definitely watching me. Someone who was incredibly fast.

I had enough. I lunged forward, quickly covering the space between myself and the tapestry, my eyes locked on the hooded figure that was frozen. He knew I saw him. He knew he'd been caught.

I made it to the side where he stood and I pulled back the tapestry, stepping behind it, reaching toward the darkened shape that now turned away. My hands closed around his arm... and went through.

I was left grasping at black smoke... my fingers trying to hold something that had no shape.

And then it was gone.

I stood there, stupefied, staring at the wall, wondering if I'd imagined the entire thing.

I felt the tapestry being yanked forward and then from behind me Frankie said, "Umm, are you having a private moment back here with... the wall?"

"I... I thought I saw someone."

"There's no one here," Frankie said gently, grabbing the sleeve of my coat and pulling me toward the stairs. "Come on. You're gonna eat some sugar whether you like it or not."

"Yeah." I agreed. "I think I will."

As we went up the stairs I gazed back. The tapestry was swinging slightly from our movements, but otherwise there was nothing there.

I looked beyond that out the glass doors and onto the sidewalk. Someone was walking swiftly away from the building. Someone in a dark coat and hat. His shoulders were hunched up around his neck and his hands were jammed into his pockets. A whisper of something—recognition?—went through me before he disappeared from sight.

At least he looked solid and real, not at all like a ghost.

Chapter Thirteen

"Reject - To refuse to accept, submit to, believe, or make use of. Fail to accept as part of one's own body."

Dex

I turned up the heat in the Roadster as high as it would go and tried to calm my tossing stomach. My hands were shaking and I felt this weird kind of pulling sensation beneath my ribs. I took a shuddering breath and ripped off my gloves, sticking my hands as close to the heater as I could, and stared through the windshield across the parking lot of the college campus. Even parked way in the nose-bleed section, it was full. This place was full of people.

But that wasn't why I didn't go through with my plan.

And it had been a good plan.

A college shooting was practically a normal occurrence these days. Apparently, violence wasn't regulated to just the streets of the ghetto anymore. According to the news on my flat screen, this world was going to hell in a hand basket. Guess I wouldn't be lonely when I got there.

I figured I could fire a couple wild shots around and "accidentally" hit Piper with a bullet. In all the chaos, I could get away, call Mr. Burns like he asked, and collect my raise and my body.

But that was before I saw she was being followed. By someone that wasn't me.

I managed to catch up with her minutes before the girl in the red coat appeared, following her with ease until I noticed the dark shape that darted in and out behind her and then appeared seconds later yards in front of her. It was odd. And it kind of pissed me off.

No one was taking out this Target but me. I had too much on the line here. I wanted my body back, I wanted to keep my car and my house, and I wanted a pay raise so I could buy whatever I wanted. So I followed and I watched.

It was interesting to me that she figured out she was being followed. This girl was no pushover. She seemed to be aware of things that no one else would be… even when she appeared deep in thought.

I watched her when her shoulders stiffened slightly, when she scanned the parking lot and then stopped to look over her shoulder. At first I was worried she'd made me. But she kept looking where the other guy was; she seemed to catch on to his quick movements. Clearly, sneaking up on this girl wasn't an option.

I followed her and the girl she spoke to, the weight of the gun reminding me of my job the entire time, all the way to the building with the double glass doors until they went inside. Then, because I couldn't help myself, I walked as close to the doors as I could and peered inside.

I saw the stalker peek out from behind that oversized blanket. I saw her see him. I wanted to laugh when she went after him, instead of running. I watched her tear back the blanket, saw her arm shoot out, and could imagine her spinning him around and demanding an explanation.

Better him than me, I'd thought.

Except then she came back out with this weird look on her face. It looked a lot like disbelief. And then her friend was leading her away, up the stairs, like she was a psych patient that needed care. I watched the blanket; I waited for the stalker to reveal himself.

But he never did.

It's like he hadn't been there at all.

Yet I saw him.

So had Piper.

My hands were shaking uncontrollably at that point. I felt like I was going to barf all over the sidewalk, yet there was this urgency inside me that seemed to push me… but I had no idea where it wanted me to go.

So I got out of there.

I had to.

And now here I was, sitting in my car with the butt of a gun digging into my back.

Did someone else want Piper dead?

I yanked the gun out of my waistband and stared down at it in my hands. There would be no shooting today. Something else was going on here and I wanted to know what it was. I leaned forward and opened up the glove compartment and tossed the gun inside. I was glad to get it away from me. Maybe shooting her wasn't the way to go. Even still, I would keep it. Just in case.

As I leaned back into my seat, something caught my eye. Something red. I ducked down, thinking maybe they'd seen me after all and her friend in the red coat was coming after me. But after long minutes of no one appearing beside my car, I rose, peeking over the dashboard to look across the parking lot.

He was there. Walking among everyone else. But he was different.

Why did no one notice? Why did no one turn to stare?

The guy was completely surrounded in red, almost as if the very air around his body had been stained with the bright color.

He had his hands stuffed into a black coat, a hat on his head, and his chin tucked into his chest. I guess he looked pretty ordinary, if you didn't count the flaming ring of color. I watched him for long moments; I watched the people around him. He didn't speak to anyone and no one spoke to him. No one paid him any attention at all. It was like he was just another student hurrying to class. I blinked my eyes, thinking they were playing tricks on me. But no matter how hard I blinked, the red was still there.

I watched him until he was completely out of sight, and then I noticed my hands were still shaking and I still felt sick. I swallowed, turning on the car, and with one last glimpse where the man had been, I pulled away. I drove slowly, staring at everyone through the windshield, watching for someone or something else bathed in red. But everything looked normal. When I turned out of the parking lot and onto the main road, the cramping in my stomach loosened and my shaking hands began to steady.

What was wrong with me? Was I going crazy? Or could the nagging feeling, my illness, and now my eyes playing tricks on me be linked to Piper? Or was it something else? What if it was this body? Maybe it was somehow rejecting me. I didn't know if it was possible, but after everything I'd experienced since I died, it wasn't that far of a stretch.

Chapter Fourteen

"News - interesting or important information not previously known or realized."

Piper

"Tell me already," I begged Frankie as I sipped the hot tea, into which she dumped half a bottle of honey.

"Not until you promise me that what I saw back there wasn't you having some kind of psychotic break."

"Said the girl with a piece of pie, a cinnamon roll, and a caramel coffee sitting in front of her."

"Hey, there's a salad too. Didn't you see my salad?" She pointed to the lettuce and carrots covered in dressing being ignored in favor of the cinnamon roll. "Besides, the craziest people I know are the ones who don't eat sugar." She stared pointedly at me.

I saluted her with my cup full of honey.

"I just want to be sure you're okay," she said seriously.

"I am. Really. I just thought I saw something that wasn't there." I sighed. "It's just been a long few days. I've been waiting desperately to hear what you would find out."

I hoped the reminder would finally get her to spill the beans about what she learned about the guy from the diner.

"You eat; I talk," she said, pointing to my turkey on wheat. I dutifully took a bite and she dug out a slip of paper from the pocket of her coat hanging on the back of her chair.

"You probably aren't going to like what I'm about to tell you,"

"He's married," I said, a hard knot forming in my stomach.

Frankie looked at me strangely. "I find it very telling that the worst news you could get from me is that this guy is married. I think you're interested in him more than just because of"—she wagged her eyebrows and leaned in—"you know."

I just stared at her. She sighed dramatically. "Because of your vision."

I leaned in and whispered, "Yes, I know." Then I straightened. "And I am *not* interested in him that way. I'm not interested in men that way at all right now. I'm too busy with school and trying to get my life together." I didn't want to live in a tiny apartment in the worst part of town all my life and since I had no family to help me, giving myself a better life was solely on me.

"Then why do you care if he's married?"

I really didn't have an answer for that.

"Just give me the paper already," I said, flustered, and snatched it out of her hand.

I looked down at it, then back up at her. "Dexter Allen Roth." I read and then looked back up.

Frankie nodded sagely. "I told you it wasn't good."

I burst out laughing. "It's not that bad."

Dexter Allen Roth. So that was his name.

"Only a girl with a massive crush would think that name was anything but a mouthful."

I suppressed a smile and looked at the paper in my hand again. "Is this his address?"

"Assuming that's really his car and his name…," Frankie said, sipping her latte.

"You think the car is stolen." I said, flat.

Frankie sighed. "I did, but I checked the stolen car list we have. None match that make or model."

"The address is in a nice neighborhood," I said.

Frankie nodded. "Yeah, maybe the guy is loaded."

"I don't care how much money he has," I said, still looking at the address.

"Yeah, I know," Frankie said, setting her coffee down. "So what are you gonna do with that information?"

I thought about that as I gathered up my tray and cup. "I'm going to go see him."

"You're going to just knock on his door?"

I shrugged. "Yeah. Why not?"

"You got guts." Frankie grinned, but then the grin fell away. "I just hope he isn't some weird car-stealing stalker," she replied as we threw all our trash away.

My eyes wandered toward the stairs and toward the tapestry where I could've sworn I saw someone. Then I thought about the figure I saw hurrying away from the building. It could've been a student rushing to class.

It could have been someone else.

I really hoped Frankie wasn't right.

Chapter Fifteen

"Anaphylactic shock - a severe, sometimes fatal, reaction to a substance to which a person has an extreme sensitivity, often involving respiratory difficulty and circulation failure."

Dex

I looked up "ways to die" on the internet. I didn't find any ways to possibly kill a Target, but I did learn I wasn't the stupidest guy on the planet. Apparently there was a waiting list for that and it was very, very long. According to one site, one of the manliest ways to die was by lighting yourself on fire. It seemed to me the manliest way to die would be to not die at all. Self-preservation is a lot harder than most people realize. Probably because more people live closer to the way I do now than the way I did before I died.

I clicked through the videos and articles, searching for something that might actually give me some ideas. I never thought in a million years as I was living on the violent streets of the city that I would need ideas on how to kill someone. And I guess I really didn't need ideas… It was just that the ideas I had weren't something I cared to live again.

I was looking through an article about asphyxiation when the doorbell rang. I glanced up past the computer screen and into the kitchen where Hobbs was cooking up some dinner.

"I will see who that is, sir," he said, grabbing his cane and going to the front door.

I returned my attention to the computer screen. "Tell them to go away." I didn't have any friends so I knew it wasn't anyone I wanted to see.

A few moments later Hobbs came back into the room, clearing his throat. "You have a visitor."

"I'm busy, Hobbs," I said, annoyed.

"*Sir,*" he said again, with more emphasis, and I looked up.

I was so shocked I almost fell out of my chair.

Piper was standing a few feet behind him and she was looking at me. "Piper," I said, getting up from the chair. "I-I... How did you know where I lived?"

Her eyes narrowed and she glanced back toward the front door. "How did you know my name?"

"It was on your nametag... at the diner."

"Oh. Right," she said, looking a little less alarmed.

Hobbs mumbled something about leaving us alone and then left the room.

"How did you know where I lived?" It was my turn to act suspicious. When, really, I was thrilled she was here.

She winced. "I had my friend run your license plate number."

I digested that. So the car was registered to me and not to Mr. Burns. He must be pretty confident I would finish the job.

I grinned, ignoring the queasiness once again building in my stomach. "You must have really wanted to see me again," I said, enjoying the way her face flushed.

"Actually, I wanted to ask you about something."

I adjusted the glasses on my nose as a wave of dizziness passed over me. My eyes darted around the room, looking for something, but I didn't know what.

"Are you okay?" she asked and came closer, her eyes wandering toward my computer screen.

I reached out and slammed the lid of the laptop closed, not wanting her to see what I'd been looking at, and then turned back to her. "Yeah, I'm fine." I lied.

Why was I feeling sick again all of a sudden?

"You don't look too good. Have you been sick?"

"Me? No. I'm just hungry. Hobbs is cooking dinner. Would you like to stay and join me?" I glanced into the empty kitchen where Hobbs had been. "Hobbs!" I yelled.

"I really just came to ask you something."

"You can ask me while we eat," I said as Hobbs came into the room.

"You bellowed, sir?"

"Piper is going to be joining me for dinner," I told him.

"Certainly. It will be ready shortly." He went back into the kitchen to finish frying some chicken. My eyes zeroed in on the bottle of peanut oil by the big pot on the stove. I could hardly believe my good luck. It was almost too easy.

Here I was trying to come up with ways to catch my prey when my prey came right to me. And to top it off, my butler just happened to be cooking with something that she was allergic to. With any luck, this job would be completed by tonight.

"Come, sit down," I told Piper and headed toward the living room. "We can talk while Hobbs finishes dinner."

Piper followed as I plopped down on the couch. She stood beside it and lifted her eyebrow. "You have a butler?"

I shrugged. "A guy's gotta eat."

"You seem kind of young to be able to afford that car and a butler."

I liked the way she crossed her arms over her chest, like she'd somehow caught me in a lie.

"Trust fund," I said with a shrug and picked up the remote control to the flat screen.

"Figures," she muttered.

I suppressed a grin. "Have a seat." I motioned to the couch with the remote.

She sat down on the end and I channel surfed. Really, I wasn't paying any attention at all to the TV. I was too busy wondering about the way my hand shook and trying not to stare at her when everything in me was demanding I look at only her.

I finally gave in and shifted my gaze. Her dark hair was long and framed her face; her brown eyes seemed to take in everything around the room. When they settled on me, the twisting of my stomach seemed to quiet.

"So what do you want to ask me?" I said.

She nodded. "I just got this feeling the other night that you maybe knew more about the accident I was telling you about."

I tried not to outwardly react. I knew I'd said too much. This girl was far too perceptive. "Why would you think that?"

"Well," she replied. "Right after I told you about what happened to me, you seemed to get upset." She paused before she went on. "I thought maybe you might have known the guy who died and me bringing it up bothered you."

"I told you I hadn't heard about the accident." In my mind I replayed everything from that night. She'd caught me off guard by bringing it all up, and then I started to feel sick… She must have thought that was because I knew more than I let on.

"I know you said that, but…" Her voice trailed away.

"You thought I lied." I finished for her, slightly annoyed.

I didn't really like being accused of lying. Even if I was.

"No," she began, but Hobbs interrupted.

"Dinner is served," he said. "If you should require anything else, please call."

"Thank you, Hobbs," I said, grateful he cut in when he did. He nodded and then went upstairs.

"I'm starving," I said, getting up from the couch. "I hope you like chicken."

"Yes, I do." Piper agreed, following me into the kitchen where Hobbs had set out several dishes full of food on the island. I grabbed a plate and piled it high with fried chicken, mashed potatoes, and green beans.

Piper followed, her plate not looking nearly as full as mine. I casually glanced behind me where Hobbs had been frying the chicken to see if the oil was still out, but thankfully it wasn't.

I went and sat down and tore into a piece of chicken. I made a sound of appreciation. "This is really good," I said around a mouthful.

"What were you doing at the diner that night if you have such a wonderful cook here at home?"

I paused my chewing. She never gave up. "I was out shopping so I stopped by for a bite. It was late and I wasn't going to come home and make him cook me something."

"That was very thoughtful of you," she said, forking up a bite of potatoes. I tried not to stare pointedly at the chicken on her plate.

"I'm a thoughtful kind of guy," I said and took another huge bite.

"I wondered if maybe you came by the diner because you knew the man who died right outside," she said, watching me.

I choked on the food as I swallowed and grabbed up a glass of water that was sitting nearby and took a drink. After several moments, I looked at her. "I don't—*didn't*—know the guy who died."

We both lapsed into silence and I focused completely on eating. Then, because I really wanted to know, I said, "Why do you care so much about this guy anyway? He's dead."

When she didn't answer, I looked up. At the same moment, her fork clattered onto her plate and she looked at me. Her breaths were coming in short gasps.

"Peanuts," she wheezed. "I'm allergic to peanuts."

As I stared at her, red welts began to appear on her cheeks and neck. She pushed her chair away from the island and tried to stand, but she stumbled and caught herself on the counter. I reached out to steady her.

"Piper? What's going on? Are you okay?" I said, trying to sound concerned, realizing it wasn't hard to do.

She tried to say something, but I couldn't understand her words. I clutched her arm and turned her to face me and saw that her lips and tongue were swelling rapidly. She made a motion with her arm, toward the front door.

"Ppputthhhh," she said.

"What?"

She said it again. I grabbed my phone off the counter. "I'm calling 9-1-1." I knew by the time they got here she'd be dead.

"Nnnoo." She pointed again toward the front hallway. "Pppuuthhh."

"You want your purse?" I said, finally understanding.

She nodded rapidly. I released her and ran into the entryway, grabbing her bag. Then I stopped. I didn't want her to realize I'd known all along about her allergy to peanuts, but I also didn't want to move so fast I ended up saving her life.

I heard a light thump and forgot my thoughts, rushing back into the room. She'd fallen or sat down on the floor and was leaning against the base of the island. Her face was completely red and her head was lolling to the side. I could hear her struggling for air.

I could see her suffer.

I saw the unfocused panic in her eyes.

I didn't like this.

I dropped to my knees beside her. "Piper!" I yelled when her head rolled away from me. "Piper!"

I dumped the entire contents of her bag out onto the floor and stuff went flying. I wasn't really sure what I was looking for and figured it was some kind of medicine. I shifted through all the stuff and none of it looked like it would be what she wanted. I grabbed her by the shoulders and looked into her swollen face.

"Tell me what you need." My heart pounded and everything inside me felt frantic. "Tell me!" I demanded.

She couldn't talk. She was too far gone.

In mere seconds she was probably going to pass out from lack of oxygen.

I shook my head. *No.*

Something inside me whispered, *Yes.*

I didn't want her to die.

Yes. Yes you do.

"Piper…," I said again. "Piper, I'm sorry."

And then Hobbs was there, pushing me out of the way with strength such a small man shouldn't possess, and he was stabbing her in the outer thigh with something.

"What the hell are you doing, Hobbs!?!" I demanded.

"I'm helping her," he replied without looking back at me.

He dropped the tube in his other hand and I grabbed it up to look at it. Epinephrine. "Is this medicine? Is she going to be okay?"

"Call an ambulance," Hobbs said, finally turning around. His face was sad.

"Hobbs! Is she going to die?" How could that idea fill me with so much dread, yet so much hope?

"No, she's going to be okay, but she needs a doctor."

I let out a breath and then started looking for my phone. In all the confusion, I couldn't remember what happened to it. I found it on the floor in the entryway underneath her coat. I went back to her side, dropping to my knees next to her head.

"I'm calling for help,"

"No," she rasped. "No ambulance."

"Piper?" I looked down, surprised she was talking.

"Good stuff," she said and glanced at the epinephrine tube still in my hand.

"You need a doctor."

She nodded. "You take me."

"Yeah. Yeah, I can do that." I felt shaky, like the time I'd almost gotten caught robbing the corner convenience store in my old neighborhood and I jumped out the bathroom window and ran for three blocks before stopping.

She grabbed my arm. "Thank you," she said.

"Don't thank me. It was Hobbs. He knew what to do."

She looked past me at Hobbs and I moved away to begin gathering all the stuff that scattered when I dumped out her bag.

Hobbs moved beside her and leaned down. "Please accept my sincere apologies. I feel awful knowing something I cooked caused such a reaction."

"I should've asked," Piper began, her voice shaky. "I usually do, I just… I didn't think of it today."

I paused and glanced over at her. She was watching me and I quickly looked away.

She'd been too busy trying to figure out what my connection was to the man who died. Her distraction had almost been my success.

I should've been disappointed that my plan didn't work.

I wasn't.

Chapter Sixteen

"Suspicious - Arousing or apt to arouse suspicion; questionable. Tending to suspect; distrustful."

Piper

I felt as if someone wound a coarse length of rope around me and then yanked, cinching up my skin, squeezing my organs, and then tying it into a knot. Everything inside me was shaking; everything inside me still felt seized by panic.

I hadn't felt this way in so long. Even still, this was a feeling I could go a hundred years without ever experiencing again and I would still be able to remember it; I would still fear it.

I was usually so careful about what I ate.

I let my guard down. I didn't think. I was so busy trying to figure out the puzzle that Dexter Allen Roth was that it nearly cost me my life. If the butler hadn't been there, I might be dead. And there would be no one to blame but myself.

Dexter hadn't known what to do. If I closed my eyes I could still see the panic on his face and that alone was very telling because his panic was able to get through mine—and mine had been crippling. So I couldn't blame him for not immediately taking action.

"You still with me over there?"

I turned my head and looked across the seat at Dexter. He was focused on the road, but then his eyes flicked to me and back. I cleared my throat. My tongue still felt thick and heavy in my mouth.

"Yeah. It's up here on the left." I directed him.

A moment later we were pulling into the clinic's parking lot and I let out a sigh of relief. I knew I was going to be okay. I had known that the very second the adrenaline in that

EpiPen coursed through my body, loosening my lungs to allow room for air.

Dexter slid into a spot and cut the engine. Before I could do anything, he opened my door and reached in to help me out. He wrapped his arm around my waist and accepted most of my weight as we made our way to the clinic doors. I hoped they weren't busy. The last thing they needed was having to tend to one of their own.

When the front doors opened, Gladys looked up from the desk. Her eyes widened and she stood. The chair she sat in rolled away behind her.

"Ohmygoodness," she said so quickly all her words ran together. Then she was yelling for Dr. Cooper and rushed toward us. "Piper, honey, what happened to you?"

"She had a reaction." Dexter tried to explain.

Gladys shot him a look. "Who are you?"

"My name's Dex," he said.

My lips pulled up. Of course he called himself Dex.

"Anaphylactic shock," I told her, drawing her attention away from him. "I used the EpiPen."

They ushered me back to exam room one and then Gladys pinned Dex with a stare. "Out."

He glanced at me and I nodded. "I'll be in the waiting room," he said, then disappeared through the door.

"Who is that boy? What happened to you?"

I shook my head. "It wasn't his fault. I wasn't paying attention to what I was eating."

She bustled around the room, taking my blood pressure and my pulse and asking me questions. Dr. Cooper let himself in the room halfway through and stood silently watching. When Gladys was done he took over and I had to sit through his poking too.

When he was done, he made a few notes in his chart and then looked at me. "Your blood pressure is a little low. Are you having difficulty breathing?"

I shook my head. "No. But my chest feels tight."

He nodded. "It probably will for a day or so. You're going to be sore tomorrow. Normally I would want to keep you here or send you over to the ER, but since you know what you're doing…" He gave me a mischievous look. "You have been going to class and paying attention, haven't you?"

I smiled. "Yes."

He nodded. "Okay, then. I'd say you're fine to go home. But if you feel any worse or experience any new symptoms or swelling, call me immediately. You have my number."

When he was gone, Gladys looked at me. "I'm going to get you a bottle of Benadryl to take home. Take some later. It'll help with those hives."

"Yes, ma'am."

"And don't come in tomorrow afternoon. Stay home and rest!"

"Oh, that isn't necessary," I said, my throat finally loosening some.

"Don't you sass me. You're going to thank me tomorrow." She went to the door. "And when I come back, I wanna know about that boy in the waiting room."

She left and I was blissfully alone. The silence was nice after all the chaos. My body was still wound tight and I felt lightly anxious. My stomach was upset and underneath it all, I was bone tired. I didn't like being the patient. I didn't like feeling helpless.

There was a soft knock at the door and then Dex stuck his head inside. "Can I come in?"

I nodded and he let himself in, closing the door silently behind him. "Everything okay?"

"I'm still a little shaky, but I'll be okay. I'm sorry about all the drama."

"I should be the one apologizing. I invited you for dinner, then fed you something that landed you here." He looked down at the floor as he spoke.

"I'm allergic to peanuts. It's a pretty severe allergy. The chicken was probably fried in peanut oil." I explained. "It wasn't your fault."

"You don't blame me?" he asked, almost like he was surprised.

"Why would I? It's not like you knew I was allergic to peanuts and deliberately fed them to me." I gave him a look. "Right?"

He looked like a deer caught in a pair of headlights. His eyes were wide and his face was frozen in fear and shock.

I smiled. "Relax. I'm kidding."

His face melted and he smiled. "At least let me give you a ride home."

"Thanks."

Gladys came back carrying a small paper sack. She stopped when she saw Dex in the room. "What are you doing in here?"

Once again, he looked like the deer.

"He's my ride," I said. "Can I please go?"

"You sure you trust this guy?" she asked, not even trying to lower her voice.

I laughed, but it hurt too much and I clamped my lips closed.

Gladys sighed. "Fine. Go. I'm going to call you later."

"I'll answer," I said, getting down from the table. Dex came to my side, but I waved him back. I didn't want to touch him and risk another vision. I hadn't had one since we first met, but I wasn't about to push it. After everything I'd been through tonight, having that vision again might push me over the edge.

When we stepped outside, I welcomed the freezing air. It felt good against my cheeks, which were still covered in hives. His car was parked right at the curb in front of the doors. He went ahead of me and opened the passenger-side door and I sank into the buttery leather seat. I could get use to this car.

He drove to my apartment without any directions and at first I thought that was suspicious until I remembered he'd already brought me home once. Except this time he didn't just pull up to the curb to drop me off. This time he found a parking spot.

"I'll walk you to the door," he said, not waiting for me to agree or deny, but coming around and helping me out of the two-seater. The walk to my front door seemed endless and when we got there, I had to dig through my bag to find my keys because everything was in a large heap at the bottom. Finally, I found them and unlocked the door, swinging it open and reaching inside to switch on the light.

"Do you want to come in for a minute?" I asked, my mind thinking maybe we could finish our conversation from earlier.

He followed me inside and I shut the door, throwing one of the locks. He was standing in the center of the room, taking in everything. "This is a nice place," he said.

I made a sound, not really agreeing or disagreeing. It was in a crappy neighborhood and was as tiny as a shoebox, but I spent some time trying to make it look nice and feel like a home.

"It's okay. I did what I could."

"I like it," he said, running his hand along the back of the couch where I kept a soft blanket. "It's real."

Real? That was kind of an odd thing to say. "Your house is really nice too."

"Yeah, *my* house."

He seemed to put some emphasis on the word.

"It is yours, right?"

He must've heard the curiosity in my voice because he glanced at me. "Yeah. I just moved there so it doesn't really feel real yet—you know? This place... it seems lived in."

I nodded. "New house and a new car." I went over to the couch and sat down, sighing in relief. "Did you just move here, too?"

"Something like that," he said, looking over at the small window to his left. "How long have you lived here?"

"About a year. It's all I could afford right now."

"It's better than the streets," he murmured as he moved across the room.

"What was that?" I said, not sure I heard him right. I pulled the blanket off the back of the couch and tossed it over my legs.

"They seemed to know you," he said, walking closer to the window and staring out into the dark. "At the clinic."

"Yeah. I intern there a couple days a week. I'm studying to be a doctor. Which explains why I can only afford this place."

He was silent a moment, then he said, "You save people."

The tone of his voice was a little odd and I wished I could see his face and not his back as he spoke. "Well, not really, but I hope to help them."

When he didn't say anything else I leaned back into the cushions and said, "I haven't done anything like what that man did for me."

"It always comes back to him," Dex said quietly.

"What's your connection with him?"

He swung around to face me. "I told you I don't have one."

"I think you're lying."

"What makes you so sure?" he said, stalking toward me. His dark-blond hair stood out around his head and behind his black-rimmed glasses his green eyes were wide.

"Call it a hunch," I replied, beginning to wonder if baiting him in this empty apartment was a very good idea. I mean, really, I didn't know him hardly at all.

He made a scoffing sound and looked up.

Everything about him changed in an instant.

He seemed to do a double take and then he stood there silently, staring like he'd forgotten we were talking.

"Where did you get that?" he said, moving toward the aqua painted chest of drawers near the door.

"The dresser? At a secondhand shop."

"No," he said. "That." He pointed at the little card with the picture of the beach that the man at the morgue gave me.

"Why, do you like it?" I asked, trying to keep my voice casual.

He looked at it for long moments, then shrugged. "It's okay. I saw something like it at the mall the other day."

"So it doesn't mean anything to you?"

He turned away. "Why would it?"

"It belonged to the man who died."

He seemed shocked. I couldn't decide why. Was it because he wondered how I had it? Was it because he was lying and knew all along whose it was?

Or was it because he really didn't know anything and didn't know why I wouldn't let it go?

"I thought you said no one knew who he was?" he said, not looking back at the picture, but looking at me.

"I went to the morgue to see if they would tell me anything. They still didn't know who he was but the doctor there, he gave me that. He said it was in the man's pocket."

"You went to the morgue?" he asked, disbelief on his face.

"Yes. I thought I might get more in person than on the phone."

"Why? Why do you care so much about someone who… who you didn't even know?"

"But I do know him. Maybe not in the sense you mean but, I…" I shook my head, letting my voice fall away. He wouldn't understand.

"But, what?" he pressed, finally looking interested in the conversation.

"I was with him when he died," I said quietly. "I sat there with him after he did something that half the people I know wouldn't do for me. I might not have really known him, but his final actions right before he died told me an awful lot about him."

"You can't judge someone off *one* thing they did." He argued.

"He stole from me, too," I admitted, voicing something I hadn't thought about until now.

"Stole?" he said, his voice hollow, but then he sat down on the coffee table right across from where I reclined on the sofa. I was right, he was more interested in this guy than he wanted me to believe.

I nodded. "When I got home from the accident that night, I took off my apron and my tips weren't in there. At first I thought maybe I lost the money on the street during the commotion, but then when I was at the morgue the doctor mentioned he had twenty-four dollars in his pocket."

"So?" He shrugged.

"So, that's how much I was missing. Before the bus came I almost slipped and he caught me," I said, watching him closely, remembering when he caught me in the diner the night we met how he said, "*We keep meeting like this.*" But he gave no reaction; his face was blank so I continued. "I think he probably picked my pocket."

"And this is the guy you think of as a hero?" He scoffed, his eyes focused on the floor.

"I don't care about the money. He looked cold and hungry. He probably just wanted a hot meal."

He stood up from the table like he was agitated and paced to the window again to look out into the night. "Maybe he was a jerk and took advantage of you."

"Maybe. But I don't think a jerk would've come back to push me out of the way."

He didn't speak for a long time and I thought he might not say anything else, but then he turned and came back over beside the couch. "I'm glad you have something of his. That seemed important to you."

"I really just wanted to know his name." I yawned. I was starting to crash from everything that happened.

"Sorry, I can't help you," he said so sincerely that this time I found myself wondering if he told the truth.

"I bought those flowers for him. Since I couldn't take them to his grave, I brought them home." I tried to force my eyes open wider, wanting to stay awake, wanting answers.

He walked over to the vase and looked at the small bunch of daisies, reaching up to finger the delicate white petals. Then he pulled one out, wiping away the water at the end of the stem on the leg of his jeans. He brought the flower over to me and lowered himself onto the edge of the coffee table, holding it out. "Well, I'm sure he wouldn't mind sharing. You've had a pretty rough day and since I kind of owe you, for feeding ya bad chicken and all, this one can be for you."

I looked at the flower. It's perfectly formed smooth petals were open and trusting. It revealed the center of itself so willingly that I found myself sighing.

"Why can't people be as easy to read as a flower?"

I hadn't realized I spoke the thought out loud until Dex answered, his voice a mere whisper.

"Because people are flawed."

I smiled and brought the flower to my nose to take in its bright scent. "Maybe that's why people like flowers so much. Because they aren't."

"Only girls like flowers," he said with a smirk. He looked cute with his preppy glasses and messed up hair.

"Especially when a guy is the one giving them." Was I flirting? I must be delirious from all the medicine.

He stood up. "I should let you rest."

"Is something wrong?" Okay, so clearly I was lousy at flirting.

"No," he turned back. "I should go."

I yawned as he moved toward the door and I saw him glance again at the little card with the beach on it.

"The doctor at the morgue said the reason they couldn't identify him was because his body disappeared. Can you imagine? Who would steal a body from the morgue?"

His shoulders tensed. "Are you serious? That's sick."

He made a face like it upset his stomach. There wasn't a hint of guilt on his face. Maybe I'd been wrong after all. Maybe he really didn't know anything. I guess it was kind of crazy to believe the guy who'd just given me a daisy was a body snatcher.

"Are you going to be okay? Do you need anything?" he asked after I said nothing else.

I shook my head. "I'll be fine."

He unlocked the door and opened it, glancing back once more. "Maybe I'll see you again."

"Maybe," I echoed, knowing full well I would.

I lay there for long moments after he'd gone and replayed our conversation over in my mind. Dexter Allen Roth was quite the puzzle. I couldn't tell yet where all the pieces fit, but once I had him all put together, I had a feeling he would make a very interesting picture.

With that thought, I went to bed.

I took the daisy with me.

Chapter Seventeen

"Ghost - The spirit of a dead person, especially one believed to appear in bodily likeness to living persons or to haunt former habitats. The center of spiritual life; the soul."

Dex

I took the stairs two at a time. I had to get out of this building. There was this draining tug and pull action going on inside my chest and I wanted it to stop. It made my stomach clench and my hands shake. Part of me was sickened with everything that happened tonight, and the other part of me was disappointed it hadn't ended in death.

I was like Dr. Jekyll and Mr. Hyde, only I couldn't tell which one was the real me.

I reached the first floor and let out a sigh of relief… Then I caught movement out of the corner of my eye. A dark shape seemed to float around the corner—the same looming shape that passed by Piper's window upstairs. I'd stood at the window, trying to catch a glimpse of it, but I never did. Probably because it was dark, just like the night—until it shifted and moved. That's the one thing about the dark. It doesn't move.

I pushed off the bottom step and took chase. When I got around the corner, there was nothing but the door leading outside. I slammed through it and ran out onto the sidewalk. The shifting shadow disappeared around the side of the building and I went after it, running into a dark, narrow space between the two brick buildings.

It was completely dark here and whatever had been there was gone. In fact, it was so still between the buildings that I began to think I was imagining things. Hell, I probably was.

I turned to go back out onto the street when someone spoke. "You're the new Escort."

I turned back, once again seeing nothing at all. "Who's there?" I demanded.

"Please don't tell him she saw me."

"Who?" I replied, looking for any kind of movement.

Then something shifted; the shadows seemed to form into a shape. A shape that really wasn't a shape. It was very familiar… "Where are you?"

"I'm right in front of you."

The muscles in my back bunched, expecting a fight, but no threat ever came. As my eyes adjusted to the darkness, I was able to make out more movement, but still no definite shape.

Then it dawned on me.

This was some kind of ghost. Some kind of in-between being, like I was before I got my new body. "What are you?" I asked.

"I'm like you, except I don't have a body."

"You're dead?"

"Sort of."

"Are you a ghost?"

"A ghost haunts. I don't haunt." He sniffed, offended.

"Then what are you doing lurking around Piper?"

"I'm working. Watching her is my job."

"Who hired you?"

"The same guy that hired you."

"You're an Escort?" I asked.

"Yes. A Ghost Escort."

"I thought you said you weren't a ghost."

He made a sudden movement and this time I saw him spread out like smoke. He looked exactly like I had before I got this body, except he wasn't purple. He was black.

"They call us that because we're nearly invisible, like a ghost. That's why we're the ones who watch the Slated."

"The Slated?"

"Yes, you call them Targets."

"So you were hired by the same guy—rich, kinda eerily cheerful—but you didn't get a body?"

"Ghost Escorts don't get bodies. The fact that we don't have bodies is to our advantage."

He was the one at the college campus. It's the reason he was able to be behind her one second, then yards in front of her the next. "So you can just appear and disappear, just like that?"

"Well, it's a little harder than that, but once you learn it's easy."

"So I'm not supposed to see you?"

"You're supposed to, but other people aren't."

Made sense. If I didn't know better, I'd think I was standing here talking to myself.

"You can see me because you're an Escort. We can all see each other. Though, I've never seen a purple one like you."

"How'd you know I was purple?" I asked, holding out my arms to make sure I still had my body.

"It's how we recognize each other. The color of your essence surrounds your body, but only fellow Escorts can see it."

"You mean like an aura?"

"No. An aura changes colors with your feelings. Your essence never changes."

I thought about the man surrounded with the ring of red. Turns out I wasn't crazy. I'd seen another Escort—another killer.

"How many of us are there?"

"I don't know. There aren't as many Ghost Escorts as there are Death Escorts."

"I don't understand why you're watching her."

"When a person is chosen to die—Slated—they basically become property of our boss. He likes to know what his property is up to. You, uh, are taking longer than expected to finish the job, so he sent me here to watch her and make sure nothing was wrong."

"Nothing is wrong," I said, my hands balled into fists at my sides. "I don't like being spied on."

"I'm not spying on you. I'm spying on her."

"Are you going to tell him I tried to kill her tonight and failed?"

"Not if you don't tell him she saw me."

That's right. Piper saw him at the college and she wasn't an Escort. "How come she saw you?"

"I don't know. That's never happened before."

"She's very perceptive."

"I noticed," he said wryly.

I wished I could see him more clearly. He actually didn't seem like that bad of a guy—for a sorta ghost. It might be nice to have someone I could talk to about all this. But not a friend. I didn't have those.

"So what's your name?" I asked.

"Storm."

"For real?"

"Something wrong with my name?"

"Nope. I just think it's kinda ironic your name is Storm and you look like a rain cloud."

"Yeah, well, I guess I was born to be a Ghost Escort." It sounded like he was grinning.

"Seriously, though, why would you agree to *not* have a body?"

"The alternative is worse," he said.

I shrugged. I don't really know why, but the idea of being sent to hell didn't scare me. Maybe because I always knew that's where I would go. Or maybe because I pretty much lived in my own personal hell all my life so it was nothing new.

"So you're going to keep watching her, huh?"

"That's my job," Storm said. "And if I don't do it, I don't get paid."

"Gotta get those Benjamins."

"Hey, it ain't all about the money," he said. "Ghost Escorts get paid in other ways too."

"What do you mean?" *What other ways are there?*

"Time off," he said meaningfully.

It took me a minute to realize what would be so great about getting time off from following people around.

Then it dawned on me.

"He lets you have a body?"

"Right outta that freaky closet of his."

I grinned. "It is pretty creepy."

"Well, I guess when you're the ultimate death dealer, having bodies in the closet it just like having cereal in the pantry."

The ultimate death dealer?

The darkness around me shifted and I felt him move. "I better get back. I'm on the clock."

I guess being reminded he could spend some time in an actual body made him anxious to finish his job. "So you aren't supposed to kill her? Just watch her, right?"

"Killing would be hard to do without any hands."

"I don't know. I almost killed her tonight without lifting a finger."

"That was a pretty good move, by the way."

"You saw?"

"Everything."

I wondered what he thought about my sudden panic. I wondered if he thought that made me less of a man... less of an Escort.

"Anyway, better luck next time."

"We cool?" I asked. An echo from my past. I used to say those words after every meeting or talk I had with someone on the streets. I guess standing out here in the dark between two buildings had a way of bringing things back.

"Yeah, we're cool."

I grinned and held up a fist. "I'd fist bump you, but that might be kind of hard."

"Like I haven't heard that before," he muttered.

I laughed. "Find me when you have a body and we'll hang."

"Soon as you get this job done, I'll get my time off."

"You don't get time off until I kill her?"

"Job won't be over 'til then."

"Right," I agreed.

The darkness seemed to absorb Storm, and everything went quiet. I tried to listen for which way he went, but all I heard was the sound of my own breathing. I walked around the front of the building and looked up toward her window. It was dark. She must've gone to bed. Something inside me twisted and tugged; my stomach turned. What was wrong with me? What was wrong with this body?

I climbed into my car and pulled away from the curb.

Only one way to find out.

* * *

The GPS in my car directed me back to where Mr. Burns lived. The man at the front gate waved me through without question, probably because he recognized the car. When I got to the house, I parked and jogged up the stairs to ring the bell. When Mr. Burns himself greeted me, I stood there gaping like an idiot because I really thought he wasn't the type of man to open his own door.

He smiled when I stared. "The staff has the night off."

That seemed to shake me out of my stupor. "You gave me a defective body," I said. "I want a new one."

He opened the door wider and motioned me inside. "It's cold, come in." Once inside, he turned to me, looking rather amused. "What is wrong with your body, Dex?"

"I think it's rejecting me."

He laughed. "Rejecting you? That's impossible."

I didn't like being laughed at. "My stomach always hurts. There's this weird tugging right here," I said, pressing my palm beneath my ribs. "And sometimes I feel shaky and dizzy. So, either this body doesn't like me, or there's something wrong with it."

"I can assure you there is nothing wrong with your body," Mr. Burns said smoothly. "Would you care for a nightcap?"

I didn't know what that was, but I was pretty sure I didn't want it. "I want answers."

"You're body is merely doing what it's programmed to do."

"You programmed it to be sick?" Maybe being a Ghost Escort and not having a body wasn't that bad if all the bodies this guy handed out were damaged.

Mr. Burns laughed, his thin lips pulling into a smile. "I programmed it to kill."

Of all the things he could've said, that was the last thing I imagined. "You what?"

"Tell me, do you mostly feel the way you described when you're near your Target?"

"Yes."

"That's because it's your body's way of reminding you to do your job."

"I don't need a reminder." And if I did, I'd set the alarm on my iPhone.

"It isn't just you; it's all the Death Escorts. You all have a physical reaction when you are around your assigned Target. That tugging sensation you described is your body's way of urging you closer, telling you it's time to kill."

He was serious.

"Do you not trust us to get the job done without your reminder?"

"It isn't a matter of trust. All my Escorts do their job because the alternative is far worse."

Once again, I wondered why going to hell was that terrible.

Mr. Burns continued. "I've found that programming the bodies this way makes it easier for the Escorts. At least for their first few kills, and then they pretty much ignore the internal signals and complete the job on their own."

"Why would feeling like I want to barf make my job easier?"

"Because instead of focusing on what you must do, you focus on feeling sick and making that feeling go away."

He used it as a distraction. Almost as a trick.

"Have you always programmed the bodies?" I asked, already guessing the answer was no.

"When I first started out in the Escort business I did not. But there were too many Escorts failing and my losses were great. So I started this and now not nearly as many fail."

"But some still do."

"Yes." He looked at me levelly. "Some fight their own bodies. Some end up warring against themselves. It's such a shame because they will never ever win." His voice held a note of warning and I knew it was for me.

Did he know I'd already failed to kill Piper twice?

"Well, now that I know that there isn't anything wrong with my body, I can focus on my work."

Mr. Burns smiled. "Wonderful! Is there anything else I can do for you?"

"No," I said, turning back to pull open the front door. Snowflakes swirled inside and landed on my shoe.

"I'll walk you out," he said, motioning for me to wait. I watched as he grabbed a long black coat and put it on. Then he reached toward a bowl on a slim table against the wall. The bowl was filled with light-colored stones, just like the ones in his office.

"What are those?" I asked as he chose two and slid them into his pocket.

"Just a little token I like to give people I visit," he replied and ushered me out the door.

We stepped out into the snow. The big white flakes fell steadily from the dark sky. Snow had a way of blanketing everything, making everything quiet. But tonight, even the heavy white flurry couldn't silence everything.

"And Dex?" Mr. Burns said as we stepped onto the driveway and headed to our separate cars. I glanced over my shoulder. "Time's a wasting."

As I walked to my car, I could've sworn I heard the ticking of a clock.

Chapter Eighteen

"Found - come upon unexpectedly or after searching."

Piper

Alarm clocks are evil and vile. They make constant noise, disrupting sleep and making it hard to stay buried under the covers away from the world.

I don't know how many times I hit the snooze button, but I do know I didn't become fully conscious until the shrill ringing of my phone finally had me throwing back my covers and searching for my bag. I didn't really care who it was, but I wanted the ringing to stop.

"Hello?" I said in relief when I finally silenced the ring. I carried the phone back to my room and climbed back into bed, pulling the covers up over me.

"May I please speak with Piper McCall?" asked the woman on the other end.

"This is her," I replied, trying to think up something evil to do to the telemarketer that would dare call this early.

"This is Nancy Holland calling from Fairbanks Memorial Hospital." I pushed the covers back and listened a little more closely. "You called a few days ago about a man who was brought into the morgue."

"Yes, that's me," I said, fully alert now.

"I have Doctor Patricks here and he would like to speak with you."

"Okay," I said, wondering if it was the same doctor I saw in the morgue.

The line was silent for a moment and then I heard someone pick it up and a man with a familiar voice came on the line. "Ma'am, I'm Doctor Patricks."

"Yes, I remember," I said, thinking of the little card still tucked in the frame of my mirror.

"I wanted to call and let you know the status of the body we discussed."

I was surprised he called to tell me anything. "Go ahead."

"It seems that…" He cleared his throat. "The body hadn't been taken… It was more misplaced."

"What do you mean misplaced?" I said, my voice rising.

"I was here the night the body was brought in, but then I left and another doctor arrived. He sent the body to be cremated. The paperwork was buried under more paperwork on my desk and I only just found it."

"The body was cremated," I said, hollow.

"Yes. Someone came forward and identified him and so the cremation was ordered."

"Who came forward? Who was it?"

"I can't divulge that information."

"But you can tell me all this," I snapped.

"I didn't want you to keep thinking someone had stolen a body from the morgue."

He didn't want the hospital to get sued and he figured this would keep me from blabbing to the press about a missing body.

"I see," I said, my mind still spinning. Then I blurted, "You can't have the picture back."

"I don't want it back. I just wanted you to know he wasn't missing."

"Thank you," I said, leaning back against my headboard.

"Have a nice day," the doctor said and then he hung up.

I laid the phone in my lap, still trying to decide how I felt. On one hand, I was happy someone claimed him and his body wasn't really missing. On the other hand, I was disappointed. Because now that I knew the body really hadn't been stolen, my whole theory that Dex knew more about it than he would admit was pretty weak. Still, what about my vision? Was it a coincidence? A fluke?

Or was it something more?

Chapter Nineteen

"Spying - secretly keeps watch on another or others."

Dex

The one good thing about never having a phone was that it could never ring and wake me up. When my iPhone wouldn't stop making noise, I dragged myself out of bed to answer it.

"What?" I demanded.

"Morning sunshine," said a vaguely familiar voice.

I was still half asleep and I didn't feel like trying to figure out who it was. "Who is this?" I demanded.

"Storm."

"How'd you get this number?" I said, falling back into the bed face first.

"I'm a Ghost Escort. Finding things out is what I do."

"I thought spying on people is what you do," I said, rolling over and pulling the covers up to block out the morning cold.

"Well, my spying saved your ass."

"What do you mean?"

"I mean I took care of the problem you had with the Target."

"What did you do?" I said, sitting up and throwing off the covers. My fingers tightened around the phone and my palms became slick with sweat. I sat there frozen while images of Piper lying dead inside her apartment tormented my brain.

"I fixed it up so the hospital found your body. They called her and told her it was all a mix-up."

"Oh. How did you pull that off?" I asked, relief turning my spine to jelly as I slumped backwards into the headboard.

"Don't sound too grateful." Storm snorted.

"Tell me what you want for this favor; then I'll decide if I'm grateful." People don't do things just to help out other people.

"I don't want anything other than for you to finish this job so we can go chill on a beach somewhere."

A beach.

His words brought to mind the perfect image of the faded card I used to carry in my pocket. I snatched it years ago from some store. I never took things I couldn't use (like clothes), eat, or trade for money or other stuff I wanted. But this… this was different. It had been one of the coldest days of the year that day. The ice was inches thick on the sidewalks and the snow banks were so high I thought they would never melt. It was impossible to stay warm no matter how many blankets I stole, where I huddled, or how much coffee I drank. Then I saw the image of the crystal-clear water, the sun, and the warm, welcoming sand, and I knew that was the place I wanted to be. That was the place I was going to leave this arctic prison for. And once I got there, I would never leave.

I took the little card and slid it into my jacket, and all winter long I would look at it every day and plan how I'd get there. *Some day,* I used to tell myself. *Some day I'll make it there.*

I never did.

And now Piper had my card.

I told myself I didn't need that card anymore. Now I had the money and resources to go to that place in the flesh. Maybe I'd buy a house and live there. Maybe I'd never come back to this frozen berg again.

"Dex, you still there?" Storm asked.

"Yeah, yeah, I'm here," I replied, shaking away the memory.

"Now that she isn't too suspicious about you being a body stealer, I figured it'd be easier for you to get closer to her."

"Why was she so suspicious of me in the first place?" I wondered out loud.

"I can't tell you all her secrets!" Storm laughed.

"I don't want to know them. I don't care where she hides the key to her diary or what color her underwear are."

Storm laughed again. "You so want to know what color they are."

I grinned. Maybe I did.

"Well, duty calls. She's up and moving around."

"Hey, ah, how does she look this morning?"

"Alive and kicking," Storm answered.

"She doesn't look like she's still beat up from last night?"

"Are you worried about her?" Storm practically accused me.

"No. I just want to know if she's weak—you know, to take advantage."

"Ahhh, I got ya. She looks pretty normal to me. You might want to get a plan. Then get a back-up plan."

"Right. I'm working on it." I agreed; then we both hung up. I pulled the phone away from my ear and saved his number to my contacts in case I needed it again. Vaguely I wondered where he kept a phone if he didn't have any pockets… or a body to put pants on. Then I wondered how he even dialed the phone. Too many questions this early in the morning.

I tossed the phone off to the side and collapsed back onto the pillows. My mind drifted back to the little card with the picture of the beach and the way it looked tucked into the frame of her mirror. It seemed important to her. She put it out where she'd see it every day.

And then there were the flowers.

She bought him—*me*—flowers and sat them near the card as her own personal memorial. I never once thought anyone would miss me if I died. I kind of liked that someone did. It meant I was more than a drifter, more than just another bum on the street. It meant someone out there thought I was worth caring about.

Really, I wasn't.

I told myself if she knew the real me, the me that was trying to murder her, she'd throw away those flowers and that picture real fast. But she didn't know. And she still had the picture and the daisies.

But I was still me.

Chapter Twenty

"1-800-FLOWERS—Elegant flowers for any occasion."

Piper

It wasn't often that I had a day off. Going in anaphylactic shock wasn't really a good way to get a day to myself, but hey, I'd take my good fortune where I could. I didn't feel as bad as I thought, but my muscles did protest when I finally crawled out of bed. Breathing came easily, but I knew better than to push myself. I knew I'd be able to get a doctor's excuse for missing classes so after a brief debate, I decided to skip.

Between recovering from the reaction and the early morning phone call, I really did just want some time to myself. After I called Frankie and invited her to dinner (Hey, if I was going to call off school and work, the least I could do was have some girl time), I took a long, hot shower and then spent some time blow-drying and curling the ends of my hair into loose waves. (I never had time to curl my hair.) I pulled on a pair of black leggings, an oversized purple sweater, and a pair of furry slipper boots before I went into the kitchen for some hot tea.

A brief cloud passed by the small kitchen window, but when I turned to look, the sun was back out. After pouring my tea I wandered into the bedroom and put the daisy Dex had given me into a small glass of water. Back in the living room, I sat it on the coffee table and studied it while I drank my tea.

The rational part of me said I was being silly for getting so melty over a flower—a flower that technically he hadn't really given me because I bought it, yet the gesture behind it got to me. No one had ever given me flowers before.

I picked up a magazine, determined I wouldn't sit here and stare at a flower for hours, and began to read. A few minutes later there was a knock on the door and when I answered I was greeted by a man in a fleece coat holding a huge bouquet of white daisies. The exact same kind I bought, except there were more and they were in a sculpted glass vase with a purple satin ribbon tied in a big bow.

I gasped a little, wanting to reach out and take them, but I stopped myself, thinking maybe the man was at the wrong door.

"Piper McCall?" he asked.

"That's me,"

"Delivery for you," he said and then the vase full of cheerful flowers was in my arms.

"Wow, they're…" My voice trailed away when the man smiled. "Oh, let me get you something," I said, turning to go into the room.

He held up his hand. "It's already been taken care of. Have a nice day."

And then he was gone.

I kicked the door closed and went over to the couch, sitting down, still holding onto the vase. I took a deep breath of the light floral scent and then carefully set the vase down on the table in front of me. The sheer size and volume completely hid the single flower I'd been staring at moments before.

There was a simple white card stuck amongst the stems and I plucked it out carefully.

Because you shouldn't have to share. Dex

If I'd been a bit melty before, now I was a puddle. I brought the card up to my lips, which curved into a secret smile, and I sat there with a goofy look on my face, staring at the gift. His words from the night he'd given me the single flower replayed through my head.

I'm sure he wouldn't mind sharing…

Hugging the card against my chest, I got up from the couch and went over to the mirror to tuck the card with

Dex's message right above the picture of the beach scene. Both cards were about the same size. Then I went back to the vase and reached around to pull forward the glass with the single flower. After plucking it from the water, I used the mirror to tuck the stem into my hair above my right ear. My slightly curled hair looped around the flower and it looked right at home.

I smiled some more. I just couldn't stop.

In that moment I didn't think about bodies in the morgue or my allergy to peanuts. I didn't think about what I did and didn't know about Dex.

In that moment, I was just a girl.

A girl who got beautiful flowers from a boy.

I went back over to the couch, sitting down but reaching out to finger the smooth satin of the large purple bow. I gave up on the magazine and sat there and stared at the flowers until I glanced at the clock and realized I still needed to go pick up dinner before Frankie arrived.

I pulled on my coat, wound a white scarf around my neck, and grabbed up my keys. Then I gave the bouquet one last smile before walking out the door.

* * *

I settled on Chinese takeout for dinner—vegetable lo mein, beef and broccoli, hot and sour soup with wantons and egg rolls. Even though I ordered from this place a lot, I still made sure to double-check they didn't use peanuts or peanut oil in any of my dishes. One reaction was more than enough for me, thank you very much. Before I left, the man at the counter added some extra fortune cookies to the bag. My stomach rumbled as I walked home and I realized it was because I'd forgotten to eat earlier.

Had I really been so caught up in those flowers?

Yes. Yes, I was.

When I got to my apartment door, I placed the bag at my feet and pulled out my keys, but when I inserted it in the lock, I noticed the door wasn't closed all the way. I didn't put my keys away. Instead I shifted them, placing the largest key between the first two fingers on my hand, letting the sharp end poke out. It was simple, but it would be an effective enough weapon if someone was in my house.

I pushed open the door, holding tight to the keys, all my muscles tense and ready to jump into action.

"Who's here?" I called into the room.

I heard a sound from the kitchen and I was about to start yelling for help when Frankie appeared. She took in my raised arm and the key and the determined look on my face and she held up her hands.

"Don't stab me!" Then she began to laugh.

My breath made a whooshing noise when I let it out and the keys fell from my grasp. "Holy crap, Frankie! You about gave me a heart attack!"

"You're the one that invited me to dinner then wasn't even here when I arrived. You're a very bad hostess."

I laughed and hauled the bag of food in and shut the door, throwing the locks. "I ran out to grab the food."

"I'm starving," Frankie said, taking the bag from my hand and over to the coffee table, beginning to pull all the boxes out. "That witch I work for about drove me nuts today."

I went into the kitchen to get some plates, napkins, and silverware, and when I came out she had everything out and was already eating the lo mein.

"Hey, save some for me!" I cried.

"Ya snooze, ya lose." Then around another mouthful, she said, "Where'd you get the flowers?"

I smiled and glanced at the centerpiece of the coffee table.

"A fancy car *and* flowers… You don't stand a chance."

"Are you implying I can be bought?" I said, slightly offended.

She lowered the lo mein toward her lap. "I know better than that," she replied. "But you have to admit it doesn't hurt."

"I don't like him for his money, Frankie."

"But you do like him." It wasn't a question.

I shrugged and reached for the white carton in her hand. She held it out and my hand brushed against hers when I grabbed it.

The vision came on fast, strong, and it took over everything else I was seeing and hearing.

And then it was gone.

But the devastation it left would stay with me forever.

"Piper?" Frankie said, pulling me away from the assaulting vision.

I pulled away and set the carton beside me on the table. "Sorry," I mumbled, still caught in the pain of what I saw.

"Did you have a vision?" Frankie asked, looking at me with curiosity on her face.

I blinked and cleared my throat, forcing what I really felt down deep. "Yeah, but it wasn't anything big."

"Well, what'd you see?"

"You know I don't like to talk about my visions."

"Yeah, but your reaction just now..." Her voice trailed off and she bit her lip nervously.

I forced myself to smile. A real smile, not something fake. "It just caught me off guard like they do sometimes. I hadn't been thinking about visions, just how hungry I am."

Frankie nodded. "So it wasn't anything?"

I shook my head and glanced at the daisies. They actually lessened the knot of panic in my gut. "Nope." I looked back at my friend and grinned. "And don't worry; you still look hot."

She smiled and fluffed her hair. "Of course I do." She grabbed up the container of beef and broccoli. "Let's eat."

I picked up the container of lo mein I'd been so hungry for just minutes before. But now, my appetite was gone. The truth was that vision hadn't been nothing. It was something.

Recalled

Something very bad.

Chapter Twenty-One

"Nightshade - Any of several plants of the genus Solanum, such as the bittersweet nightshade, most of which have a poisonous juice."

Dex

All through my typical breakfast of bacon, eggs, and coffee I thought about what Storm said. I did need a plan. Seeing Piper's reaction to the peanut oil had given me an idea, but I wasn't sure if it would work or not so I pulled out my laptop and typed the word *nightshade* into Google.

I smiled as I read. It was possible to die from ingesting the poisonous berry, and it could cause adverse effects like dizziness, trouble breathing, and nausea. If I acted fast I could somehow get it into her system and then say she was having complications from the anaphylaxis.

Brilliant.

Now that I had a plan, all I needed was a way to get the deadly nightshade. I could probably find it online, but that would take forever to get here and I needed it fast.

There was one way…

It was in a place I never planned to go again. A place I was all too happy to be rid of.

I guess the old saying that history sometimes repeats itself was true. To get what I wanted I was going to have to go back… back to where I came from.

Back to the streets.

* * *

I hadn't been to this part of town since I died. The streets seemed dirtier, lonelier, and colder than ever. Probably because I'd been spending all my time in a spacious, heated townhouse cleaned by my butler.

I shoved my hands deeper into my coat, wondering what I was thinking to wear such a nice leather coat. I was hoping maybe my ripped jeans and Converse sneakers would be enough to not mark me as some rich kid looking for some fun in the wrong part of town. Maybe to the watchful eyes of the people that lay in wait in the shadows, I would look like one of them who got lucky enough to steal a nice coat.

The streets here were familiar to me, but I didn't feel like I was coming home, because even though I once lived on the streets, they weren't my home. I hadn't had a real home in years.

I looked at the sidewalks, which had patches of ice every couple feet. In this part of town no one bothered to lay salt. The city had long ago given up.

It seemed there was a different set of rules on this street and the few that ran beside it. The people here weren't governed by the same laws everyone else lived by. Here it was eat or be eaten, live or die, steal or be stolen from. Yes, the police still patrolled here, the city still wanted to claim they were doing all they could to keep every street in Fairbanks safe, but the truth was even they had given up.

I passed a few places where I used to spend a lot of my time. The narrow alley between two rundown apartment buildings looked exactly the same with the shell of an old rusted out car sitting on blocks. It reminded me of all the nights that I'd climb into the front seat and use the frame to block the snow and what I could of the icy air.

There were a few people hunched around a large barrel with flames glowing out the top. I heard a few laughs and the sound of something hitting the side as they threw it into the fire to keep it going. I ducked my head and kept walking, not wanting them to see me stare. That was considered a challenge in these parts.

I walked past a small convenience store where I used to loiter, picking pockets of the unfortunate people who had to be in this part of town and hadn't thought to get gas before they came. It smelled the same—burnt coffee and stale cigarettes with a hint of gasoline.

I saw some people I knew, people who weren't quite my friends but might've wondered what happened to me when I disappeared and never came back. Not that they would've cared. They knew I was always looking for the next big score, my ticket out of here, and maybe they assumed I found it. That or I died trying. By now, my minimal stash of clothes and personal items had been found and raided, probably fought over and won.

The truth was I hadn't thought once about anything I left behind. I didn't miss it here and having to come back only reminded me why I so desperately wanted out.

I came to an abandoned brick building, a building probably considered condemned by the city. For the people here on the street, it was a refuge. A refuge from the harsh temperatures Alaska was famous for.

I flicked my gaze around the sidewalk in front of the building and looked across the street. No one seemed to care what I was doing so I ducked into the building through two loosened boards that were hammered over a broken window.

It was dark on the very bottom floor of the building, completely stripped of whatever it used to be. Bare concrete floors, empty cracked, yellowed walls, and crumpled trash made up the inside of this refuge. It wasn't much, but there weren't many windows so most of the snow and wind didn't make it in. There was a room in the center that was pretty much what most of us considered a suite because it blocked out all the elements and housed a small heater that ran on batteries. But most of us were never permitted entrance.

No, it belonged to a guy who staked his claim on this street years ago. He was essentially the boss around here. Nothing happened without him knowing about it, and the bigger deals that would bring in the most cash were always run by him. If you tried to run a big deal without him knowing he killed you, plain and simple.

I'd run a few deals, earned a few dollars, but mostly I tried to stay out of his way. He was the kind of guy who lived by his own rules and expected you to live by them too. When one of his rules inconvenienced him, he changed it and that left the other person out in the cold. Literally.

But he was the guy who would get me what I wanted. And he would get it now.

As I approached the room in the center of the building, someone came out to meet me. A very big someone. I knew he would. Joey Malone, AKA The Bouncer was the boss's right-hand man. He did exactly what his name implied— bounced people that weren't supposed to be around.

"Who the hell are you?" he said, narrowing his eyes.

I pulled my hands slowly out of my pockets and dropped them to my sides. "I heard this was the place to come when you needed something fast," I said.

"Yeah? Where'd you hear that?"

I shrugged, keeping my cool. "Around."

"I've never seen you *around*," The Bouncer said.

"That's because you wouldn't see me unless I wanted you to," I replied, injecting enough attitude for him to know I wasn't a stranger to the streets and he wouldn't intimidate me.

He made a grunting sound and said, "Wait here."

I stood there, appearing casual but really ready for any kind of fight. I just hoped this new body had reflexes and skills like my old one did because if not, Mr. Burns might not like the condition in which this body is returned to him.

The Bouncer appeared and gestured for me to follow him. He led me into the room we all used to covet. Now, as I looked around, all I saw was a place in the middle of the ghetto that was no better than the rooms I'd just walked through, except maybe it was warmer.

The little heater was running and there were two metal chairs set up in the center. Off to the right there was a bare mattress pushed up against the wall with a blanket that was rumpled and dirty.

"What's a guy like you doing in this part of town?" the boss asked, looking me over.

I guess my beat-up jeans and Converse sneakers weren't enough to give the new me a street approved look. "I want something. I heard you can get it."

The boss lifted an eyebrow and proceeded to light a cigarette. "Yeah? What do you want?"

"Nightshade," I said, trying not to make a face at the smoke. Smoking was one thing I never did. It was nasty.

He coughed a little and then squinted up at me through the smoke. "Nightshade?"

"Yeah." I didn't bother to define it further. He knew full well it was a poison. Insulting his knowledge of lethal substances would only tell him I didn't belong on the streets. But I did. He might usually deal the hard stuff, but I knew he could get this. Anyone who could get kilos of cocaine could get me a little bag of nightshade.

"What do you want that for?"

"Does it matter?" I retorted.

"Are you a narc?" he asked, and I wanted to laugh. He thought I was a narc? I was the furthest thing from a tattletale he would ever see.

"If I was a narc I wouldn't be trying to get nightshade from you," I replied, flat.

"I don't have any."

I reached into my pocket, noting how The Bouncer stiffened, expecting me to pull out a weapon, and pulled out a fat wad of cash. "I got something here that says you do."

The boss ground out his cigarette on the floor and then stood. I counted out quite a few crisp hundred-dollar bills and held them out. "How about you suddenly find some?"

He took the money and it disappeared in his pocket. "I'll be back." He stepped around me. "Watch him, Joey."

We stood in the tiny room, with the battery-operated heater working overtime, for endless minutes that dragged into an hour. During that time a girl with greasy dark hair came into the room and collapsed onto the mattress. I recognized her. We hung out a couple times in the alley and one time I got her some food. She was young, probably no more than sixteen, and the streets hadn't been kind. She was the kind of person that the streets would eat for dinner if she didn't find a way to survive. I tried to convince her to go back home once, months ago. A few weeks later I didn't see her around anymore and I thought maybe she'd listened.

I guess she hadn't.

And now, from the way The Bouncer acted like seeing her here was nothing new, I'd guess her way of surviving was getting involved with the boss.

I must've stared at her too long because she turned her head to look at me. "What?" she demanded.

I looked away.

The Bouncer shoved me in the shoulder. "Eye's off," he warned.

After that I just stared at the floor.

The boss finally came back with a little bag in his hand and he held it out to me. "You didn't get this here."

I took it, nodding, and barely glanced at the dark berries in the sack. I shoved it into my pocket and left. I breathed a sigh of relief when I was out of the room and walking away. From out in the hall, I heard the raised voice of the boss and then a sharp slap followed by a light cry.

My steps faltered before picking back up again.

Then I heard the scrape of a chair, a loud bang, and another cry.

Sounded like the price of being at the top was pretty heavy. She should've gone home like I told her to. Now she wouldn't go anywhere without the boss's permission.

He shouted again and she began to sob, and without thinking, my feet pivoted and I walked back toward the room. The Bouncer was standing outside the door, his face impassive. When he saw me coming, he straightened. I didn't hesitate before plowing my fist right into his nose. Blood spurted and he doubled over. I pushed open the door to the room and saw the boss standing over the girl, who was hunched on the mattress, shielding her head. They both looked up when the door hit the wall.

"What the hell are you doing in here?" he yelled.

I picked up the metal chair and swung it at him, knocking him against the wall. I reached down and grabbed the girl by the elbow and yanked her up. She had a bloody lip.

"You should've went home," I told her, shoving her toward the door.

The boss charged me and I hit him with the chair again. This time he fell onto the mattress with a loud shout.

"Go!" I yelled and was surprised when she listened.

"You messed with the wrong guy," the boss growled, getting up from the floor.

"I know a guy who hangs bodies in the closet. You're nothing," I told him calmly. Then I slammed the chair into him again, knocking him out cold.

I dropped the chair and left the room. The hallway was splattered with blood, but was otherwise empty. I jogged to the front of the building where I heard the sound of a struggle and when I got there I saw The Bouncer trying to keep the girl from leaving through the boarded up window.

When he saw me, he shoved her away, causing her to hit the wall, where she slid down onto the floor. He came at me hard and fast and there was nowhere for me to go.

But up.

I grabbed a low hanging wooden beam and prayed it would hold my weight, and I pulled myself up, swinging my legs a bit for momentum. The Bouncer was charging so fast that when he tried to stop and turn back, he tripped and stumbled. I let my legs swing out toward him and kicked him dead center in the back. He sprawled out on the floor, and the beam I was holding broke and I fell onto the ground.

Rough hands grabbed me, yanking me to my feet, and I looked into the eyes of The Bouncer. The skin beneath them was already darkening from his broken nose.

I twisted in his grip, dropping back onto the floor, then springing up, bringing with me the beam I'd been hanging on.

I swung it and it connected right across his abdomen. All the air whooshed out of him and he hit the ground.

The girl was watching us with wide frightened eyes, so I dropped the beam and hustled her out the window and onto the street. I walked fast, pulling her along with me until we were behind the convenience store in the dark.

"Why did you do that?" she cried. "He's going to punish me now."

"No, he won't because you aren't going back there. If you do, you'll end up dead." I looked her straight in the eye. "Do you want to die?"

She was silent a moment. "No."

I knew she'd say that. No one ever wanted to die. Piper probably didn't want to die either... I shook the thought and reached my hand into my pocket for the rest of my cash. "Here."

She looked at the money with hungry eyes.

"Take it. Go home. And if you can't go home, go somewhere that isn't here."

"Who are you?" she asked, still looking at the money.

"Let's just say I know what it's like to live on the streets."

She took the money and turned away.

"Hey," I said, gripping her elbow, spinning her back around. "I'm serious. Leave here. I won't be here next time."

She nodded and I released her.

"There's a phone inside. Call someone to come get you."

She went through the back door of the convenience store and I stood there for a long time, wondering what possessed me to behave that way. Antagonizing a well-known, highly feared drug dealer and his body guard, helping a girl who was living on the streets and too stupid to go home, then giving her all the cash in my pocket... something I never would've even thought about doing when these streets were my home.

But I didn't live here anymore.

Those drug dealers didn't scare me because they didn't make my rules.

And the girl… I didn't even know if she would listen to me. She hadn't when I told her before. She might take that money, waste it, and then end up right back where I found her. But at least she had a chance now. It was more than anyone ever gave me.

If I wasn't careful I might start thinking I was a decent guy. I stuck my cold hands deep into my pockets, one of them colliding with the bag of nightshade. My previous thought was blown out of the water. No, I wasn't a decent guy. I was still the same as always.

* * *

Snowflakes rained from the sky, looking angry, and they blew with the wind and slashed into my windshield with the tenacity of a starving man at a buffet. I struggled to pay attention to the road because my mind wanted to go to other places. Like to everything that had happened back there on the streets.

Never once in my entire life had I stepped in like that to try and help someone else. Well, except for the night I died.

Look where that got me.

So why now? Why this girl? Why try and help someone I couldn't care less about?

Because you can't save the one you really want to.

The thought caused me to swerve a bit on the road and I righted the Roadster and then scrutinized the idea. Did I want to save Piper? Is that what this was about?

I shook my head. It couldn't be. I knew I had to kill her. I knew she had to die. There was no escaping that.

I guess I could admit to myself that the more I was around her and got to know her, the more I realized the world would be worse off without her in it. Is that why I tried to save someone else today? To make up for what I was taking out of this world.

I sighed heavily. As hard as I thought the streets had been, everything seemed easier back then.

And now, everything always seemed to come back to Piper.

It was beginning to piss me off.

I slammed into the house and kicked off my shoes. Then I grabbed the baggie out of my coat pocket and slid it off, throwing it into a heap on top of my shoes. I walked into the kitchen where Hobbs was busy cooking up something and I sat down at the island, hunching my shoulders forward a bit.

"Bad day?" Hobbs asked, lifting an eyebrow.

"You don't have to wear that uniform, you know," I said, motioning toward his dove-gray coat and bowtie.

"I have a distinct feeling that my choice of wardrobe is not what put you in such a nasty mood." He sniffed, turning toward whatever he was cooking.

I watched him add a few things onto a platter and then slide it in front of me. "Perhaps a cookie will help things?"

I didn't think so, but I shoved one in my mouth anyway. Chocolate and sugar melted onto my tongue. "These are good," I mumbled around another.

"Yes, well, chewing them might actually make them taste better," he said with a frown.

"I need some milk," I said.

"You need some manners," he muttered, but he got me a glass of milk.

I took a gulp and looked down at the cookies on the plate, then down at the bag in my lap. "Hobbs," I began. "I need you to make me some more cookies and this time add these to the batch." I put the bag on the counter between us and snatched up another cookie.

This time I chewed. He was right. It tasted even better.

Hobbs picked up the bag and looked at it closely. Then he looked back at me. "Where did you get this?" he asked.

"The store," I lied.

"One does not buy nightshade at the grocery store."

I choked on my cookie. "Nightshade? What's that?" I said, trying to play dumb.

"Please," he said, rolling his eyes. "I'm a butler, not stupid."

"I don't think you're stupid." I didn't, but I hoped he'd think I gave him some exotic berry.

"It is not in my job description to help you kill others," he said, still holding onto the bag.

"Who said I was going to kill someone?" I asked, feeling slightly alarmed.

Hobbs actually looked a little alarmed by what he said too. "I apologize, sir. That was very... inappropriate to say."

I shrugged. "So you'll make the cookies?"

"We both know nightshade is poison, so whatever you plan to do with these cookies is clearly not something respectable."

"I'm not a respectable guy, Hobbs," I told him, putting down the cookie I held.

"Respect is earned, sir. Perhaps if you want it, you should earn it."

"Maybe I don't want it."

"I think you do," he said knowingly.

"Just make the cookies," I demanded.

"I will not," he said in his dignified yet offended tone. "Whatever you have planned with this poison, you will have to do without me."

"I'll fire you," I growled, rising off my chair.

"Then that is your choice." He sniffed.

Some of the steam went out of me and I dropped into my seat. "I don't have a choice."

"You always have a choice." His voice held a note of finality.

"Not in my world."

"In all worlds. Some choices are harder than others. Some choices seem impossible but aren't always as difficult as they seem."

His words sounded good. They made me wish he was right. But he didn't get it. No one did.

"So what is your choice, sir," Hobbs asked me. "Shall I pack my things?"

I looked between Hobbs and the bag of nightshade. "You do make damn good coffee," I said finally.

Hobbs smiled. "Well, yes, I do." When I didn't say anything else, he picked up the bag and glanced at me. "I'll just get rid of this."

I watched as he threw the bag into the trash. Everything I went through to get that stuff and here I was allowing my butler to throw it all away.

I must be crazy.

"You made the right choice," Hobbs said like it was over.

I left the kitchen and headed upstairs. What Hobbs didn't understand was that I might've made the right choice today, but tomorrow would be a whole new set of choices.

Chapter Twenty-Two

"Cupcake - A small cake baked in a cup-shaped container."

Piper

I couldn't get the vision out of my head. No matter how hard I tried to distract myself, no matter how much Chinese I ate, I still kept coming back to the picture that only lasted seconds in my brain.

Frankie was going to die.

No, I reminded myself, *the future can change. It doesn't have to happen.*

God, please let it change.

Sometimes having the gift of sight didn't feel like a gift at all. Many people say they'd rather know when they were going to die... not me. I don't want to know. Knowing was too hard. It was too stressful because then life would be reduced to the ticking of a clock. Of how many hours, seconds, minutes you had left. There's no way you could fit in everything you wanted to do, and I think the knowledge of your impending death would be crippling and keep you from actually living anyway.

Frankie wasn't just my best friend. She was my family, the person I counted on most, and the only person in this world I really trusted. Since the death of my parents it sometimes felt like it was Frankie and me against the world. I depended on her. If she died I'd be completely alone.

"Piper," she said, interrupting my worried thoughts. "Are you sure you're okay?"

I mustered a smile. "Yes. I ate way too much." I put a hand to my stomach like I was about to burst.

"Well, you know what the cure for that is," Frankie sang, getting up and going into the kitchen.

"Don't say it," I warned.

A few seconds later she came out of the kitchen carrying a pink box and a smile. "Sugar!" she exclaimed, pushing some of the half-empty cartons of Chinese out of the way and setting down the box.

"Is that what I think it is?" I asked.

"Yep." She flipped open the top of the bakery box and lifted out a perfect-looking cupcake. It had a pink baking wrapper around the bottom, the top was piled high with white icing and pink sugar sprinkles.

I snatched it out of her hand. "You went to The Iced Princess!"

She laughed and reached into the box to get another perfect treat identical to mine. "I figured after everything you've been through you need a little royal treatment."

The Iced Princess was the best bakery in all of Alaska. It was also way on the other side of town. In the rich district. Everything in the store was pink. Pink couches, pink rugs, a pink counter, and it even had a pink crystal chandelier hanging from the ceiling. They had a big poster just inside the door that read: *The Iced Princess: Where everyone gets the royal treatment.*

The place was so popular she usually had a line around the corner by the time she opened the doors at eleven o'clock every day.

It was one of my favorite places in town, but we rarely went because it was so far and because it was definitely not cheap.

"You didn't have to do this," I said as she reached under the box and pulled out a DVD. *Magic Mike.* It was a movie about a bunch of male strippers who basically paraded around in very little clothing the entire time. Or so I heard.

"I figured we princesses needed a little bit of naughty to go with our nice," Frankie said, waiving it around in front of my face.

Tears sprang to my eyes as I clutched the cupcake in my hand.

She sighed and set the movie down on the table, then placed her cupcake on top of it. "Tell me what's wrong."

I shook my head and blinked back the tears. "It's nothing. I just love you is all. Thank you for all of this."

"Well, it isn't flowers," she said, glancing at my bouquet.

"It's better," I whispered.

"Oh, don't start blubbering," she said, getting up from the couch to put in the movie. "No tears on girls' night."

I swallowed and the vision replayed in my mind.

Frankie lying on the floor, her glassy eyes staring upward—seeing nothing. The curls of her blond bob created a halo and her face was pale except for her red lips.

There was no blood.

There was no screaming or crying.

There was no sense of urgency.

I remembered nothing about the background or her surroundings—only her and the overwhelming sense of sadness and loss.

How would I live with that image forever burning a hole in my mind?

What would I do without her?

I blinked and looked up when I felt a hand on my arm.

"I know something's wrong. That vision was bad, wasn't it? That's why you're upset."

"Upset? How could I possibly be upset?" I said. "I got the entire day off, a delivery of flowers, Chinese food, the best cupcakes ever, and I'm about to watch a thoroughly entertaining movie with my favorite person in the world."

She nodded her head once. "You got it good girl. And to make it even better, I propose a slumber party."

"We haven't had one of those since high school."

"We're overdue." She grinned, but I saw the brief cloud of worry in her eyes. She only wanted to sleep over to be certain I was all right.

I liked the idea of having her here tonight. I might not worry as much. I nodded. "That would be fun."

She rolled her eyes. "I know." She grabbed her cupcake and settled back onto the couch, picking up the remote to start the movie. Just as the credits were rolling on the screen, she hit the pause button.

"Oh, I forgot. Some guy came by to see you earlier."

"A guy?" I asked, automatically thinking of Dex. "Was he wearing glasses?"

She shook her head. "Nope. And he looked like a Ken doll. Perfect hair, clothes, and teeth."

"Well, that's not Dex," I mumbled to myself and Frankie laughed. "But he is good looking," I added.

"Well, he can definitely pick out flowers." We both looked at the daisies. "Anyway, it was before you got here with the food and I answered the door. He must've thought I was you because he was being all slick and charming. When he called me Piper, I laughed and told him he had the wrong girl. Turns out Ken isn't so perfect after all. All that charm went right out the window. He was arrogant, sarcastic, and rude," she said with a *how dare he* tone to her voice. "I took great pleasure in throwing him out."

I laughed. "What did he want?"

"I have no idea. He was probably selling a vacuum and when he figured out I wasn't buying he decided he didn't have to be nice."

"Well, I'm glad you had to deal with him and not me," I said, using my finger to swipe some of the icing and pink sugar off the top of the cupcake. It melted the second it hit my tongue.

"Yes, well, I figure since I had the job of tossing him out I deserve two cupcakes." She leaned forward to pull out another cake and held them both up, one on each side of her face, and grinned.

"There better be another one in that box for me."

"You know it, sister," she sang, then looked at the TV. "Now hit play. I wanna see some abs!"

I hit play and with the help of some very hot guys and some tasty dessert, I was able to forget about the vision. Even still, I knew the time would come when I would begin to worry again.

Chapter Twenty-Three

"Babysitter - A person who cares for or watches over someone or something that needs attention or guidance."

Dex

I was upstairs enjoying the comfort of my king-sized bed and the flat screen when the sound of the doorbell echoed through the townhouse. I ignored it, knowing it was probably just some kid selling Girl Scout cookies and Hobbs would answer it anyway. When it rang a few minutes later, I pushed up onto one elbow. "Hobbs! The door!"

I knew he was down there. I could smell dinner cooking. Just because he was cooking dinner didn't mean he couldn't answer the door too. He was, after all, a butler. He was probably trained in things like this.

I focused back on the TV and the bell rang again, three times in a row. Whoever was at the door was very impatient. I tossed the remote on a nearby pillow and jumped off the bed and made my way downstairs, muttering the whole time about finding better help.

I walked past the kitchen, where Hobbs was nowhere to be found, but noted that dinner looked done. He was probably at the door right now. Made me sorry I'd gotten up. I walked around the corner and into the entry way where Hobbs wasn't.

I shook my head and opened the door, expecting to snarl at some little kid, but it wasn't a kid.

It was a man with a strangely bright red pulsing cloud around him. It was exactly like what I saw at the college.

"About damn time. It's freezing out here," the man said, pushing past me to let himself into my house.

"Who the hell are you?" I said, zeroing in on the black duffle bag he carried.

"Your babysitter," he replied, taking in the entryway, and then spun to look at me.

He was tall, a few inches taller than me, and had dark hair that was styled a little too perfectly. His green eyes watched me as he set down his bag to unbutton his black coat.

"I'd invite you to make yourself at home," I drawled, "but you aren't staying."

He smirked and took his coat off the rest of the way and hung it on the nearby coat rack. Then he walked away, farther into my house.

"Did you not hear what I just said?" I told him as he went into the kitchen.

"Yes, I'm not welcome here. But you don't make the rules," he said as he lifted the lid to the pot on the stove. Then he glanced at me. "Honey, you cooked," he said in falsetto.

"Get out."

"Here's the thing. You might live here, but this isn't your house. Yet," he said as he looked through all the cabinets. So he was an Escort, like me. Storm had been right about us being able to identify each other.

"What are you talking about?" I said, pretending not to hear the meaning behind his words.

He sighed dramatically and looked at me. "We have the same employer and since you seem to be having trouble completing the job you were assigned, G.R. sent me here to make sure you did it."

"He gave me two months," I said, crossing my arms over my chest.

"One of which is already gone." He'd resumed his cabinet searching and made a face when he found what he wanted, reaching in to pull out a large white bowl.

"So?" I prompted.

He took the lid off the pot on the stove, grabbed the nearby ladle, and began scooping homemade chili into his bowl.

Where was Hobbs? Why had he suddenly disappeared? Clearly I was going to need help getting this guy out of here. Of course, I was also glad he wasn't here to listen to the truth behind my income.

"So, a job like this should've taken a week, tops," he said, smug. "My first job took me two days." He spooned a huge amount of sour cream onto the chili and then added an equal amount of shredded cheese.

Part of me was curious. I wondered about the other Escorts and what it was like to essentially kill people for a living. I also had some questions that I hadn't thought to ask when I was given my job. I'd been a little preoccupied with the new body and the shiny car. Maybe I could get some answers before I kicked him out.

I went farther into the kitchen and made myself a similar looking bowl of chili and sat at the opposite end of the island.

"So you're an Escort and you were sent here by G.R. to make sure I did what I was told." It wasn't really a question, just me summing up the reason he was here.

In response, he shoved a huge bite of food into his mouth. He certainly didn't have a problem making himself at home.

"How long have you been an Escort?"

He paused and glanced at me. "A very long time."

"How many bodies have you had?"

He took another bite and seemed to think it over as he chewed. "A few," he replied after a while.

We ate in silence for a few minutes, but there was something I really wanted to know. "How many people have you murdered?"

He lowered the spoon toward his bowl. "I've lost count."

I digested that along with my chili. It was good chili, but I wasn't sure how it would settle with death. Even though I'd tried to "Escort" Piper to her death several times now (and not very successfully), I still couldn't quite wrap my head around the fact that I was basically an assassin for hire. I had a pretty crappy life, but even to me, that stuff only happened in movies.

I mean, why would a man make a business out of killing people? What did he gain? How did he never get caught? Was this some sort of modern day mob? A crime ring? I'd lived on the streets long enough to know that this wasn't a gang. It was too upscale to be a gang.

I put my spoon down and looked at my visitor. It was hard to really focus on him because all I saw was red.

"Did you die too?"

He stopped eating and put his spoon in the bowl. "All of the Escorts died at some point."

"But why?"

He gave me an *are you serious* look and rolled his eyes. "How am I supposed to know why we all died? If there's one thing I've learned all these years it's once you're fated to die, you die. You can't outrun death."

But that bus wasn't aiming for me. It had been aiming for Piper. Did that mean she was really the one meant for death? Or had it been me all along?

"But why didn't we end up in heaven? How did G.R. find us?"

"People that die violent or sudden deaths don't cross over right away. I guess it's because their spirits are too shocked to realize they're dead. Sometimes they're good candidates to be a Death Escort and G.R. finds them and makes them a deal, like he did with you."

I made a good candidate because I was easily seduced by money. Anyone who never had anything would be. Add that to the fact I became a killer as a child and you had a perfect match.

"What's your name?" I asked, turning away from the heavy topic for a minute.

"Everyone calls me Charming," he said with a smirk.

"Charming," I said, deadpan. "Are you serious?"

"I come by it honestly." He got up and filled his bowl with another serving of chili.

"People think you're charming?" I scoffed. I thought he was an ass.

"I have a way with people."

I made a rude sound. "Do people thank you while you're killing them?"

"I give the friendless a friend, the depressed hope, and the rejected acceptance. When their time is up, they go happier than they were."

I looked at him again, looking past the red, trying to see what he claimed others saw in him. All I saw was white, perfect teeth, wide shoulders and a sarcastic grin. He was wearing dark jeans and a heavy grey sweater with a zipper near the neck. It had a collar, which was flipped up around his jaws.

To me he looked like a soap opera actor.

I watched one of those shows today and I thought it was ridiculously cheesy. But the ladies must like them, so maybe they liked him too.

But really, dude? You let people call you Charming?

"So basically you get close to people, get them to trust you—like you—and then you Escort them."

"Pretty much." He flashed me a grin that said he liked his job.

To do what he did, I wondered if he liked himself.

That thought brought me up short—I'd never thought about that before. About liking myself. I guess I always knew where I stood in the world. At the bottom. And I did what I could to survive. I never really had the luxury of self-worth. But sitting here now, it seemed self-worth wasn't a luxury; it was something everyone should have.

Charming pinned me with a hard look. "Are you having second thoughts about the job?"

I sat up a little straighter. "Me? No."

"Then why isn't it done?"

"It's been harder to kill her than I thought it would be."

"Yeah, well, not finishing the job would be harder."

"What do you mean?"

He smirked. "Seriously? Did you not ask what would happen if you didn't do the job?"

No. I hadn't. G.R. (when had he become G.R. to me and not Mr. Burns?) hadn't really given me a choice about completing the job. It was this or an eternity in hell. It wasn't a hard choice.

Charming rolled his eyes. "You were given an amount of time to do the job. To prove yourself as a Death Escort. If you don't do the job, you get recalled."

"Recalled?" I asked.

"As in that pretty purple spirit of yours gets sucked out of that body and you get sent into a fate I hear is worse than hell. An endless world of emptiness, caught between places, still thinking and feeling but being completely lost in a void of nothing."

Hell actually sounded preferable. I shrugged. "I'm not worried about being recalled," I said, the word sounding weird on my tongue. "I'll get the job done."

"You better. I'm very invested in this assignment. I'm going to be watching you."

"Why would you care?"

"Let's just say there's something in it for me when she dies."

Something inside me wanted to tell him to stay far away from Piper. The thought of him near her made my skin crawl. But I didn't let it show. It would reveal more than I wanted to. And I didn't really understand what those feelings meant anyway.

"What do you get out of this?" I pressed.

"Did G.R. tell you nothing?"

I shrugged. I was beginning to wonder that myself.

"Sometimes the Escorts get more than payment after eliminating a Target. Sometimes we get powers."

"Powers." I scoffed.

"It's the reason we just don't go around killing anyone. It's the reason we have Targets."

"So some lives are more valuable than others."

"Exactly. Some of them have tons of money—those are mostly my Targets." He flashed a grin and I got a glimpse of the charm he bragged about. It dawned on me he was used to charming people out of their money and then killing them. "And some," he continued, "have abilities that are beneficial to us."

Well, I knew Piper didn't have any money. That meant she must have some sort of ability. What could it be?

I pushed that thought away because another was forming. "How could someone take another person's ability? How would you even know who had one?"

"You don't know?" Charming said, grinning like he had a secret no one else knew.

"Know what?" I growled. He was an irritating ass.

"Who you—who *we*—work for."

"Yes, I do. You know I've met him."

"But he didn't tell you who he was, why he has the power he does."

"Just spit it out already."

"Well, maybe knowing who you're dealing with will speed up the job completion."

I gave him a *just spit it out* look and he grinned wider.

"Your new employer is none other than the Grim Reaper. The ultimate dealer of death."

"The Grim Reaper," I echoed, disbelief in my voice.

Charming spread his hands wide. "Who better to run a death ring? With a single touch he can claim a life. No one has the power to stop him and no one would even believe it to try."

I sat there, partially stunned. I never in a million years imagined this. I knew he had to be powerful. I had known there was something I was missing... but this. This was not what I expected.

Yet I believed it. He went by G.R., mere initials for his full title. He kept bodies in his closet and radiated power, yet he seemed almost jolly. Of course he would be. Because he knew he'd never be stopped. He didn't have to be mean and vile. If he wanted someone dead all he had to do was touch them.

And now I worked for him.

I worked for the Grim Reaper.

Chapter Twenty-Four

"Crush - a strong positive emotion of regard and affection."

Piper

I crept through the darkened apartment toward the couch where Frankie insisted on sleeping. I hoped she was comfortable, but I wasn't sure my couch would be. I didn't have a sleeper with a pull out mattress so she had to settle for the lumpy cushions. I tried to make her take the bed, but she refused, saying I needed more rest than she did.

I peeked over the back of the faded red velvet to see she had a couple blankets piled on her and all I could see was the top of her white-blond hair. At least she managed to sleep. Before creeping back to my room I glanced at the daisies still sitting in the center of the coffee table. They were still as gorgeous as yesterday.

It was early, still dark outside and very cold. I could hear the howling of the wind outside the window. Mornings like this I hated the opening shift at the diner. But on Friday's, my classes didn't start until later in the day so that left room for an extra shift, and it was money, which I needed. And since I had the day off yesterday, I didn't really need to be complaining.

As I pulled on my uniform and then a sweatshirt on top of that, I thought about Dex and how I hadn't seen him since he brought me home from the clinic. I was still unsure about who he really was and the more I got to know him, the more I wanted to find out. At first it had all been about the man who died in the street. I was positive he knew something. But I wasn't so positive anymore, and even though I began to suspect he knew nothing, my desire to get to know him was still strong.

Maybe my attraction to him hadn't been all about the man who died after all.

Maybe I just had a crush on him.

His messy blond hair, the thick-framed glasses, and the green eyes… I couldn't deny I thought he was handsome. Never mind the fact his jeans always had a rip in them and he wore those black Converse sneakers every time I saw him. His look was an absolute contradiction to his expensive sports car and fancy townhouse (with a butler!). I smiled to myself thinking about it all.

"Why on earth are you smiling that like at this ungodly hour?" Frankie grumped from the doorway of my bedroom and I gave a little shriek and dropped the ponytail I was pulling my hair into.

"Crap! You scared me!"

"Well that's what you get when you creep up on a girl who's dreaming about a hot actor sweeping her off her feet."

I grinned. "Who was it this time?"

"Patrick Dempsey," she said as she trudged over to my bed and fell onto it face first.

I laughed. "I'm sorry I woke you." She grunted into a pillow as she pulled the covers up around her. "Make yourself at home," I said, amused. Really, I wished I was still in bed. It was too cold for work this morning.

"What are you all smiles about?" she mumbled. "I know it isn't because you have to go to work."

"Nothing," I replied, going into the bathroom to brush my teeth and throw on some minimal makeup.

When I came back, she lifted her head from the comfort of the blankets and said, "Mmmhmmmm, it's Dex, isn't it?"

"Maybe." I smiled.

"I'll never understand it. Crushing on some guy who fed you chicken with peanuts."

"He didn't mean it," I said, trying not to remember the reaction I had. My body was still sore from the panic. It was probably why I still felt tired even after a full night of sleep.

"I'll meet you here later and drive you to class."

"Don't you have to work?"

"Yes, but not until an actual decent hour. And I'll take an early lunch to come drive you."

"You don't have to do all that." I protested, knowing it was useless. I covered up my reaction to touching her last night, but she still knew me well enough to know something had thrown me off. I'm just glad she didn't seem to realize that whatever it was had been about her.

"Girl, don't make me get out of this bed," she warned. "After everything that's been going on, it'll make me feel better to know you actually made it to class. And that peanut boy won't be driving you."

I rolled my eyes, but then said, "Thanks, Frank."

She was a good friend—sleeping on my couch to make sure I was okay and then driving me all around town.

"Must sleep," she groaned.

I laughed. "There's coffee in the kitchen if you want to make some later."

She grunted and I slipped out the bedroom door and into my boots. As much as I hated riding the bus these days, it was too cold to walk. As I waited at the bus stop, my thoughts went back to Dex. I wondered when I would see him again and I found myself hoping it would be sooner rather than later.

Chapter Twenty-Five

"Disappointment - a feeling of dissatisfaction that results when your expectations are not realized."

Dex

It was time to get serious about my job. That was the thought that kept me up half the night. Well that and the fact that Charming was sleeping down the hall. I didn't want him here looking over my shoulder and watching my every move. I didn't sign up for a babysitter; I was too old for that.

'Course working for the Grim Reaper wasn't really what I planned either.

I lay there in my huge, almost too comfortable bed and stared up at the ceiling. It was still dark out, the winter night lasting a long time here in Fairbanks. I didn't really want to get up. I knew the air would be icy as soon as I pushed back the covers. Sure, we had the heat on—I kept it up high (the luxury of having money to pay the heating bill)—but I usually always felt cold.

With a heaving sigh I shoved the covers off anyway and rolled out of bed. I reached for my glasses, finding them on the nightstand, and pushed them onto my face. The room came into clearer focus as my arms prickled with goose bumps as I made my way into the bathroom for a hot shower. I didn't bother to shave, but I did use the wall mounted hair dryer to blast my hair, because walking around with a wet head only made me colder. I pulled on a pair of jeans (without holes because that would be freezing) and a long-sleeved thermal T-shirt, grabbed my converse, and went downstairs to hopefully find breakfast. Hobbs never did reappear last night and I hoped it didn't mean he quit.

At the end of the hallway I paused at Charming's door, noticing it was slightly ajar, so I pushed it open. The room was empty and I had a happy thought he left. But then I noticed the clothes lying across the foot of the bed and knew he was coming back.

Feeling disgruntled, I went downstairs. Thankfully for Hobbs, he was in the kitchen and the coffee was made. I went quietly over to the counter and poured some into a mug. I growled when the creamer was nowhere to be seen. It appeared at my side and I uncapped it and poured it into my mug.

"Trouble sleeping?" Hobbs asked.

I grunted and took a gulp of the coffee. I loved that creamer stuff. "Where were you last night?"

"I had to make an impromptu trip to the store to get your beloved creamer."

"Did you just say 'impromptu' and 'beloved' in the same sentence?" I wondered out loud.

"Yes, sir, I did," he said dryly. "Will you be having your usual bacon and eggs this morning?"

"Heavy on the bacon," I said, taking my coffee to the bar and sitting down.

Hobbs began putting together my breakfast while I drank half my coffee. "Where's Charming?" I asked, suddenly remembering he wasn't around.

"I assume you mean your houseguest?" Hobbs asked, his back to me as he cooked the bacon. It smelled really good.

"More like my jailer," I mumbled.

"What was that?" Hobbs said over the sizzling of the meat.

"Yeah, that's him."

"I heard him leave early this morning," Hobbs replied.

"Quick, change the locks," I said sarcastically, knowing full well if G.R. wanted him in this house the locks wouldn't matter.

"You jest, sir," Hobbs said, placing a plate with some eggs and a heaping pile of bacon in front of me.

"I what?" I asked, not understanding half the words out of his mouth.

"You joke," he clarified.

"Yeah," I agreed. "I was just kidding." Kind of.

"Tomorrow is my day off and I was wondering if it would be okay if I took the following day off as well. I'd like to visit my sister a few towns over."

"Sure, take off as many days as you need," I said around a mouthful of food.

Hobbs refilled my coffee and sat the creamer beside my cup. "Thank you. Two days will be plenty. I'm afraid you'll starve before I come back."

"I'll eat out," I said, dumping the cream into my coffee. I looked at the bottle. "Where do I get this?"

"I stocked the fridge. You will have plenty until I return."

"You're the best, Hobbs."

I finished off the rest of my food. I felt better already. Bacon has a way of putting a man in a better mood.

I was ready to get down to business. The fact was, I could've had this done by now. Dumb accidents and coincidences kept ruining things, but I couldn't let that go on. Finding out your boss is the King of Death himself, well, that has a way of lighting a fire under a guy. That and the knowledge I would be recalled if I didn't complete my job. None of this was really what I wanted, but like a lot of my life, these were the cards I'd been dealt. All I could do was play my hand.

It was time to amp things up. To get the job done. The Target wouldn't even know what hit her. Grim would be satisfied and Charming would be off my back and out of my house.

"Put my coffee in a travel mug, Hobbs. I have somewhere I need to be." I got up from the island and went to grab my coat and keys.

"Do you have an appointment, sir?"

"As a matter of fact, I do," I zipped up my coat and pulled a black knit cap over my head. "I'll be gone all day. Go ahead and get a head start on your vacation."

Hobbs handed me my mug and I thought I saw some worry pass behind his eyes.

"Sir, you remember that talk we had not so long ago?"

"The one about my job?"

"Yes, that's the one."

"What about it?"

"I hope you have given what I said some thought."

I actually had. Quite a lot. But the fact of my situation was that I really didn't have the luxury of choice. Well, I guess I did. I could choose to be sent to a lonely, empty existence—an existence that promised to be worse than hell itself. Or, I could suck it up, do my job, and preserve my humanity, my life.

I pushed away the voice that whispered my life would come at the cost of someone else's.

"I did, Hobbs," I told him, turning away. He didn't say anything until I reached the door that led to the garage.

"Remember," he said quietly but loud enough that my hand froze on the knob, "with great sacrifice sometimes comes reward."

I stood completely still for long moments as his words kind of wrapped themselves around me. They echoed through my ears with some kind of meaning I didn't understand. Then I blinked and the feeling was gone.

"Thanks for the advice," I called and left the townhouse, backing my little Roadster out onto the street.

I pushed away the feeling that I somehow left a very disappointed butler behind.

Chapter Twenty-Six

"Bully - A person who is habitually cruel or overbearing, especially to smaller or weaker people."

Piper

As if getting up early on a freezing cold morning, riding a bus that makes you feel like a traitor, and worrying the whole ride about your best friend's life wasn't enough, I get to work and find out I'm stuck with Emilio.

Yay.

Emilio is a new addition to the diner's staff (any other time I might've said family, but I would rather get poked repeatedly with a sharp object than call that guy family), and he has to be the hardest person to get along with I've ever met.

Frankly, he's a bully.

None of us like him, but we all have to tolerate him.

I was the first waitress to arrive, on time, but Emilio was already there, standing on the sidewalk in a thin coat with his hands shoved into the pockets. The minute I stepped on the sidewalk, he started complaining about us waitresses and how we were never on time. He blamed me for his frozen toes and nose the whole time I unlocked the diner and he was still complaining after I let us in and flipped on all the lights.

"I'm sorry you had to wait. I know it's very cold this morning," I said to be polite. Really, I wanted to tell him it wasn't my problem he showed up early and had to wait. I guess I should be glad he showed up at all.

"I think I might call the boss and let him know you didn't show up on time. Made people wait on you."

I didn't say anything as I started the coffee makers. When I tried to move past him toward the back and the ice machine, he blocked my path, staring down at me with a sour look on his face.

"Excuse me," I said, holding on to my temper. Giving this guy a reaction is what he wanted. I wasn't about to play into his hands.

Just then the other waitress working the morning shift walked in and behind her was our first customer of the day. He stepped aside and I went past to get the ice. I let out a deep breath. If the start to my morning were any indication, this was going to be a very, very long day.

Chapter Twenty-Seven

"Fight - To engage in a quarrel; argue. To attempt to harm or gain power over an adversary by blows or with weapons."

Dex

I got a spot in front of the diner, probably because it was still early. I sat there with the engine running for a few minutes and looked through the windows and into the restaurant. Piper came out from around the counter, holding a plate of food and a pot of coffee. She went across the room to deliver the meal. She moved a little slower than normal and I figured it was because it was early and she was probably still half asleep.

I realized I was smiling.

I stopped.

Then I climbed out of the car and headed for the diner. The bell on the door was offensively loud when I pushed open the door, and the few customers looked up from their food. I went to the bar and sat on a stool, waiting for Piper to notice me.

She did and she smiled.

I cleared my throat and she came over and stood behind the counter in front of me.

"Here," I said and shoved my travel mug at her.

"We have coffee here," she said, amused.

"Yeah, it tastes like mud. This'll actually wake you up."

Her lips curved and she took the mug and lifted it to her lips. Her eyes sparkled over the rim as she tipped it against her mouth. Just moments before my lips were in the same spot. The thought made me feel a little… well, *warm*.

She made a face and handed it back to me. "Do you want a little coffee with that creamer?" she said, reaching for the pot.

"Don't mess with my coffee, woman," I warned.

She laughed. "So what are you doing here so early?"

"Breakfast," I lied. "Hobbs has a few days off."

"Does that mean you actually made that coffee?"

"He set the timer," I lied again.

"Figures." She rolled her eyes. "So what are you having?"

"Pancakes."

She walked toward the line and spoke to the cook. He made some remark and she rolled her eyes and said something rapidly. He made a motion at her with a large spatula.

"Just make the order," she spat.

"Write it down and hang it up like you're supposed to," he shot back.

She shook her head and pulled out a little notepad from the pocket of her apron and began to write.

"Pancakes," she said and ripped off the paper and hung it on a little carousel by the cook's head. "Now you make it."

He made a reply, but it was too low to hear. Piper made a face and grabbed the coffee and went around filling cups. On her way back by I grabbed her wrist and spun her around. Gently, she pulled away and sat the almost empty pot on the counter.

"Is that guy bothering you?" I asked. I hadn't liked the way he acted toward her.

"No. He's new and he doesn't like me is all. It's fine. I deal with it." She picked up the pot again, then smiled. "I can't believe I haven't thanked you yet."

"Thanked me?"

"I got the flowers. They're beautiful."

Was she blushing? "I'm glad you liked them."

"I really do," she began, and it looked like she might say something more when the cook interrupted.

"Order up!" he yelled.

She took a breath and moved off to put the coffee pot back and deliver the plates of food to a nearby table.

A few minutes later she handed me a plate of pancakes and a glass container of syrup. As I poured the dark liquid over the stack, I thought about her tired eyes this morning. Maybe the reason she looked a little run down wasn't from lack of sleep or an early morning. Maybe she was still feeling sick from the reaction she had before.

I felt a little stab of something in the center of my chest, but I ignored it. I didn't have time for feelings. I had to complete this job. My life depended on it.

I took a bite of the pancakes, not really tasting them, as my mind worked to formulate a plan. I needed to get out of town. I needed away from Grim, from Charming… I needed a vacation.

Bingo.

I glanced up to see Piper hanging an order slip for the line cook. I watched as he knocked into her with his side and she fell sideways, nearly losing her balance.

She put her hands on her hips and made a face as the guy yelled, "Watch where you're going!"

My fork clattered against the glass of my plate as I shoved off the stool and went around to the employee side of the counter.

"Employees only, sir," the other waitress on staff told me as I shouldered my way past her.

Piper looked up from behind the register. She looked worse than earlier. Something inside me snapped and I shoved the line cook, causing him to pitch forward. He caught himself before landing face first onto the piping hot griddle.

"Hey!" he shouted and turned. "What the hell's your problem?"

"I don't like the way you treat the waitresses."

"It's none of your damn business!" he said, waiving an oversized spatula around.

"Apologize," I demanded.

"Dex, just let it go," Piper said from behind the angry cook.

"Yeah, Dex, let it go," the cook mocked.

My fist shot out and nailed him right across the jaw. He flew backwards, knocking over a container full of utensils and they all clattered to the floor. He gave a grunt and came at me, and instead of sidestepping like I should have, I stayed still and took his fist right to the left side of my face.

A guy had to do what a guy had to do.

I felt my cheek split open and my skin began to sting. Shouting erupted around me. Piper ran forward, trying to make it to my side, but the cook held out his arm, clothes-lining her behind him. She slipped on something and fell backward onto her butt.

My hand shot out and grabbed the cook's wrist and forced his hand down onto the griddle. He yelled in pain when his skin sizzled. I didn't hold on to him long—I wasn't trying to melt all his skin away, just some of it—and I let go to help Piper when I felt something heavy hit me over the head. I fell to the floor, and just before passing out, I noted that Piper was unharmed.

Chapter Twenty-Eight

"Stupid - men." (Definition provided by Piper and many other women across the globe.)

Piper

Stupid. I was pretty sure if I were to look up the definition for the word it would say "men." Why did everything always boil down to some sort of fist fight when they couldn't agree on anything? Granted, I did secretly enjoy watching Emilio get punched in the face by Dex, but the rest of the drama, I could have done without.

You'd think the place would be loud and alive with people shouting and taking sides, but it was eerily quiet in here. A quick glance around showed me that the morning regulars were enjoying the show. They were all sipping their coffee and giving the unfolding scene their undivided attention.

Figures. Most of the customers were also men.

The smell of burnt flesh violated the air as Emilio's hand was ruthlessly burned. Then the silence was shattered with his screeching in pain. And then Dex was falling to the floor, passing out from the hard hit Emilio delivered with a frying pan.

Despite his stupidity, I rushed to his side, calling his name, but he was out cold.

It was then that everyone decided to cause a commotion.

Mary, the other morning waitress, was standing there with wide eyes and when I glanced her way, she seemed to shake herself out of it. She looked at Emilio who was still wailing and said, "I'll call for an ambulance."

Emilio stopped long enough in between wails to yell, "I'm not getting in one of those things."

"Well, then you can walk 'cause no one here wants to drive you," she snapped.

I would've laughed had I not been feeling for Dex's pulse, which thankfully was strong. I shook his shoulder, but he still didn't stir. I was considering dowsing him in water when Emilio rounded on me, cradling his injured hand at his chest.

"This is all your fault!" he growled.

"Mine?" I said incredulously.

"You and you're better than everyone attitude, coming in here with your boyfriend and causing trouble."

My boyfriend. My stomach flipped a little at his words. Dex wasn't my boyfriend, but it was a little shocking to realize maybe I wouldn't mind if he was.

But now wasn't the time for those kind of thoughts.

"He's not my boyfriend. And the only person with the attitude around here is you." I snapped, glancing down at Dex. He was still out.

Apparently Emilio's burned hand was momentarily forgotten because he launched himself at me. His eyes were wild and he reached out with his good hand and grabbed me around the arm, just beneath my elbow, and yanked. I planted my foot into the ground and tried to jerk my arm free, but he didn't let go. So I kicked him. The heel of my boot caught him in the knee and finally he let go, howling.

Mary pushed him backwards and he fell onto his butt. There was a bucket nearby, half filled with ice, and she reached in and grabbed a handful and threw it on the downed cook. "Sit there and cool off until help arrives."

My chest was heaving when he glared at me. I wanted to kick him again, but I didn't. The customers in the diner had seen enough. I could only imagine what the owner was going to say. I prayed I didn't get fired.

I leaned down beside Dex again and shook his shoulder, brushing the hair back from his forehead. He began to stir and then he was blinking open his eyes and looking up at me.

His glasses were slightly askew and I reached out to adjust them.

"We keep meeting like this," he said, his eyes still kind of unfocused.

Memories assaulted me of sitting in the street with snow falling all around. The chaos from that night suddenly mirrored the chaos of tonight. It was just him and I sitting in a bubble, the two of us a part of the room, yet somehow separate. Activity hummed around us, but the air that encircled us was still. Just him looking up at me.

Except this was Dex.

This wasn't the man who died.

Right?

Sitting here now, in the middle of the diner, I felt a connection… some sort of familiarity between us.

I reminded myself that this wasn't the night of the accident. Dex was hurt and needed medical attention.

"Dex, how do you feel?"

"I'm fine. How's the other guy?" he replied groggily.

"Burned and pissed off," I said, watching his eyes, checking for any sign of a concussion.

He grunted in response and I wondered if that meant he didn't feel well enough to speak or only that he didn't really care about Emilio. Most likely the latter.

The chaos of the room was breaking into the bubble I imagined surrounding us, and I was grateful Mary was trying to calm everyone down.

"Come on, you need a doctor," I told Dex, reaching down and grabbing his arm to help him up.

I shouldn't have touched him.

Maybe it was the way I was feeling. Maybe it was the memories flooding back to me or what Dex said only moments before, but the vision came over me and it was exactly as it always was.

The man from the accident, the one with the serious eyes and knit hat, flooded my head. All I could see was him. He wasn't wearing a hat and he had almost black hair. Hair that was either slightly curly or just really messy fell onto his forehead. He was smiling, a beautiful smile, and I imagined it was me he looked at.

And then it was gone as fast as it came.

For some reason I felt bereft. Robbed of a certain warmth.

Why? Why of all days did I have to have this vision today?

"Piper? Are you okay?" I heard Dex ask and then I felt his hand on my arm.

I pulled my arm away from his touch, not wanting a replay. "Yeah," I replied. "Give me your car keys."

He needed a doctor and suddenly this room seemed way, way too small.

"You want to drive my Roadster?" he asked me like I suggested he run down the street naked.

"Well, you aren't driving it." I retorted. I was still unsure if he had a concussion or not.

He fished the keys out of his pocket and handed them to me. I took them, hoping he didn't notice how hard I tried not to touch him. I wanted to run from the place, but I couldn't. I had responsibilities.

I turned toward Mary who was refilling the customers' coffee and working to calm everyone down.

"He needs a doctor, stitches, I think," I told her when she came close enough so I didn't have to yell.

Behind us Emilio was still crying about his hand and how no one was even worried about him.

"Just go," Mary said. "The EMTs are on their way to help him. I'll call for another waitress and a cook in a sec. I can handle things. It's still early, and the crowd is small. Better to get him outta here anyway."

"I owe you one, Mary," I replied.

"No. It was payment enough watching this guy get what was coming to him. I'll do my best to cover for you, but I can't promise anything."

"Thank you," I told her again and headed toward the door, hoping Dex would follow. He did and soon we were outside on the sidewalk in the wintry air. As we headed to the Roadster, I did my best not to look at the spot where the accident happened. Instead, I looked toward Dex.

Blood ran down the left side of his face. It caught in his eyebrow, the thick hair diverting it around his eye where it then continued its dark trail.

See? I told myself. *He's completely different from the guy in your vision.*

I knew this was true. It was obvious they were two different people.

So why did something inside me keep whispering they were the same?

Chapter Twenty-Nine

"Suture - thread of catgut or silk or wire used by surgeons to stitch tissues together."

Dex

I didn't really start to notice everything around me until I was sitting in the passenger side of the Roadster. The cold air outside acted like a wakeup call and really brought some clarity back into my head. I must have been completely out of it to agree to let her drive my car. I was about to tell her that I was the one who would be driving when she started yelling at me.

"What were you thinking?" Piper demanded as she put the car in drive and pulled away from the curb.

I calculated the odds I had of getting her to pull over and let me drive. I didn't think they were very good and besides, I was comfortable.

"I didn't like that guy's attitude," I said in response to her question. And my answer was actually true. Sure, I needed a reason to get her out of the diner, and sure, this would buy me some points for what I had planned, but when I saw him shove her, anger slammed through me.

"Well, I'm probably going to get fired," she said, flat. "And you're bleeding all over yourself and this car."

I was such a hypocrite. Beating on a guy with a bad attitude directed at Piper when all the while I plotted her death. I didn't have a right to be angry at anyone for what they did to her… yet I felt strangely territorial when it came to her. No one was allowed to hurt Piper. No one but me.

I was a world-class ass. I deserved an eternity of floating through an empty void.

For a moment I imagined what it might be like there. Maybe I should just cut my losses and let myself get recalled.

"Dex!" Piper demanded, worry in her tone.

"I'm sorry," I mumbled.

"Hey! Stay with me. We're almost there." She flicked some switches in the dash and directed the heat vents toward me except they weren't blowing heat yet and the air was icy cold.

"That's freezing!" I complained.

"It will keep you awake." She retorted. "And don't be sorry. That guy had it coming. In the couple weeks he's been at the diner he's done nothing but torture us all."

I didn't say anything else as she pulled into the parking lot of the clinic where she interned. She got out and came around to open my door and I looked up at her. "What are we doing here?"

"You need stitches. He hit you with a frying pan."

A frying pan. My plan worked a little too well. I knew there was a joke in this somewhere but I just couldn't find one. This didn't feel funny.

"Come on," she said and I followed her into the side door of the clinic. She called out a greeting to one of the nurses who exclaimed over my bloody face and we were ushered into an empty exam room.

"We're pretty backed up," the nurse said, apparently this is a morning of accidents for everyone. "Unless you want to stitch him up?"

Piper shook her head. "My hand is too unsteady this morning. How about I get him cleaned up a bit then I will go out there and help out while you stitch him up?"

"Are you all right? You look pale." The nurse said, reaching out to feel Piper's forehead.

She smiled. "I'm fine, Jackie."

"Well when I come back I want to hear about what happened," she said, giving me a pointed look.

"It was the other guys fault," I told her.

"It always is," she said around a sigh then disappeared out of the room.

Piper began going through cabinets, pulling out supplies and creating a small pile on the rolling table beside her. Then she washed her hands, pulled on some plastic gloves and rolled her tray over beside me.

"Hold still. This might hurt,"

I watched as she ripped open a little pack of wipes and stepped closer to me. She smelled like coffee and pancakes. She gripped my chin in her gloved hand and titled my face upwards and brought the pad down near my hairline. I winced when she wiped it.

"That's cold!" I growled.

"Serves you right," she snapped and wiped me again. The cut began to sting and I let out a growl. She pulled back and dropped the pad, now covered in red onto the table. She reached for another then looked at me. "We need to check you for a concussion."

"I don't have one," I denied.

She half smiled and said, "Okay tough guy."

She positioned herself between my legs and lifted the wipe once more. She was so close I could hear her breathing. It was a soft sound and her chest rose and fell steadily. Her free hand brushed through my hair, pushing it away from the cut, but instead of short quick strokes, her hand moved slowly and went through my hair all the way to the back of my head.

I heard her clear her throat, but I didn't look up. My stomach was bouncing around and my heart was pounding. I told myself I might have a concussion after all... but deep down I knew that wasn't it. It was her closeness affecting me.

I liked it.

Once more the voice programmed inside me—inside this body—whispered, *Kill her now.* I could. I could reach over to the table and grab something sharp. I could use it to take away her life.

But then she would stop breathing.

And I liked that sound.

I told that voice to shut up and I listened once more to the breaths that filled her lungs.

"Almost done," she said low, reaching for another wipe. "Does it hurt very much?"

"Yes," I whispered and my eyes widened.

She lowered her hand and looked at me. She was so close I could see all the different colors that made up the depth in her eyes. I don't know why I said yes. My head didn't hurt. In fact, I didn't even think of it at all.

"I meant to say no," I said, still looking in her eyes. The room around us seemed hushed; there were no other sounds but the ticking of the wall clock and Piper's slow, even breathing.

"You hit that guy for me," she whispered.

I felt myself nod. I might have needed an excuse to get her out of the diner, but I'd hit that guy because he hurt her.

She brushed at my hair once more and I leaned a little closer, my eyes closing.

"It wasn't the first time you did something to protect me," she whispered again.

I nodded again, my hands coming up to grip the sides of her waist.

She looked down at me and I pulled her even closer. I could now feel the heat radiate from her body and into me. Her face leaned closer to mine and I lifted mine up.

Inches… mere inches…

"Tell me who you really are," she said, the words practically touching my lips.

My hands tightened around her and it took a minute for her words to actually make it to my brain. When they did, some of the haze I felt ebbed away and my eyes widened.

"What do you mean?"

And just like that the moment was lost. The corners of her mouth fell and she looked at me with some kind of disappointment in her eyes. The door to the room opened, and she jumped back like she was caught doing something illegal and turned away.

"His wound is all clean. His pupils seem responsive so I don't think he has a concussion. He's ready for stitching."

"Doc could use you in exam three," the nurse said, coming in and grabbing a pair of gloves.

Piper disappeared from the room without a backward glance. The nurse pulled up a stool holding a needle and thread. "Did she numb you?"

"No," I said. "Just do it."

"It's going to hurt," she warned.

"I don't care."

"You got it bad," she said, shaking her head.

"What are you talking about?" I ground out as she directed me to lie back.

"Piper. Only a lovesick fool would refuse numbing."

"I'm not lovesick," I demanded as she stuck the needle in and began to stitch me up. It hurt so much I almost asked for that numbing shot.

She made a sound like she disagreed, but I gritted my teeth against the pain.

I wasn't lovesick. I'd never loved anyone in my entire life. I wasn't about to start now.

* * *

When Piper let herself back into the room, the nurse was applying a bandage over my stitches. The whole upper half of my face hurt and I was rethinking my plan of getting her out of the diner. Why did my plans always end up with me getting hurt?

"I hear you had some morning!" the nurse exclaimed to Piper.

Piper glanced at me, then back at the nurse. "How much did you tell her?"

"When a woman has a needle in your head, you tell her whatever she asks," I said, wincing and pushing myself into a sitting position.

Piper shifted and I noticed she was holding something in her hand. She came farther into the room and handed it to me. It was a cold pack.

"Here, this'll help with the swelling."

I took it gratefully.

"Now, tell me why you look so tired," the nurse questioned her.

"It's nothing," Piper protested.

"Working too hard. Between school, work and this place, you never have any time to breathe." She nodded her head.

I took advantage of the moment to set my plan into action. "I think she needs a vacation. After today, I think I need one too."

"Ooh, yes! A vacation is what you need."

I almost forgave her for jamming a needle in my head repeatedly.

Piper smiled. "That would be nice, but I don't have time for that."

"It's the weekend. Why don't we drive up to that resort I keep hearing people talk about… you know, the one northeast of Fairbanks…?" I snapped my fingers like I was trying to remember.

"Chena Hot Springs Resort?" The nurse supplied the name.

"That's the one," I agreed.

"I hear that place is nice. You can see the aurora borealis up there."

"The what?" I said.

Piper smiled. "The northern lights. They're supposed to be beautiful."

"Good, let's go," I said, shifting to stand up.

"We can't just go there," Piper said.

"Why not?" the nurse demanded, putting her hands on her hips.

"I have work at the diner and here at the clinic."

"I'll cover for you here," the nurse replied.

I was starting to like this lady.

"I really think lying low after what happened at the diner this morning is a good idea," I said, trying to sound convincing while holding an ice pack on my head. "Besides, you should probably watch me for at least twenty-four hours in case I do have a concussion."

"I thought you said you were fine," Piper demanded.

The nurse snorted.

"I am. But just in case…" I looked at her and grinned. Maybe I could be charming too. "And you should probably drive. And I'll pay for the entire weekend."

"A free vacation?" the nurse exclaimed. "If you don't go, I will."

Piper laughed. "Okay, you convinced me."

"Let's go," I said, jumping up, wobbling a little on my feet.

"Slow down," Piper said, holding out her hands as if she might need to catch me. "I need to go home and pack a bag."

"I dug some money out of my pocket and handed the nurse a couple hundred-dollar bills. "Will this cover the bill?"

"Sure will," she said, taking it and then waving us away. "Don't come back until you've had all the fun you can stand."

My stomach tightened. I wondered what she'd say if she knew Piper wouldn't be coming back at all.

Chapter Thirty

"Phone - To impart (information or news, for example) by telephone."

Piper

She answered on the first ring.

"Hey, I'm running a few minutes late. I'll be by soon to drive you to campus."

"I don't need a ride anymore, Frankie," I replied, holding back a wince, waiting for the inquisition to begin.

"What do you mean? Are you riding the bus?"

"No, I'm actually not going to classes today."

Here it comes… three… two… one.

"What happened?! Oh my God. Did you almost die again?!"

"No, Frankie, I didn't." I sighed. "I just… Dex came by the diner…"

"I should've known he was involved." Frankie snorted. "What did he do?"

"He's taking me away for the weekend. We're going to that resort on the outside of town to see the northern lights."

She gasped. Then she squealed. "I knew it! You got it so bad," she yelled into the phone.

I slid a glance at Dex who was standing nearby, acting like he wasn't listening. I'm sure he was. But I sure hoped he didn't hear Frankie.

"I just wanted to let you know I wouldn't be home so you wouldn't worry," I said into the phone, trying not to smile.

"Uh-huh. I want a full report when you come home."

"Deal," I agreed.

"Oh, and Piper," she sang. "Don't do anything I wouldn't do."

It was my turn to snort. But then I sobered. "Frankie. Take it easy this weekend, huh? Stay in."

"Oh, sure, you can go out, but I can't?"

"I don't want to worry about you," I said low. Maybe it wasn't such a good idea that I leave after that vision I had.

Frankie sighed dramatically. "I don't have plans anyway. I have to work half of tomorrow and then Sunday I'll probably sleep all day and await your juicy phone call full of details."

I smiled. That made me feel a little better. "I'll call you, 'kay?"

"Yeah. Have fun. You deserve it."

I hung up the phone and came around the nurse's station where Dex was leaning on the counter.

"You ready?" he asked.

"Yes," I agreed, butterflies dancing just beneath my ribcage. I'd never spent a weekend away with a guy before.

"We'll go to your place so you can pack a bag and then mine so I can pack one too. After that we'll hit the road," he said as we walked to the door.

At first I wasn't sure if this trip was a good idea, and I guess I was a little nervous, but it did sound like fun. Plus, it would give me a chance to spend a little extra time with Dex. Maybe, just maybe, by the end of the weekend all my questions about this guy would be answered and the "report" that I owed Frankie would be overflowing with information.

Chapter Thirty-One

"Warning - An intimation, threat, or sign of impending danger or evil."

Dex

I took the stairs two at a time and didn't pause at his bedroom door. I didn't really want to talk to him and was hoping if I moved fast enough I wouldn't have to deal with him at all. I found a duffle bag in my closet and began shoving in a few pairs of jeans and other necessary items I would need. Whatever I forgot I'd just buy once we got there.

Now that my plan was in action, I was motivated to see it through. The sooner I got this over with, the sooner I could move on.

The thought made me drop the rolled-up socks in my hand. Moving on implied that I would be upset, that this was something I was going to have to move past. It wasn't. This was a job, plain and simple.

Then why do you have to remind yourself of that? a voice in the back of my head argued.

I picked the socks up and shoved them in my bag as I saw a cloud of red out of the corner of m eye. Suddenly, I didn't mind so much talking to Charming. It was preferable to thinking.

"Is that the Target I see sitting out there in your car in the driveway?" he asked, leaning against the doorjamb.

"I'm taking the Target out of town for the weekend."

"You do realize you're supposed to kill her, not date her, right?"

This guy really had a way of getting under my skin.

"I'm going to finish the job this weekend."

"I could just go outside right now and take care of that quick," he said, pushing away from the door and coming farther into the room. "Smile my handsome smile, get her to roll down the window, and the minute she does I could just reach inside and snap her neck." As he spoke he held out his hands like they were really reaching for her. "It would be over in two seconds."

Without any kind of warning I swung the duffle up and around, catching him in the side of the face. He stumbled and fell into the closet door, which buckled so he fell into the closet, knocking several hangers off the rack.

"Keep your hands off my Target," I ground out, dropping the bag.

He righted himself quickly and looked at me with flashing, angry eyes. Then he smiled a cruel smile and turned for the door.

He was going after her.

I launched myself at him and leaped onto his back. He fell forward onto his knees and I took the chance to punch him in the kidney. His breath made a whooshing sound and then he hit the floor. As he hit, he rolled so he was on his back, facing me. I was straddling him from when I jumped onto his back and so I drew my fist back to punch him again.

He caught my fist in his hand and squeezed.... He squeezed so hard I thought my bones might break. How much strength did this guy possess?

I wasn't willing to find out. So I kneed him.

I climbed off him and stood as he rolled into the fetal position, cupping himself.

"Don't you know there's a guy code about never nailing another guy in his family jewels?" Charming said with a strained voice.

"There is no guy code where I come from." I spat. Then I leaned down in his face. "And if you threaten me or my Target again, you'll find out what other dirty tricks I learned from the streets."

He sprung up, hitting my shoulders, and I fell back but caught my balance. He stood in the center of the room with a red face and a heaving chest. I calmly grabbed the duffle bag and slung it over my shoulder.

"Don't be here when I get back."

"You better kill that girl this weekend," Charming said, his voice unnaturally calm and low. I stopped in the doorway to hear what he would say next. "Because if she comes back, you're going to wish she hadn't. I'll go after her and use every single one of my ninety years' experience to make sure she suffers. And then I'll come for you."

He's been killing people for ninety years?

That would explain his sense of entitlement, but not his lack of patience. I glanced over my shoulder, pretending his words didn't bother me at all.

"I thought old people were supposed to be wise. You aren't very wise at all because making an enemy out of me is the stupidest thing you could ever do."

Then I walked away, down the hall and toward the stairs. From behind me he called out. "This weekend. Finish the job or I will."

This time I didn't look back. I was afraid if I did he'd see genuine fear on my face.

Chapter Thirty-Two

"Ominous - threatening or foreshadowing evil or tragic developments."

Piper

My favorite song was playing on the radio when Dex pulled into the driveway of his townhouse. As Snow Patrol's "Chasing Cars" played, I mouthed the words. After a few minutes of us just sitting in the driveway, the car idling, I realized he wasn't moving. I turned my head and looked at him. He was watching me. I felt my cheeks heat under his gaze.

"What?" I asked.

"You like this song?" He smiled.

"No. I just mouth the words to songs I really hate," I said sarcastically but with a smile on my face.

"I do that all the time too." He grinned. "Why is it the worst lyrics always get stuck in your head?"

I laughed. "I don't listen to songs I don't like."

"Huh. Now there's an idea."

I shook my head.

"If I leave you out here in the car with the engine running, you aren't going to steal it and run away are you?" He teased.

"I don't know. I might. This is a pretty amazing car."

"It won't be as amazing once I get out of it." He wagged his eyebrows.

"I think that bump on your head has done more damage than we realized," I said seriously.

He pulled on his glasses and looked at me over the black rims. "I assure you, I'm thinking perfectly clear."

I laughed and a new song drifted through the speakers.

"I'll be right back. I'm just going to grab a few things. That's all that'll fit in the trunk with the fifty pounds of stuff you brought."

"I did not bring fifty pounds of things." I sniffed. "Only forty-five."

"Close enough," he replied and got out of the car, slamming the door behind him. I watched him run up to the front door and let himself into the townhouse.

I really couldn't believe the way my life had been going lately. It was so full of unexpected twists and turns. And now, here I was, about to go on a weekend getaway with a guy. It was kind of surreal.

The song that was playing on the radio was not one of my favorites so I leaned forward to turn the volume down and when I did, some movement in the upstairs window caught my eye. I looked up, and there was definitely something or someone there. But the person—a man?—was standing back from the glass, not right up behind it so I couldn't make out who it was. Plus, there were sheer curtains hanging and they were almost pulled together, only giving me a glimpse at the dark shape through the crack.

I doubted it was Dex. Why would he stand in the window and look out when he was supposed to be packing? Then I grinned. Maybe it was him and he was really looking to see if I had taken off with his car.

I leaned forward even more and waved up at him.

He didn't wave back. In fact, he stepped away, the curtains swaying slightly from his movements, and then he disappeared.

Maybe it really hadn't been Dex. Maybe it was the butler… Hobbs, I think.

But hadn't he said Hobbs was off for a few days? I shrugged it off and leaned back in the seat.

A few minutes later Dex appeared, slamming the front door behind him and carrying a black duffle bag. I would never understand how guys managed to pack so lightly.

Especially when here in Alaska we had to wear like a hundred layers just to keep from freezing.

He tossed the bag into the trunk and then hurried to get into the car.

I smiled at him, but he didn't even look my way. Instead, he threw the car into reverse and backed out of the driveway suddenly.

"Is everything okay?" I asked him, concerned.

He barely glanced at me. "Everything's fine."

He put the car into drive and as we drove away I looked back at the house. There was someone standing in the window again, closer this time. I could see the looming shape of the man as he watched us drive away.

I shivered a little.

There was something creepy about the person standing there. Something ominous.

Dex must've noticed my shiver because he turned up the heat and when we turned the corner and headed off his street, he finally looked at me.

"This guy"—he hitched his thumb at himself—"is ready for a vacation."

I smiled and nodded.

Who was that person in the window? Maybe this wasn't a sudden vacation. Maybe Dex was running from something. Or someone. But whom?

Chapter Thirty-Three

"Alone - Being apart from others; solitary."

Dex

I rented a small one-bedroom cabin with promises I would take the couch. It seemed even colder here, if that were possible, probably because there were no tall city buildings to buffer the frigid, whipping wind. When I rented the cabin, the man at the desk went on and on about the hot springs, the northern lights, and the many activities available to us here. I just looked at all this as my opportunity to finish my job.

True, I'd thought about maybe just going into the void for all eternity (the unprogrammed side of me), but that idea really wasn't that appealing so it was back to plan A.

I let us into the small wooden cabin and shut the door against the cold, looking for a light switch. The small room flooded with light when I found it, and Piper went around pulling open the heavy drapes to reveal wide views of bare landscape and snow. Off in the distance was some water that looked icy even from here.

There was a very large couch in some kind of Navaho print in red and blue with two large leather chairs off to the side. A wood-burning stove sat directly adjacent from the couch and across the room was a pine table with seating for four. There was also a small kitchen in the main room with a fridge, stove, and a row of cabinets above the sink. Basically, the cabin was all one room, with the exception of the bedroom over to the right and the bathroom beside it.

"I heard, of course, how nice it was here, but I never really gave it much thought. It really is nice," Piper said, standing in the center of the room.

I set down our bags and went over to the woodstove to build a fire.

"You probably need more pain medication. Is your head bothering you?" she said, coming to stand next to me.

"It's fine," I said, glad there was already a fire set up. I lit a match and got the kindling burning. I sat there and watched it burn for a while, long after I was sure the fire would stay lit. The truth was, I wasn't really sure what to do now. I managed to get her alone. I managed to get her away from her friend and coworkers. Now all I had to do was kill her. Something I hadn't been very good at up to this point.

I was also realizing I didn't really know how to be alone with her.

Yes, we'd been alone before, but not completely alone, like it seemed now. Before, we were a door away from other people, just passengers in a car on a road full of other drivers, people in the diner who talked with others in earshot...

But now, now we were shut up in a small cabin at a resort with vacationing couples and families. No one would come walking through the cabin door.

"Let's get out of here," I said, feeling claustrophobic.

She laughed. "We just got here."

"Yeah, but this is just a boring cabin. Let's go do something." I brushed my hands together and stood.

"Sure, why not? That's why we're here."

As soon as the cabin door was behind us, I felt lighter; some of the tension inside me eased.

"Are you okay?" Piper asked, eyeing me.

"Of course. We're on vacation." I shot her a grin and she giggled.

"Let's go to the Ice Museum," she said, looking down at one of the pamphlets in her hand.

It advertised a museum completely made of ice. People could go there for tours and a martini at the ice bar.

"Okay, but you do realize we're underage. That means no sitting at the bar for us. I can't have you getting me drunk and then trying to take advantage of me,"

She hit me in the ribs with her pamphlet. "Oh, please. Like that would happen."

"Right," I muttered. "I forgot you're still hung up on the dead guy."

She gasped and narrowed her eyes. "Don't talk about him that way! If it weren't for him I'd be dead."

Great. Now I'd gone and made her mad. *Good going, Dex.* With my luck she'd leave and never want to speak to me again. That would only make things harder.

I shook my head, not even knowing where that comment came from. It seemed that suddenly I had a shot of jealousy. I felt the need to compete. Against myself.

What an idiot.

"Look, I'm sorry. That was really crappy of me to say." I apologized, trying to inject all the meaning I could behind my words.

She didn't look at me. She looked everywhere but at me.

"Piper?" I asked. "I really am sorry."

She sighed. "Yeah, I know." She uncrossed her arms. "Look, I'm not hung up on him, okay?"

"Yeah, okay." I agreed even though I thought she was totally hung up on him. I saw it in her eyes every time she mentioned him. And sometimes when she got this far away look in her eyes I knew she was thinking about him—*me*—and wondering what would've been if they met in a different place and time.

I kind of wondered that too.

I cleared my throat and held out my arm. "To the Ice Museum?"

She slid her arm into mine, her gloved fingers resting on my forearm. "Let's go."

We didn't say anything until the house came into view.

"Huh," I said, "it really is made completely of ice."

"It's so beautiful," she said as we made our way inside, where it was just as cold as it was outside.

The place was pretty awesome and it featured a ton of life-sized ice sculptures like jousters on horseback and an animal-themed chess set. There was also a two story observation tower and a spiral staircase all made completely of crystal-clear ice.

"I love the lights," Piper said as we made our way through some of the rooms. It was almost like a light show, with the lights all in neon colors like green, blue, and pink. Some changed periodically and others stayed the same. Some of them seemed to light the ice from within and I marveled that they found lights that wouldn't produce enough heat to melt the sculptures.

There were four bedrooms here—all made of ice—and of course the bar with carved barstools and martini glasses made of ice.

"Dex, look!" Piper said, pulling me toward a carved vase full of ice flowers. "This one looks like that daisy you gave me."

Inside the vase was a yellow light giving all the flowers a cheerful cast.

"You want this one too?" I asked, raising an eyebrow and wiggling my gloved fingers, and I reached toward the ice flower.

She laughed and rolled her eyes. "Sure, and the minute we get back to the cabin it would turn into a melted mess."

"Well, I'm not cleaning up any messes." I scoffed.

"I think it's best left here, where it belongs."

Something overhead caught my attention and I looked up. It was a very large ice crystal chandelier hanging from the ceiling. An idea began to form in my head...

Nearby, there was a man on a very tall ladder, leaning against one of the ice walls, using some tools to carve out what looked like the makings of a window. He had a tool belt on and some kind of pick in his hand. There was another tool, something electric that had a very long cord that dangled all the way down and went behind the bar, where it was likely plugged in.

I left Piper still admiring the ice flowers and casually wandered over toward the ladder. There was another ice display nearby with a few people admiring it. As I walked closer to get a good look at the sculpture, my foot "lost" its holding on the very slick ice and I began to slip and slide, flailing my arms.

I called out a warning, but it was too late. I bumped into the people near the sculpture and sent one of them careening toward the ladder. I watched as the man plowed into the bottom and sent the ladder falling back, away from the icy walls.

The man above gave a startled shout and jumped as it fell over and landed on the upper story of the observation deck. But the ladder continued to fall and it crashed into the crystal chandelier, causing it to crack and a big section of it went hurtling toward the ground… right where Piper stood.

"Piper," I shouted, the sound ripping from my throat. It startled me at the amount of fear I heard as I watched the unfolding scene before me.

My feet began moving, rushing to get to her—for what I didn't know. But the floor was slick and I didn't move as fast as I wanted. I watched, actually horrified, as the big chunk of ice fell, effectively cutting off my view of Piper.

People were shouting, a few were crying, and the sound of ice splintering echoed along the walls, bouncing around, creating a deafening roar. I scrambled around, trying to get to the other side, shoving people out of my way as I tried to see if Piper had been crushed.

Crushing her had been my intent, but now, faced with the aftermath, I felt a little mournful and panicked.

Finally I made it around to the opposite side and heard a crunching sound beneath my feet. I looked down and my stomach twisted uncomfortably. There was a broken piece of the ice daisy beneath my boot. Piper's flower was crushed. I bent and picked it up, turning it over in my hand. The crystal-clear ice was still beautiful even though it was broken. What had I done?

I looked up. There was a man lying on the ground, his body limp, and it was draped over something, someone I couldn't see.

I looked a little closer and saw a foot, a boot, sticking out from beneath him. It was white with fur trim and purple laces. *Piper.*

Piper was the something that was underneath the unmoving man. Her foot was slightly askew and she didn't move at all.

I swallowed.

My plan had clearly worked.

She was crushed.

Job complete.

Chapter Thirty-Four

"Marshmallow - spongy confection made of gelatin and sugar and corn syrup and dusted with powdered sugar."

Piper

It all happened so fast. One minute I was standing in the Ice Museum admiring the ice daisy and then the next there was this sound and I was being pushed onto the ground and something heavy was coming down on top of me.

I couldn't see what was happening, but from my position on the floor I heard the commotion and worried yells. It was hard to breathe; the weight pressing in on me was suffocating and I felt panic begin to build within my chest.

I tried to push myself up, but my arms were shaking and I couldn't. I wiggled my foot, trying to find a place to dig my toes into the floor, to help push me up.

A low groan filled my ears and I stilled. The mass on top of me was a person. Most likely a man. And he sounded hurt.

Dex! "Dex," I said, my voice muffled and I lifted my head to try to say his name louder.

I heard some crunching ice behind me and then blissfully, the weight was lifted and I could draw in a deep breath.

"Piper, oh my God, are you all right?" Dex said as he grabbed me by the elbow and hauled me to my feet.

I swayed a little, trying to get my bearings.

"Yes, I think so. What happened?"

"You didn't see?" he asked, studying my face.

I shook my head. "It happened so fast."

"The chandelier on the ceiling… it fell. The sculptor over there had an accident with his ladder." His face was a mix of emotions ranging from relief to fear. And maybe something else I couldn't quite identify. Before I could think more about it, he continued. "That man must've fallen on top of you. Probably saved your life."

I looked down at the man still unconscious on the floor and gasped. I bent beside him and felt for his pulse. It was strong and I let out a relieved breath. I couldn't take it if anyone else died for me.

"Sir!" I yelled, shaking his shoulder. "Sir, please wake up."

A few moments later his eyes fluttered open and he looked at me.

I smiled. "There was an accident, but you're okay," I told him.

He sat up and put a hand to his head. "Damn chandelier almost crushed us! I pushed you out of the way. Are you hurt?"

"No. I'm fine, thanks to you."

He grunted. "That's good." Then he pushed himself to his feet. He was dressed in a heavy flannel shirt and snow pants with boots. He had a knit hat pulled low over his eyes and thick gloves covering his fingers.

"Oh, please be careful. You might have a concussion." I reached out to steady his arm.

"I've been through worse," he said, then looked at Dex, who was watching us. "This your boyfriend?"

"Uh, no," I replied, glancing at Dex. "We're just friends."

The man snorted. "Well, where were you when the giant piece of ice almost crushed your *friend?*"

Dex cleared his throat and looked at me. "I wandered over there." He gestured to the other side of the room. "To look at another sculpture a few feet away. I never should have walked away."

"You couldn't have known that thing was going to fall!" I insisted.

Dex didn't say anything; he just looked around at the mess of shattered ice.

Movement at the door caused me to look and I saw a few EMTs coming in the door.

"You should go get your head looked at. Just to be sure you're okay," I told the man.

He nodded.

"I can come with you," I offered.

"No, that's not necessary. I'll be fine."

I hesitated, not really wanting to leave him, but then a small woman in a heavy coat came rushing over and took the man's arm.

"I've been looking everywhere for you! I heard the sound from the other room and then I couldn't find you…" Her voice faded away as she looked him over.

He smiled and put his arm around her shoulders. "Now you know ain't nothing going to hurt this hard head of mine."

The woman looked at Dex and me standing so close beside them.

I smiled at her. "He pushed me out of the way of the chandelier when it fell. He's a hero."

She smiled. "I'm glad no one was hurt."

"Well, he needs to have his head looked at," I told her.

She nodded knowingly. "I'll make sure he does."

He began to refuse, but she wasn't having any of it and dragged him off toward the EMTs.

Dex grabbed my shoulders and spun me to look at him. "Are you really okay?" he asked.

"Yes, really."

He nodded and then put his arm around my shoulder and turned us toward the exit that was being flooded with people. "Come on. Let's get out of here."

Once outside, we didn't stop walking; we just kept walking until we arrived back at the little cabin. I was taking my coat off when Dex spoke behind me.

"I'm really sorry." His voice sounded heavy.

I turned, coat in my hands. "It's okay. You couldn't have known that was going to happen."

He frowned at my words and I realized he was more upset about the accident than I thought. I hesitated, not knowing what to do. I thought about hugging him, but I wasn't sure if he'd like that—or if pressing my body against his would trigger another vision. I had enough of my visions lately to last me a long time. I decided against hugging him, instead setting down my coat and heading toward the kitchen.

"How about some hot chocolate?"

"Only if you put marshmallows in it," he said, his voice back to normal.

I smiled. "Can't have hot chocolate without marshmallows."

Marshmallows always do the trick.

Chapter Thirty-Five

"Aurora borealis - an atmospheric phenomenon consisting of bands of light caused by charged solar particles following the earth's magnetic lines of force."

Dex

The aurora borealis, also known as the northern lights, are naturally occurring lights that can be seen on clear nights in some parts of Alaska. Here, at Chena Hot Springs Resort, they are a huge attraction. When Piper suggested we go and see if they would light up the sky tonight, I jumped at the chance because it was preferable to being alone in the cabin with her.

We made our way to the vast clearing where people gathered in hopes of seeing them, both of us dressed in countless layers because it had to be at least minus twenty degrees. But it was a crystal-clear night and when we arrived, there was already a crowd of people hoping to catch a glimpse of the light show.

Piper and I found a place amongst the people and lay down with our backs against the hard packed snow. I didn't look at her, but instead looked up at the darkened sky and watched as my breath came out in white puffs and then floated upward until it disappeared.

"Do you think we'll see them?" Piper asked hopefully, and I glanced in her direction.

She was smiling, looking up at the night sky, waiting for something spectacular to happen. You wouldn't know by looking at her that just a few hours ago someone tried to kill her.

That I tried to kill her.

I was still feeling a little… confused since this morning, but she seemed to put it out of her mind. I guess I should be thankful for that.

In some ways I wished it would've worked today. That any of my plans to kill her had worked. Because then it would be over and maybe I wouldn't feel so mystified by my own feelings.

I closed my eyes off to everything and took a breath of cold air. I don't know how long I lay there with my eyes closed, but they opened when I heard her gasp. Ribbons of color were lighting up the night. Long bursts of brilliant color shimmered across the sky, creating curtains of green and yellow.

"Oh look, Dex," Piper said, reaching out and laying her hand on my arm. Her voice was hushed as if the view was so spectacular her words might disrupt it.

I turned my head to watch her. She was completely enthralled by the lights, and the colors of the sky reflected onto her skin, giving her a neon glow.

She was so beautiful.

How could you hurt something so beautiful? a part of me asked myself, and in that moment I wouldn't have been able to come up with the answer to save my life.

"Dex?" Piper turned her head to look at me. "You're missing it!" she said, her hand tightening on my arm.

"No, I'm not missing anything," I replied, my voice the same hushed tone as hers.

She smiled and even though it was dark, I saw her eyes soften. The pull between us was so great in that moment I felt like I was in the sky and the ribbons of light were what stretched between us, shimmering and dancing, holding us together, yet still keeping us apart.

"You know," Piper began, tilting her head back toward the sky, "the guide book in the cabin said there's a legend saying some people believe the lights are actually flaming torches carried by departed souls who guide travelers into the afterlife."

I liked that. I looked back up at the sky at the twisting and turning patterns of color and I thought how they reminded me of the way I looked without a body. I was nothing but color without form, a mist that floated in the air. I wasn't green or yellow, but my color had been neon and vibrant. When I died, where was my guide? Maybe if someone would've been there to show me the way, I wouldn't have ended up working for the Grim Reaper.

I looked back at Piper and realized that maybe where I was now wasn't so bad.

"So what do you think?" I asked her. "About the legend?"

"I don't know what to think," she said, her gaze colliding with mine.

From the tone of her voice I knew we were no longer talking about the northern lights and the legends behind it. We were talking about something else. Something deeper.

"Can you feel it?" she asked, turning her body so she was lying on her side in the snow, facing me. Her hand released my arm so she could bring it up to pillow beneath her cheek.

"Feel what?"

"There's something between us, but I don't know what it is."

"Maybe you think I'm hot," I said, flashing a grin.

She burst out laughing, disrupting the quiet of the night. She broke it off abruptly but continued to giggle lightly. "It's those glasses. Men with glasses are hot."

"You knocking my glasses?" I asked, smiling.

"No!" She gasped. "I was telling the truth."

Without thought I reached toward her. Noting the thick glove on my hand, I used my teeth to pull it off, then reached toward her again to brush my fingers across her cheek.

"You're fingers are warm," she said with a sigh.

I got a little bolder and cupped my palm around her jaw. Her eyes closed, but she didn't jerk away so I left my hand against her skin.

Moments later, through the dark, she whispered, "Sometimes you're like two different people."

I stilled. "What do you mean?"

She was quiet a moment and I felt her shake her head beneath my hand. "Never mind."

"Tell me," I said, ignoring the way my heart beat faster.

"I can't explain it. Sometimes I just feel two different people when I'm around you."

"And yet the two people you feel in me can't compete with the one you lost."

Her eyes opened and she looked at me. If she was shocked, she didn't show it. "You feel like you're competing for me?"

"Sometimes," I admitted, turning my body so I was also on my side, facing her. In more ways than she knew. I was competing against my old body, the guy she viewed as a hero. I was competing against this new body as it tried to carry out my job... and then there was the other side of me... the side that didn't want to hurt her at all.

That was the side I tried to hide from most of all. I couldn't understand that part of me. I mean, really, what did I care if this one girl lived or died?

I pulled my hand away from her cheek and the frigid air immediately blew away the warmth that was left behind on my palm.

"I never meant to make you feel that way," she said, still looking at me. "I never really meant to get close to you at all. I just..." Her voice fell away.

"Just what?" I urged.

"I just couldn't figure you out. You're the one person in my life that I've never been able to figure out."

"You got everybody else's number, huh?" I said, trying to lighten the conversation and ignore the way my stomach flopped.

"Their addresses too," she quipped.

"And how do you manage that?" I asked, wondering if this had to do with whatever ability Charming wanted.

She paused and then said, "It's not that hard, if you really pay attention."

"I don't think that's it." I pressed. "What's your secret?"

"My secret?" she asked, and I felt her retreat ever so slightly.

"Yeah." I flashed a grin, trying to pull her back in. "You're secret to reading people." Before she responded, I quickly added, "Or you can just tell me any of your other secrets."

She laughed lightly. "Who says I have secrets?"

"Everyone has secrets."

"Do you?"

"Maybe. Most likely."

"I'll tell you mine if you tell me yours," she sang lightly.

"I like to sleep naked," I lied.

She laughed. "Not tonight you don't."

"Oh come on. I'll be on the couch; you won't have to see."

"You are so wrong," she said, turning her face away to look back up at the sky.

I only joked because I felt like she was getting too close, because part of me wanted to tell her my secrets, but I knew I couldn't. I hadn't wanted to lose the moment.

"Hey," I said, reaching out my hand to her. She caught it in hers and fit our fingers together. Her gloved hand against my bare one.

"Look," she said quietly. "They're fading."

I glanced up at the sky at the vanishing northern lights. We both rolled so we were once again on our backs, staring up at the endless sky. Except this time our bodies were closer; this time we were pressed together and our hands intertwined. We watched the colors until they were barely a memory, until they were almost completely faded away.

Something in me felt lonely watching them go… like the disappearing lights represented the loss of something more. Something important.

We lay there long after the sky turned black and we could see the stars. Eventually, we got up, our hands no longer touching. And as we walked away I realized what I lost.

This moment.

This chance.

Maybe if I'd said something more, admitted just one of my secrets, something might have changed.

But I hadn't and now it was gone.

Nothing had changed.

Chapter Thirty-Six

"Secret - Something kept hidden from others or known only to oneself or to a few."

Piper

He wanted to know my secrets. I almost told him. I almost told him everything. Lying out there in the Alaskan snow hadn't been cold. It was warm. We'd never been that close before. Sure, I always felt a little pull between us, but tonight it seemed stronger. I felt like I might get a glimpse of the man he seemed to hide.

I almost admitted my secrets. I thought about it. But I knew in that moment I wouldn't be able to stop at one. They all would've come tumbling out of my mouth. The way he looked at me through the dark… I could feel his stare. And even though my hands were gloved, I swear I could feel the heat of his skin against mine.

For a moment, when he touched my cheek, I thought he might kiss me, lay his lips upon mine, and that the northern lights would've become just background to the show of colors and feelings swirling within me.

But something held him back. Just as something held me back.

I wasn't quite sure what it was, but I wanted to find it. I wanted to erase it so the only thing between us was the beating of our hearts and the barrier of our skin.

I knew what held me back was the missing pieces of the puzzle that was Dex, but the more I got to know him, the harder it was to remember I was trying to piece him together. I was beginning not to care about the things I didn't know. I was beginning to only think about the things I did know.

He said he felt as if he were competing with the man who died. That might have been true in the beginning, but now the tides were turning. What Dex didn't seem to realize was that everything else was beginning to have to compete with him.

And he was winning.

Chapter Thirty-Seven

"Asphyxiation - the condition of being deprived of oxygen (as by having breathing stopped)."

Dex

That night I couldn't sleep. It wasn't because I was in a new place. I'd slept in far worse places before. It was because of her. She was one room away, nothing separating us but drywall and paint. Her light went out hours ago and I knew she was sound asleep, but still, her presence unsettled me.

How could one girl have so effectively tied me up in knots? Never in all my life had anyone gotten under my skin like this. And that's where she was. Somehow she wiggled her way beneath the surface; she wormed her way into my mind.

I couldn't allow that. I had a job to do, a debt to fulfill. It should've been an easy job, but it was proving to be much harder. I got up and paced the room in the dark, back and forth across the rug, trying to make sense of it all. And then something struck me. A single word that whispered ever so quietly through my mind.

I stopped mid-stride, halting with the force of the thought.

Love.

Even as I heard the word, I shook my head, denying it. This wasn't love. It couldn't be. It was sick and twisted and probably somehow part of G.R.'s trial assignment before making me an official Death Escort.

Besides, I'd never been in love before. I hadn't even loved my own mother. The day I turned fourteen I walked out of her apartment and never looked back. I couldn't care less where she was today and she was the only family I had. Sure, I had friends, people that shared the street, guys that I sometimes worked with, but no one I wouldn't have sold out for the right price. A guy like me didn't know how to love. He only knew how to survive.

And this girl was making it hard to survive.

On impulse I grabbed up the white pillow off the couch and made my way to her room. I wanted to stomp with determination. I wanted to shout with pride, but I didn't.

I moved silently, stealthily, and with purpose.

The door to the bedroom was slightly ajar, and I pushed it lightly, testing to see if it would creak. It didn't so I pushed it open some more. The room was darkened, but I could still make out the basic shapes in the room, the bed in the center. I crept closer, gripping the pillow close to my chest.

She lay on her side, facing me, and the covers were pulled up under her chin. Her dark hair was a mere shadow against the white of her pillow and her body was completely relaxed into the mattress.

Do it now, part of me whispered. The part that was programmed to do my job.

The pillow twisted in my grip and I knew this was probably the easiest way to do it. All I had to do was reach out, mere inches, and cover her head with my pillow. All I had to do was smother her in her sleep and it would be over. She might not even know what was happening. If she did, it would be very brief and confusing and then she'd be gone.

And with the pillow covering her face, I wouldn't have to watch her die. I wouldn't see the panic on her face—the fear. I would completely avoid seeing the light in her eyes go out, or face the realization that I was the one betraying her.

I pulled the pillow away from my body and held it out, lowering it toward her still, sleeping form.

Do it now.

My heart was beating so hard in my chest that I thought the sound would surely wake her and then my secret would be exposed. That she would know what a monster I truly was.

I took a shuddering breath and looked down, ready to complete my act… She looked smaller in sleep, more fragile somehow.

I dropped the pillow. It hit the side of the bed on its way to the floor.

What was wrong with me? Why couldn't I do this one thing?

I hunched forward to pick up the pillow and then slowly backed toward the door. I couldn't do this. Not right now. I would find another way. Tomorrow. Things would seem easier in the daylight.

"Dex?" I heard from the darkness. Her voice was sleepy and low. "Is that you?"

"Yeah," I said, hoarse. "I couldn't sleep. I was just checking on you."

"That couch is probably uncomfortable," she said, her voice still heavy. "The fabric is itchy."

"No, its fine. Go back to sleep."

"Does your head hurt?"

My head? Then I remembered the stitches. I'd only got them that morning, but it seemed like days ago. "My head doesn't hurt."

I thought that would be the end of the conversation. It wasn't.

"You could sleep with me."

I stopped cold in my tracks, wondering if I was hearing things. She couldn't possibly have offered to share her bed with me.

"Dex? There's no use in you being uncomfortable. You paid for this room."

"I don't care about the money," I said, realizing it was true. Money didn't seem important like it used to.

"I won't be able to sleep until I know you can."

I let out a sigh and went back into the room, going to the opposite side of the bed. I left my flannel pants and shirt on and lifted the corner of the covers.

"Are you sure?" I asked again.

"Yes," she groaned. "Hurry up. You're letting in the cold air."

I slid between the sheets and shoved the pillow that I'd contemplated using as a weapon just moments ago beneath my head.

Piper didn't turn toward me. She stayed in the same position, but her body remained relaxed.

Would she be so relaxed if she knew who was really in her bed?

"Is that better?" she asked through the dark.

"Yes, thank you."

"Mmmm, good. I'm going to sleep. No funny business." She warned, the words hardly sounding like a threat around her wide yawn.

I felt the side of my mouth tip up. But then it fell away. I'd done a lot of crappy things in my life, but lying here in this bed felt like the worst. I didn't deserve her trust, yet I had it. I wasn't fit to breathe the same air as her.

I waited until I heard her quiet snore and knew she was asleep. Then I got out of the bed, tucking the blankets back around her, and let myself out of her room, pulling the door around on my way out.

I went back to the living room and the itchy couch. Even that was better than I deserved.

Chapter Thirty-Eight

"Fun - pleasure, gaiety, or merriment. Playful, often noisy, activity."

Piper

I rolled over onto my side, facing the place on the mattress where Dex lay last night, and I opened my eyes. He was gone. I couldn't help but be a little disappointed. Part of me wanted to see what he looked like first thing in the morning. I smiled, thinking he'd probably look the same, minus the glasses, because I don't think he ever combed his hair.

I stretched like a cat beneath the blankets and then threw them back and stood, pulling on a thick pair of socks and a sweatshirt over my pajamas. Dex was already up and when I entered the room, he turned from the window.

"Coffee," he said in a desperate tone.

I laughed and went into the kitchen to get a pot started. "You know these things are really easy to use," I said, pointing at the coffee maker.

He grunted like he didn't agree and turned back to look out the window and the beautiful expanse of land and snow. When the pot was about half full, I pulled it out and poured two cups. The only thing in the fridge was a container of creamer and I dumped about half in his mug. When I tasted what he was drinking at the diner the other day, I figured that much was about right.

I grabbed both our mugs and went across the room to where he stood and he took his and drank about half in one great gulp. He groaned appreciatively and I shook my head and took a sip of my less-creamer-laden brew.

"Let's go do something," Dex said, his voice full of enthusiasm as if the coffee turned immediately into energy.

"Like what?"

He finished off the rest of his mug and smacked his lips together, then turned from the window and went toward his bag sitting in the corner.

"Layer up," he said. "You'll see."

"What about my coffee?" I asked, smiling. I liked this energetic side of him.

"Drink up, woman. There's fun to be had!"

He bustled around the room, putting on layers, a coat, and a knit hat. Then he went to the door of the cabin and looked over his shoulder. "I'll be back."

"Where are you going?"

"To get the fun. I'm going to bring it right to you."

"I'm intrigued."

"I know," he said dramatically. "Be ready when I get back!"

Snow swirled through the door when he opened it and went out. I finished up the coffee in my cup, sat it in the sink, and then went to layer up. I had no idea what he was up to, but I really wanted to find out.

By the time I got dressed and was pulling on my coat and gloves, I heard something outside. I went to the door and peaked out the little window beside it. Our "fun" was parked right outside.

I stepped back just as Dex flung open the door, his cheeks pink from the cold.

"Let's go!" Keys were in his hand.

"*That* is your idea of fun?" I asked dubiously.

He nodded, not noticing the doubt in my voice. "Come on, get out here!" he said and then disappeared through the door.

I sighed. There was no doubt in my mind that I liked Dex—was falling for him even. But this. I wasn't so sure about this.

Even still, I went warily outside.

Chapter Thirty-Nine

"Hypothermia - An abnormally low body temperature, often caused by prolonged exposure to cold."

Dex

"Are you sure you should be driving?" Piper asked warily, staring between me and the keys in my hand.

"I'm fine. I didn't have a concussion and I don't even have a headache anymore."

She looked at the snow mobile I'd rented and frowned. "I don't know about this."

I sighed. "Didn't we come here to have fun?"

Somewhere between Charming showing up and my vow to finish this job, I forgot the reason I made the deal in the first place.

Yes, for money.

But it wasn't the actual money itself. In fact, hadn't I just realized last night that I really didn't care about the money at all? But I still cared about what the money would bring me. More experiences, a better life—that's what I really wanted. I wanted to have fun and do stuff I never got to do because I was too busy surviving.

So I rented a snowmobile.

Sure, this was probably a good way to kill my Target, but couldn't we have some fun first?

"I've never been on a snowmobile before," Piper said.

I could see her warming to the idea. I'd never been on one either, but admitting that probably wouldn't inspire confidence in my driving so I kept my mouth shut.

I handed her a pair of goggles and then strapped a pair over my glasses. I didn't waste time but climbed onto the machine and turned toward her.

"Well? Are you coming?"

"Fine. Just don't kill us."

I pretended not to hear her.

Seconds later, she climbed onto the back of the snowmobile and wrapped her arms around my waist. It was a shame we had so much thick clothing on because I suddenly found myself with the urge to feel her pressed against me.

But that thought was followed by the familiar feeling of sickness that I always got when I was close to her. It was my body's way of reminding me what I needed to do. I wished it recognized I was trying and gave it a rest.

Sometimes it felt like two parts of me were at war.

So I stopped thinking and I gunned the engine. I smiled when Piper's arms tightened around me. I took off across the snow, starting slow at first, getting used to the feel of the machine and the way it handled. I aimed it up the trail the rental company outlined for me, ducking a little farther into my heavy coat. The wind was fierce today and I was glad we had goggles or I knew I wouldn't be able to see.

I increased the speed a little and out of the corner of my eye I saw white spray flying up around us. Snow dust surrounded us as we cut through the thickness that layered the ground. There weren't any other sleds out here on the trail with us. Well, none that I could see, and I was glad. I felt the weight of my life slip right off my shoulders and mix with the snow that blew behind us. I felt free and I wanted more.

I gunned the engine and tore up the path. In my ear Piper squealed and I knew she was having a good time too. Up and down we went on the mounds of snow. I weaved in and out of trees and whooped into the wind. We did figure eights on an open stretch and then I skidded to a stop, throwing snow in the opposite direction.

I could hear her laughing over the engine. I looked over my shoulder at her pink cheeks and wide smile.

"Again!" she screamed and gave me a thumbs-up.

We took off again, racing through the white. There was a large stretch of flat land ahead and I went for that, thinking I could really open it up and see how much speed we really could gain.

It was awesome.

I pushed the vehicle until it shook and it felt like we were flying. Then I made a wide turn and brought us back around and slowed just a little so I could think.

Maybe I could manage some sort of accident while we were out here. Maybe I could pretend to lose control of the vehicle and jump off right before I hit a tree. That would complete my job, and Piper would die without knowing what a real jerk I was.

I don't know when that became important, but all of a sudden it did.

She began tapping me on the back and yelling for me to stop, so I cut the engine. When the sound died away, we were met with sudden silence.

"Can I drive?" Piper said, her voice overly loud as if her ears hadn't adjusted to the quiet yet.

I laughed. "Think you can handle it?" My voice was also too loud.

"Oh, I know I can!" She swung her leg over the side and stood, jumping up and down a little. "My legs feel like Jell-O!" She laughed.

I laughed too. This was perfect. I never thought about letting her drive. Maybe I could somehow make it so she crashed and killed herself. Then it wouldn't be my fault at all, and the job would still be done.

I climbed off, leaving the keys in the ignition. My legs were wobbly from sitting on such a vibrating force for so long. I walked around a bit, trying to get the feeling back into them and I saw Piper doing the same. Occasionally she would jump up and down and shake her arms.

I looked toward the sky. It never really looked this blue in the city. It was a bright day and there were big white clouds moving rapidly through the azure. I figured it was the wind causing them to drift so quickly. I inhaled a deep breath of the cold, crisp air. I'd never been a fan of winter, but today I understood why so many liked it.

There was a sharp cracking sound off to my left and I turned just as Piper made a sound.

"Dex!" she called warily, as if yelling too loud would be a danger.

"Piper," I said, answering her call.

"We're on ice! This is a lake!"

As she spoke, another deafening cracking sound ripped through the silence. I hadn't seen any signs posted about the lake… Sure, I knew one was here, but it was miles and miles away. Had we really driven that far?

"Dex," Piper said again. This time it was a little more than a whimper.

"Stop moving," I told her, holding out my hands. "Slow and easy," I directed. "Make your way toward me…"

I looked around, trying to see where the water ended and the land began, but it was an endless sea of white. I had no way of knowing which way to go or how far it was to safety.

Piper took one shaky step and then another. Her movements were agonizingly slow and I wanted to scream for her to hurry up, but I knew I couldn't.

"There you go; you're almost here," I said encouragingly when she was about halfway to me.

She nodded, keeping her eyes trained on me as if I were her lifeline. That sick feeling came back over me, but I couldn't decide which part of me it came from.

"Almost there," she whispered and I nodded.

And then the ice spilt.

One minute her eyes were trained on me and the next I couldn't see her at all. The lake seemed to open up and Piper was falling… plunging right down into the unknown icy depths of the lake.

"Piper!" I yelled, stepping forward, desperately seeking some kind of sign that she was still there. I saw the red of her hat bob up from the water and heard her cough.

I watched as she reached for something to grab onto, anything to pull herself to safety.

But there was nothing. The ice around her had shattered, leaving her in the center of a circle of water. She could maybe swim to the edge and pull herself up… if she didn't die of hypothermia first.

Die.

Death.

Dead.

This was it. This was what I'd been waiting for. This was the perfect opportunity to let her die. Chances were I wouldn't be able to save her anyway.

"Dex," she sputtered, her red head bobbing to the surface again. I looked up as she reached her gloved hand toward me. "Dex!"

She would be dead in minutes… if not seconds.

All I had to do was wait.

And then the ice split beneath me.

Icy water hit me and it felt like a million sharp needles stabbing me at once. It was so cold it stole my breath and then made me cough. Coughing delivered a frigid dose of water down my throat and then I was floating…

Floating in a dark sea of ice, my body completely numb.

And then my eyes opened. Through the water I could see something flailing around. Something struggling to live.

My survival instincts kicked in and gave me a burst of adrenaline.

I pushed my arms upward, hoping to break the surface, and when I did, I gulped in the air like a starving man. My glasses were gone, claimed by the lake, so my vision was blurry.

But I could still make her out.

We were closer now. The current must have pushed me closer, or maybe it was the force of my fall. Whatever it was I pushed myself toward her, the weight of my wet clothes making it nearly impossible. I made it to her and latched onto her arm, seeing her lips were already turning blue. Out around her floated a red scarf and I yanked it away from her body and drug myself and her toward the edge of the ice.

The edge was brittle, but it was our best chance. I tried to hoist her up onto the solid sheet, but she was heavy and my arms were weak. The snowmobile was so close, but it felt so far away.

"Help me, Piper," I told her. "Help me help you."

She wasn't as responsive as I needed her to be. She was sluggish and felt like dead weight to my shaking, heavy arms.

Holding on to her with one arm, I used my free arm to reach toward the snowmobile. Maybe if I could get a hold of it, I could use it to pull myself up out of the water. Every time I leaned on the ice to pull myself up, it broke off a little more, plunging us back down into the water.

It looked like I was, in fact, going to kill my Target.

But I was going to die with her.

I threw my arm out again, giving it one last try, when something latched on to me and I felt myself being pulled upwards. I looked up and saw nothing but blackness…

My vision was going. I was losing consciousness.

"Come on, man," a familiar voice said, and I looked again.

My vision wasn't darkening, I wasn't passing out. It was Storm. Somehow the black translucent mist that made up his form had grown solid enough for him to grasp me. He was trying to help me.

He was pulling me upward.

"The ice, it's going to crack," I warned.

"Not when I don't weigh anything," he said and gave another yank.

I was pulled up, free of the water, and collapsed onto the ice. I wanted to lie there and catch my breath, but Piper was still half in the water and I knew the ice I was lying on could crack at any moment.

I looked down at Piper who was completely unresponsive; then I looked at Storm who nodded.

I let go of Piper's hand.

Chapter Forty

"Struggle - to move about strenuously so as to escape from something confining."

Piper

When I realized the sound of splitting ice was coming from beneath my feet, I knew true fear. All I could think about was the glacial, dark water that churned just below me, waiting to swallow me whole.

I called out to Dex, knowing he was too far away to help me, knowing if he came any closer he, too, would be captured by the ice, but I couldn't stop my lips from forming his name.

At first he looked confused. Like me, he hadn't realized we'd driven onto a frozen lake. Then he looked scared, like watching me drown would be too horrible to experience. And then I was falling, thrust into the shadowy, subzero water. The layers of my clothes acted like an overzealous sponge that soaked up the water as fast as it could, and then the weight of the wet layers seemed to drag me down. Down, down, down I went until I thought I would never go up again.

But then my arms started working and my brain started screaming.

I have to get out!

When my head broke the surface, I gasped, taking in air, air I knew was cold but actually felt warm compared to the rest of my body. My lungs filled painfully, almost as if the warm air was too much to breathe.

"Dex!" I tried to call, but I got a mouth full of water that I had to spit out. "Dex!" I called again. This time my voice was stronger.

Finally I caught sight of him. He was still in the same place he had been when I fell and I wondered why he was still standing there. It felt like I'd been fighting this water for hours.

The rational part of me knew it probably had been only a minute, but when the water was this cold minutes might be all I had.

I glanced at him again as I struggled to stay afloat, my arms straining under the weight of my layers, and he had the strangest look on his face. Almost like resolve. Almost like he was watching something he didn't quite like but was still going to do nothing about it.

I heard another jagged cracking sound and then Dex was gone—my only hope of survival swimming with the ice as well.

In that moment my arms stopped cooperating and my thoughts became sluggish. It became harder and harder to stay afloat and I felt myself sinking… sinking down into the depths of a frozen world. A world where nothing would be warm again.

Chapter Forty-One

"Drown- To kill by submerging and suffocating in water or another liquid."

Dex

I spent a lot of time in medical facilities these days. It seemed ironic that, since making a deal to essentially give me a life, I've done nothing but get into freak accidents and almost die.

I was beginning to wonder about that…

The door to my room opened and a man wearing a white coat came in. "Ah, you're awake."

I nodded, pushing myself into a sitting position. I had about ten blankets piled on me so it took a minute.

"Your body experienced an extreme cold shock. We estimate your time in the water at about four to five minutes. You were lucky to get out quickly and it likely saved your life. Your thinking may be unclear for the rest of the day, but that is normal. Sometimes after a shock like this your brain can be slow to work. That's normal and no cause for alarm."

I nodded again, looking around the room and wondering where Piper was. Then I remembered letting go of her hand and watching her slide slowly back into the water…

"How are you feeling?" the doctor asked. "Are you warm enough? Do you have feeling in your extremities?"

I nodded. "I think so. I feel fine."

He proceeded to check my fingers and toes and check my core temperature. Everything looked good because he called the nurse to get me some forms to fill out before I could be released.

"I want to see Piper," I said before he could leave the room.

"Of course," the doctor replied. "I was just going to her room next. Give me a few moments and then you can see her. She's right across the hall."

"She has her own room?" I asked, making sure I heard him right.

The doctor nodded. "Your clothes are over there. The nurses had them dried for you."

I came so close to killing her. But as she was sliding back into the glacial water she moaned. She was awake. I couldn't let her go back into that dark, lonely water. I couldn't let it swallow her whole.

I had been in there. I knew what it was like. How could I sentence her to a death as horrible as that? And so I grabbed her, I pulled her free, and then I raced down the mountain with her in my lap. She made no more sounds and her lips and face had long turned blue. From the dead weight of her body against mine, I truly thought she was dead.

The last thing I remembered was waving down a patrol vehicle and them rushing to help. Then I passed out. When I asked to see Piper just now, I thought I'd be visiting the morgue. I thought I'd only be seeing her body.

But she was alive.

"How long have we been here?" I glanced around for the clock.

"It's late morning. You were here all night. Bringing the core temperature back to stable levels can take time. But you both look great." He smiled. "You were very lucky."

I nodded as he let himself out the door. Funny, I hadn't felt good that my job was finally complete. I hadn't felt any kind of elation.

I told myself that was because I'd been half frozen as well. I could hardly call G.R. and announce a job well done when I was ready to pass out.

And knowing she was alive, I was disappointed. Wasn't I?

I threw off the fifty blankets and began dressing. Halfway through putting on my layers, the nurse brought in a million and one forms for me to fill out as well as my release papers. She looked alarmed when I told her I had no insurance. But when I slapped my credit card into her palm, she seemed a little less frazzled.

"I'm taking care of the woman I was brought in with too," I said, not overthinking my need to make sure Piper was taken care of.

"Sir, are you sure?" the nurse began. "The bill…"

"The card will go through. Don't worry about it," I snapped.

That shut her up and she went on her way. I finished dressing and shoved my feet into a new pair of boots. They weren't the ones I'd been wearing. I had no clue what happened to them. I had no clue where these came from, but I didn't really care.

I did, however, miss my glasses with their thick, black frames. Having blurry vision wasn't fun. Because I could barely see the forms, I only filled out two and made sure to sign the release. Something told me they didn't care about their records, only the payment.

I left the clipboard on the bed and went across the hall to Piper's room. She was sitting on the edge of her bed, partially dressed in jeans, a long-sleeved shirt, and socks. She had an oxygen mask up against her mouth and nose. I pushed down the funny feeling I got in my stomach as I shut the door behind me.

"Are you having trouble breathing?" I asked.

She pulled the mask down and shook her head. "I was when they brought me in. My lungs were too cold to breathe right. This is just warm, humidified oxygen they've been giving me to help bring up my body temperature. The doctor wanted me to take a few more breaths before releasing me, just to be on the safe side."

"How are you?" I asked, coming to stand beside her.

"I'm fine," she said, hooking the mask near the machine. "That was pretty scary."

Her voice dropped on the last part and something inside me squeezed. "Yeah. I didn't realize we were on a lake. There was no sign."

She nodded. "The patrolman said it got pushed over by the snow and then buried."

"The patrolman?"

She nodded again. "He came to visit me earlier this morning, to see if I was okay."

He hadn't come to my room, which told me he wasn't just worried about her health; he wanted to see her. Maybe cash in on the fact he saved her life…

She was watching me so I nodded and stepped toward the chair on the other side of the room. I didn't have any reason to feel jealous. If I wasn't trying to kill her, I wouldn't be spending this much time with her anyway. Besides, she wasn't my type.

And she's too good for you, something whispered in the back of my mind.

It was true. Even if I wasn't trying to kill her, I still wouldn't be good enough.

"So, they said we could go. You feeling up to leaving?" I asked.

"Yes, please. I go on vacation to get away from work and I end up in a clinic just like the one I was trying to get away from." She shook her head and smiled.

"Why aren't you mad at me?" I blurted out.

She stopped in the middle of pulling on her sweatshirt and looked at me. "Why would I be mad at you?"

Because I stood there and debated if I should let you drown. Because the only reason I pulled you out was because I figured you would die on the way down the mountain.

I didn't say those thoughts out loud, though. Instead, I replied, "Because I was driving recklessly."

She finished pulling on her sweatshirt and pushed her feet into a pair of boots.

"If it wasn't for you, I probably would've died. You saved my life."

I held back a wince. Thank God Charming and G.R. weren't around to hear that. I'd probably be recalled on the spot. "I don't think it was me. It was the patrolman."

"He did warm me and give me CPR," she began.

No, he just wanted to cop a feel. I thought bitterly as she continued.

"But the doctor said the only reason we're alive is because you pulled us out of the water so fast."

"I got lucky," I mumbled, hoping she'd been so out of it she hadn't seen who really pulled us out.

"You can call it luck," she said, "but I'm going to say it was your quick thinking."

I didn't argue. If she wanted to believe I was the hero I wasn't going to stop her. It only added to the trust between us so the next time I tried to kill her it would work.

I was running out of chances.

I was running out of time.

"The cabin isn't far from here. The nurse called someone from the rental place to give us a ride back there," Piper said, not picking up my preoccupation.

I nodded. "You need to drive home. I lost my glasses."

"We can stop and get some new ones," she offered.

"I have an extra pair at home."

"Oh. Good. Well, then, let's get out of here,"

Suddenly I wasn't in a hurry to get home. Charming would be waiting and Grim would be wondering why he never got a call to come see the body.

I had a very bad feeling it was going to be a very long day.

Chapter Forty-Two

"Suspicious - openly distrustful and unwilling to confide."

Piper

Dex was being very quiet. Since we got in the car and headed back toward Fairbanks, he'd barely spoken two words. When I tried to talk he would just nod his head or turn up the radio. It's like he couldn't even look at me.

Normally his silence wouldn't bother me. Dex wasn't really a talkative kind of guy. He didn't talk just to talk, but this time his silence was different. It was sort of charged and uncomfortable.

"Almost drowning was pretty scary, huh?" I said, not looking at him, keeping my eyes on the road. The way he acted earlier at the hospital, thinking I would be mad at him and mumbling his responses when I spoke, he probably thought I blamed him. What a horrible experience it was, and I think I got lucky. Lucky because I passed out; I couldn't remember everything. But him… He was awake the whole time. He lived the entire horror of it.

"It wasn't fun," he said, his voice low.

I was shocked he actually replied at all so I wanted to keep the conversation going.

"I told you I don't blame you. You believe me, right?"

"Yeah," he said, his voice almost sad. "Yeah, I believe you." He still didn't look at me when he spoke.

I drove on in silence, not sure what else to say. If he knew I didn't blame him and he knew that we were both okay, then why was he still acting so broody?

My thoughts were swirling so much I almost didn't hear what he said next. "Maybe you should."

I looked over at him. "What?"

"Forget it." He shook his head and stared out his window.

"I won't forget it. Why would you think I should blame you for something you had no control over?"

"Because you almost died!" he yelled, his voice echoing through the quiet car.

My hands tightened on the steering wheel. Was that what this was about? Was he this upset that I almost died?

"But I didn't," I said quietly.

"I thought you had. When we were on the mountain, I thought…"

I felt a rush of emotion. I don't know if it was from him or from me or a combination of us both, but it was intense and it filled the tiny space of the car and pressed in on me. Impulsively, I pulled the car over to the side of the highway, putting it in park but leaving the engine on.

He didn't react to the fact we were sitting along the road; he didn't even look at me.

I took a chance, turning toward him and reaching out, laying my hand on his arm. "Dex?" I whispered.

He flinched.

I pulled my hand away.

"I didn't die," I said again. "I'm still here."

And then he was turning, his arms reaching, and I was pulled against him. He tucked my cheek in the crook of his neck and one arm wound around my back while the other pressed my head into his shoulder. I could hear the thundering of his heart; it sounded like a herd of wild horses running through an open field.

"When the doctor said… when he said you were across the hall… I realized you weren't dead and I… God help me, I was so relieved."

His chest rose and fell with his breath and with his emotion. He almost sounded ashamed that he felt relief.

"It's okay," I told him, my voice muffled against his neck.

"No," he said. "It's not." Then he pulled me back, took my face in both hands, and penetrated me with his green stare. "I don't know what to do."

His voice carried so much I didn't understand. "Do about what?"

"You."

I felt like we weren't talking about almost drowning anymore. The conversation took a turn, but I had no idea where. I covered his hand with one of mine and whispered, "You don't have to do anything about me."

His thumb stroked over my cheek and then slowly he pulled his hands away. My fingers curled around his and our hands rested on the center console between us.

"We should probably get going," he said.

I could feel him withdrawing again.

"Why are you acting this way?" I asked, desperately wanting to know, to pull him back.

"You said it yourself," he answered, untangling our fingers. "I'm like two different people sometimes. Maybe this is just a side you haven't seen before."

I shook my head and looked at him for long moments, frustrated. Those few moments when I felt the wall between us slip away were gone; his guard was back up and he wasn't going to let me in. I sighed and turned back to sit straight in the driver's seat. After checking the mirrors for traffic I pulled back out onto the road. We didn't speak any more, but this time I barely noticed the silence. I was too busy thinking.

There was something going on that I didn't know about. But what?

I thought back to the man standing in the window at his townhouse and the feeling Dex was running away from something. Maybe now that we were going home, he was worried about whatever was waiting for him.

But that still didn't explain what just happened between us. He implied that whatever was going on had to do with me. He said he didn't know what to do about me. He acted as if he were caught. Caught between something or someone and he didn't know a way out.

I glanced away from the road once more. He was staring out his window, watching the scenery pass. Both his hands were in his lap and his jaw was set.

I wouldn't get any more answers. Not today.

But I would get them.

He might not want to admit it, but there were feelings between us. Strong ones. But there was also more going on here. Something other than just feelings, and the farther I drove, the more suspicious I became.

Chapter Forty-Three

"Rule - An authoritative, prescribed direction for conduct, especially one of the regulations governing procedure in a legislative body or a regulation observed by the players in a game, sport, or contest."

Dex

I knew Hobbs wouldn't be home when I got there. As I pulled into the garage, I hoped Charming wouldn't be either. I didn't know what kind of car he drove, but there wasn't one in the driveway so I took that as a good sign. He didn't know when I was coming home so maybe he wouldn't be here and maybe I'd get lucky and could avoid him the rest of the day. I knew eventually I would see him, and since I didn't kill Piper, I knew there was probably going to be a fight between us.

The first thing I did when I entered the townhouse was go upstairs and put on my spare pair of glasses. I breathed a sigh of relief when my vision cleared. Thankfully, the trip between my house and Piper's hadn't been too long and since I knew the roads, I didn't have any problems.

I had a headache, probably from my eyes, so I dug out a bottle of pain reliever and swallowed a couple tablets with tap water. Then I changed into a pair of Nike sweatpants and a long-sleeved T-shirt. I really wanted some coffee so I went down to the kitchen to see if I could figure out the coffee maker. It couldn't be that hard.

I managed to find the coffee grounds in the cabinet and was trying to figure out where to put them when I heard the front door open and close.

"Hobbs!" I called. "Get in here. I don't know how to use this damned thing."

Seconds later a figure walked around the corner. "Who is Hobbs?"

The muscles in my back tightened at Charming's voice. "Shouldn't you be out riding a white horse or something?" I asked.

"Ha," he said. "Very original."

He came into the room, filling my vision with red (not good for a headache) and took the bag from my hands and began making the coffee. I decided he could stay for a few minutes.

"So where's the body?" he asked as he filled the glass pot with water from the sink.

"Body?" I asked, playing dumb.

"The Target. You were going away to finish the job. Don't tell me you failed. Again."

I didn't answer right away. I waited until he hit the brew button on the machine, then said, "It didn't go as planned."

He spun, his eyes narrowing and all traces of the charm he claimed nowhere to be seen. "She isn't dead?"

"It's under control."

"Like hell it is," he said, advancing on me. "Let me tell you something. I have made a career out of collecting power and money. I will not have some inexperienced, wet behind the ears kid mess this up for me. I want what's mine," he growled.

I stood my ground, refusing to back away even a centimeter. "So, what do you get?" I asked coolly.

"Get?"

"Yeah, if you weren't getting something out of being here, you wouldn't stick around. So what do you get?"

He grinned, showing both rows of his perfectly straight teeth. It wasn't a friendly kind of smile. "You've been spending weeks with this girl, trying to kill her and failing miserably, and you mean to tell me you haven't even figured out she has an ability?"

"I know she has an ability. I just don't know what it is," I said.

"You are a complete loser!" Charming spat, moving even farther into my personal space. "An idiot who can't even take out one girl."

"Get out of my face." I warned. His insults were beginning to piss me off.

"You know what this means, don't you?" Charming taunted. "I'm going to take care of this my way."

I plowed my fist right into his jaw and I enjoyed watching his head snap back on his shoulders. "Maybe I'll get bonus points for giving Grim two bodies instead of one."

"Go ahead. Try and kill me. We'll just see who comes out on top," Charming spat and lunged, hooking me around the waist and pushing me backwards into the island.

I punched him in the side of the head and he backed off, only to come at me again. Before he could make contact, we were both restrained midair by an unknown force. Our bodies were pivoted around and we both stared at the Grim Reaper, who was standing in the center of the room.

"I don't have many rules in my company. But you are breaking one of them right now."

I didn't know anything about any rules.

"What is the rule you are well aware of, Charming?"

"No fighting with other Escorts," Charming replied.

"And yet, here you are."

"He hasn't finished the job! The Target is still alive!" Charming burst out, frustrated, and I looked over to see him fighting against whatever held us.

"My time isn't up," I said, defending myself.

Charming went on with a slew of curses, and I began to feel a strange pulling feeling, a feeling that was unpleasant yet vaguely familiar.

I watched as the swirling purple mist began to pull away from my body. My heart started hammering in my chest, panicked because G.R. was taking my life back. He was recalling me too soon. I looked over at Charming, to hopefully find help, but he wouldn't be any help to me either.

He was being recalled too.

I actually enjoyed seeing his life force being ripped out of him.

I watched the red floating out around him, and he struggled within his confines, trying to snatch it back. But I already knew he couldn't and I watched as his hands went right through it, scattering the mist like smoke.

"Stop!" he yelled.

Everything stopped. Just like that, I watched as the purple mist that curled around me was suddenly sucked right back into my skin, filling me up and making me whole again.

"I take it we have ourselves under control again?" the Grim Reaper asked.

I nodded, and from next to me a low voice said, "You would treat me, your best Escort, this way?"

"You can only be the best if I allow you to be," G.R. replied in cool tones.

That shut Charming up.

I thought about offering G.R. a high-five but figured it might not be a good idea.

I settled for glancing his way and letting my amusement show through my eyes. But he wasn't looking at me. He was looking at the ground with his chest heaving, his fists balled at his sides.

"I want to speak with Dex. Alone," G.R. said, dismissing Charming.

Charming stepped closer to me and leaned in to whisper, "This isn't over. I will have what's mine," before stepping away.

He glanced at G.R., anger flashing in his eyes, before disappearing around the corner.

"Don't forget your sword," I called after him, unable to resist one more Prince Charming joke. Then I winced and looked back, wondering if I'd gone too far.

I guess I hadn't because he actually smiled. "He makes it too easy," G.R. said. "I certainly wouldn't want to be named after a fairy tale character."

I sighed in relief.

"So what's this about you not completing the job?"

"It's been harder than I thought," I said, not bothering to make excuses. I was hoping my honesty would buy me some time. I was nervous for Piper now that Charming knew I hadn't killed her yet.

"Is that coffee fresh?" he asked in response to my admission and stepped around me toward the pot.

"Yes, help yourself."

He did and then he extended a mug to me, which I took. Then I went to the fridge and pulled out the creamer that Hobbs stocked and offered it to G.R. He shook his head and sipped his black coffee. I poured the rest of the bottle into my mug before taking a drink.

"That's good coffee," Grim said, setting his mug on the counter. "Now, about the job. You are running out of time."

"I know, I—"

He cut me off. "I don't listen to excuses. You have everything you need at your disposal. I gave you more than enough time to eliminate your Target. I see now that you are one of the recruits that require more information."

"More information?" I asked. I did want to know how he managed to transfer the abilities from one person to someone else. And I also wanted to know what he did with the bodies (besides hang them in his closet)… and their souls. "I do have some questions," I said.

"You know all you need to know!" he spat. "What I do with my bodies and their souls is none of your concern."

That meant it was really bad.

And how did he know that's what I wanted to know? How much power did he really have?

"What you need is to learn what it would be like if you don't complete the job. You need a taste of what it's like to be recalled."

"No, I don't," I said, shaking my head. Feeling my life force pulled even partially out of me was bad enough.

"Yes. Then you will fully understand what is at stake."

I didn't say anything else because I couldn't. For the second time that hour, my life force was being pulled out of my body, leaking from every pore of my skin. The purple mist oozed out and around me, curling around my body like smoke. The tendrils rose upward and out toward a black gaping hole that suddenly appeared.

There was no resisting. All I could do was stand there and feel my body become less and less until it dropped to the floor like a ragdoll and I was hovering above it, staring down as I was slowly and completely being pulled into a void.

Chapter Forty-Four

"Stranger - One who is neither a friend nor an acquaintance."

Piper

"That's it. I'm moving in," Frankie said from the hallway just outside my door.

I smiled and motioned for her to come in.

"I mean, really, how many times have you almost died lately? I swear it's like you have a death wish!" she exclaimed as she came inside and I shut the door behind her.

"I don't have a death wish, Frankie," I said, sinking back onto the couch with my blanket as she threw off her coat to reveal a beautiful teal sweater. It looked new, yet something about it seemed familiar.

"Then maybe someone else has one for you," she said dramatically as she paced by the window. Momentarily a cloud moved over the sun, creating a shadow on her face.

"You're just being ridiculous now," I told her, patting the couch so she would come sit down.

"Tell me everything that happened," she said, finally sitting down and giving me her full attention.

I decided not to tell her about the accident and the Ice Museum because that would only make her even more worried but focused instead on falling through the ice on the lake.

When I was done Frankie was shaking her head. "I don't know, Piper," she began. "Every time you're around that guy something bad happens. I think you should stay away from him."

"It's not his fault we fell through the ice and I ate peanut oil." I said in Dex's defense.

"Maybe not, but that guy is bad news, Piper. Why are you even hanging around him anyway? Because of that vision? You need to let it go."

"It's not just the vision," I said, readjusting with the blanket covering my legs.

"Piper!" Frankie gasped, slapping her hand on my foot. "Tell me you *do not* have feelings for this guy."

I didn't say anything at first because I was beginning to think I did. Okay, I wasn't beginning to think that; I already knew. Finally, I sighed. "Who cares if I do?"

"I need to meet this guy. I need to see what you see in him."

"I don't know if that's a good idea, Frank. It's not like we're dating or something. He probably doesn't even like me like that."

"Of course he does! Why else would be take you away for the weekend?"

"He hasn't even kissed me," I said, my voice dropping like I was telling her a secret.

She made a choked sound. "Now I know there's something wrong with him."

I laughed and smacked at her. "There is not!"

"If I were a guy, I would totally kiss you," Frankie said and we both burst out laughing.

Our good time was interrupted by a knock at the door. Frankie looked at me, lifting a blond eyebrow. "Maybe that's him now."

"Be nice!" I demanded in a loud whisper as she got off the couch and headed for the door.

She motioned dramatically and wagged her eyebrows before grabbing the knob and pulling open the door.

"What are you doing here?" she said, exasperated, when the door was open.

I turned to look over my shoulder, the smile falling from my lips. It wasn't Dex. It was a man I'd never seen before. He was very good-looking and dressed in an expensive wool coat buttoned all the way up around his neck. He had dark hair that was artfully arranged to look messy (not like Dex's, which actually *was* messy) and green eyes that held a light of mischief.

"Don't you have a home?" the man sad, his eyes settling on Frankie.

"If I did I wouldn't give you the address," Frankie retorted.

"Can we help you?" I said, ignoring the obvious undercurrents of dislike between my best friend and this man.

"Piper, this is that guy I told you about, the annoying one who came by the other day when you weren't home."

I got up off the couch, wondering why someone I didn't know would come here to see me.

"I'm sorry, do we know each other?" I asked. Maybe he was someone I had a class with and didn't remember.

"No. We don't. We have a mutual friend."

"Who?" I asked as he stepped through the door into the apartment. A feeling of unease came over me.

"Dex." He replied around a smile that didn't quite reach his eyes.

"Oh," I said. "You know Dex?"

I noticed Frankie had yet to close the door but was walking farther into the room, watching him. "I don't know, Piper. If Dex is anything like this guy here, you should get out now."

He glanced at Frankie and grinned. This time it seemed more genuine but also very annoyed. Then he glanced back at me.

"I'm afraid it's too late to get out."

"What?" I said, confused.

He began to pull his hand out of his pocket and I noticed there was something in it.

"Look out!" Frankie yelled. "He has a gun!" She threw herself at me and we both went sprawling on the floor Frankie landing on top of me.

"Get up," the man said, annoyed, reaching down to pull Frankie to her feet. "I can't get a decent shot with you in the way."

"Did you just call me fat?" she said, offended. "I am not fat. I'm curvy."

He snorted and as I was getting up off the floor Frankie swung at him.

It didn't work out too well for her. He grabbed her arm and twisted it around her back, making her cry out in pain.

"You have to be the most infuriating girl I've ever met."

Frankie stomped on his foot with her heeled boot.

He howled in pain but didn't let go. Instead, he pointed his gun at her.

"Wait!" I cried. "Please don't hurt her."

He glanced at me and I thought what a shame it was that such good looks be wasted on a monster.

"Didn't you come here for me?"

"Yes. Yes, I did. I seem to have gotten distracted by this loud lump of a girl."

Frankie stomped on his foot again and this time he released her. "Ouch!" he yelled.

She dove at him, trying to knock the gun from his grasp, but he pushed her back and then leveled it right at her chest.

All at once I understood why the sweater she was wearing looked familiar. It was the one she wore in the vision I had. The vision where she died.

"No!" I screamed and threw myself at Frankie, knocking her out of the way as the gun went off, the shot going wild and shattering the glass of the window.

Before Frankie and I could jump up, I was yanked to my feet by the man and he was dragging me out the door.

"Look what you've made me do. Now I'm going to have to kill you somewhere else. Someone's probably already called the cops."

Kill me?

I dug my feet into the floor, trying to slow him down, but it was no use. He lifted me off my feet and put my body firmly against his as if I were his shield. Then he brought the gun up to my temple and looked at Frankie, who was about to charge like a bull.

"Come any closer and I will kill her now, cops be damned."

Frankie looked between me and the gun, her eyes filling with tears.

"It's okay, Frankie. I'll be fine."

I could tell by the look on her face she didn't believe me.

And as the man with the gun dragged me out the door, I didn't believe me either.

Chapter Forty-Five

"Void - A feeling or state of emptiness, loneliness, or loss."

Dex

I couldn't say there was no color here because everything was black and black was the presence of all color. Yet, for a color that should be so full, it was maddeningly empty. It was almost as if there were too many colors and they all drowned one another out until there was nothing… nothing but darkness.

I felt as if I were Alice in Wonderland and I'd fallen down a rabbit hole, falling still. There was no bottom to this place. There was no beginning either. I was just falling endlessly.

I didn't know which way was up or which way was down. There probably was no direction here, because I wasn't going anywhere. I knew I wasn't alone, but I saw no one, yet I heard them. Tortured wails, distorted moans came out of the darkness and pummeled me. It sent me spiraling, spinning in all directions. I felt as if I were being pulled apart, but still I stayed together.

There was no end to the constant noise. I tried to call out to them to stop, but I had no voice. I had no mouth. No one would see me, no one would hear me, but I would be here.

Forever floating.

I tried to call upon a memory, a thought to keep me sane. Something to hold on to. Something to envision.

But they were all out of reach. I had no memories. I had no thoughts. All I had were the screams, the echoes of anguish, and the constant feeling of nothing.

I began to envy those cries in the dark. Because at least they had something. They had a way to show their pain.

They, too, knew something had been taken away from them. They mourned for the things they couldn't remember. They mourned for the emptiness that encompassed us.

I didn't even have that.

All I had was the taunting, fleeting knowledge that I'd lost everything and gained nothing.

I did have a second to wonder when it would end.

But then I realized it would not.

* * *

I woke with a shuddering breath, the kind that pulls you up off of what you're lying on. And for me, that would be the kitchen floor. I steadied myself, bracing my palms on the cold tile and took another deep breath.

Feelings and sensations rushed over me. It was almost overwhelming. I sat there for I don't know how long trying to make sense of them all. Trying to sort out everything.

When I tried to think about what happened, all I got was this empty blackness that seemed to open up inside my chest and try to pull me in. I jumped up onto my feet, trying to get away from whatever it was that wanted to claim me.

"Ah, you're back," called a voice from the living room.

I spun and walked toward the couch where G.R. was lying on his back, his hands across his abdomen and his eyes closed. He was so bony he looked like a corpse.

"What happened?" I asked, my voice low and scratchy like I hadn't spoken in days.

"I gave you a taste of what it was like to be recalled," Grim said, opening his eyes to stare at me. "How was it?"

Panic seized my chest and I gripped the back of the couch. "Please don't send me back there." I begged. It was a place far worse than hell.

G.R. threw his legs over the side of the couch and sat up. "I see my message was received."

"Your message?" I said, confused. The empty void of that place was still swirling through my mind, making it very hard to think.

He stood and looked at me. "That the Target will be eliminated."

Piper. Death. Job.

"Right," I said, drawing in a shaking breath. "I'll do the job. I swear." Anything to avoid going back there.

"I trust that you will. You're time has dwindled. Finish the job."

I looked toward the window. It was dark.

"How long was I… was I gone?" I asked, trying desperately not to think of that place.

"Several days," G.R. said, stepping away from the couch.

"*Days?*" I asked, shocked.

"Yes, now I really must be going. I have other Escorts and deaths to attend to."

I stood there in shock as he seemed to create a doorway out of thin air and step through. Then it closed behind him, leaving me alone.

I suddenly had a *very* strong aversion to being alone.

There was a noise behind me and I turned to see Hobbs coming down the stairs. I'd never been so happy to see the butler in all my life.

"Hobbs," I said, the relief clear in my voice.

"What has happened? Who was that man?" he asked, leaning more heavily on his cane than I'd ever seen before.

"You wouldn't believe me if I told you," I said, staring at the spot where Grim had disappeared.

"I am very good at the unbelievable," Hobbs replied.

I shook my head and swayed a little on my feet.

"How long's it been since you have eaten?" Hobbs asked, going into the kitchen. "You look horribly drained."

I was drained. Every single thing inside me was completely emptied and then replaced. All to prove a point.

I sank onto a stool at the island.

Hobbs picked up the pot and smelled the black liquid that looked more like mud. "Um, sir. How long has this been here?"

"I have no idea, Hobbs," I said. "Probably days."

He made a noise and then began moving around the kitchen. I barely paid attention to anything he was doing. I kept slipping back into that world of nothing. The next time I looked down there was a steaming cup of coffee, practically white with creamer.

I picked it up and drank about half in one great gulp.

"I would apologize for being gone longer than expected, but it seems you haven't noticed," Hobbs said, refilling my cup.

"It's been a strange few days," I muttered, drinking more. I noticed the sound of sizzling bacon and the smell of scrambled eggs. My stomach growled loudly.

"Does this have anything to do with the dilemma we discussed before?"

"Something like that," I said, running a hand through my hair.

"Maybe it's time you explain everything to me."

"I can't."

"Maybe I can help you," he said, setting a full plate in front of me. For the first time ever, the bacon wasn't appealing.

"No one can help me," I said.

"I don't believe that."

"Believe what you want," I muttered, shoving a bite of eggs in my mouth. It didn't taste as good as usual, but I ate it anyway because my stomach felt like it might consume itself.

Hobbs said nothing else and I continued to eat in silence, trying not to think of where I'd been. Grim made his point. Being recalled was the worst thing I could ever imagine. Actually, it was worse than anything I ever imagined.

I couldn't go back there.

"I have to finish the job," I said to myself.

"What job?" Hobbs asked.

I stood, my chair clattering to the floor. "I have something I have to do."

"Wait!" Hobbs called behind me. "What is it?"

"I have to do it," I told him.

I grabbed my keys and went out the garage door.

"There is *always* a choice," Hobbs yelled after me.

He didn't understand. He didn't know what it was like there… floating for days. If he did, he would understand. I couldn't go back there. I wouldn't.

This time I had no choice.

Chapter Forty-Six

"Fight - A confrontation between opposing groups in which each attempts to harm or gain power over the other, as with bodily force or weapons."

Piper

When we got to the sidewalk outside my apartment building the man had to pull the gun away from my head. Relief washed over me just because I didn't have to feel the cold metal of the gun against my skin. But I knew I was far from danger.

He jammed the gun into my side and in low menacing tones he said, "Act normal or I guarantee I'll shoot you right here and leave you to die on the pavement. Then I'll go back upstairs and shoot your friend."

I couldn't let anything happen to Frankie. After that vision I had, I knew if this guy got anywhere near her again she really would die. I nodded and began walking. He nudged me along down the sidewalk a bit and when we passed by the small space between my building and the one next to it, I swear I saw something in the shadows move. I averted my eyes because I was afraid I would be too tempted to call out for help.

We came to a nearby alleyway and he told me to turn so I did and saw he had a car parked in the center. I didn't pay attention to the make of the car because I was looking around for something I could use as a weapon.

Once we were out of the way of prying eyes, he shoved me to the side of the car, to the back door, and he flung it open. "Get in," he said.

I shook my head.

"I said get in!" he demanded.

"And I said no!" I yelled and kicked him in the knee. He moaned and bent forward and I lunged passed him, running farther into the alley. I knew I should be running in the opposite direction, but I'd never make it past him. I just really hoped this didn't turn out like a bad horror movie where the dumb chick gets it.

But I had to try. I had to at least attempt escape. I knew if I got in that car I wasn't getting out alive. And his threat to Frankie was probably no good by now. She was probably already out of my apartment and on her way for help. If I could stall him or get away… that would be my best chance.

At the very back of the alley was a chain-link fence. When I reached it I skidded to halt but rammed into it and it made a loud clattering sound. My noise alerted two great big Doberman pinschers on the other side and they began barking and snarling. I swear one began foaming at the mouth. One of them tried to stick its head through a large cut in the bottom of the fence, snapping at my foot.

I looked over my shoulder. The man and his gun were dashing this way.

I had a choice to make. The dogs or the man with the gun.

I was going with the dogs. I dropped down on my butt and pried the fence up as high as it would go.

"Nice, doggie," I tried but quickly realized that wasn't going to help me.

"Git!" I yelled and kicked at one of them. They moved back and I began shimmying myself under the fence.

The man behind me made a sound, kind of like a growl, and I tried to move faster. But my shirt got caught on the fencing and one of the dogs bit at my shoe. And then he was on me, grabbing me roughly and pulling me back into the alley. I was still half lying on the ground when he leaned over me, snarling.

"You've been nothing but trouble, you know that?" he ground out and then he hit me in the head with his gun and everything went black.

Chapter Forty-Seven

"Determination - Firmness of purpose; resolve."

Dex

I drove to Piper's apartment because I figured there was nowhere else she would be besides work, and I knew she was off. Hobb's words echoed through my head with every mile I drove.

There is always a choice.

Maybe in his world, but not in mine. He didn't understand what I was caught up in. He probably never even considered that the Grim Reaper was even real. I never gave it much thought either until I met him and saw for myself.

Remnants of my time being recalled rattled around inside me and caused me to press down on the gas. I never wanted to go there again. I finally understood what Storm meant about there being worse things than not having a body. If I had to choose between not having a body and being recalled, I would've made the same choice as him.

I couldn't even think of the words to describe that place. I wouldn't even be able to begin to make them up either. There was simply no word or description that could give meaning to what I experienced.

I turned onto Piper's street, steely resolve settling over me like ice on the ground, and looked for a place to park.

But there was nowhere.

Half the street was blocked off by police cruisers and people standing on the sidewalk. They were all in front of Piper's building. My heart rate picked up a little and I told myself it was because the police made me nervous. Still, my eyes went up to the window that I knew was Piper's.

It was shattered.

Jagged pieces of glass hung awkwardly from the sides and there was nothing left of the center.

I couldn't park my car so I just slowed it to a crawl. I couldn't help but notice how people turned to look and I realized this was not the kind of car that people drove in this neighborhood. This was the kind of car that would draw attention.

Just as I was about to take off down the road and ditch the car to come back on foot someone broke away from the crowd and came running. I was going to ignore her, but then I took another look… She looked familiar. It was the same girl I saw with Piper that day at the college. I think Piper said Frankie was her name.

I stopped the car and rolled down the passenger-side window as the woman with chin-length curly hair looked inside.

"Are you Dex?"

"Yeah. What's going on?" I hitched my chin toward the building.

"Some guy who claimed to be a friend of yours came here tonight, pulled a gun, and kidnapped Piper."

Shock and anger sliced through me. I felt my hands curl tightly around the steering wheel. Charming had threatened her, but part of me thought he wouldn't do it. I didn't think he would go against G.R. like that.

My thinking got my Target kidnapped.

"How long ago was he here?"

"An hour ago. Maybe more."

"Get back," I growled.

She barely stepped out of the way as I burned rubber all the way down the street.

Chapter Forty-Eight

"Trapped - in a tight corner, in a tight spot, with your back to the wall."

Piper

I opened my eyes and then blinked to be sure they really were open. It was so dark here that for a minute I was fooled into thinking I really hadn't opened them. I felt disoriented and confused, not really understanding what was happening. Then in a rush of panic and memory it all came back. The man with the gun, Frankie, and the dogs. He'd hit me and then put me here.

But where was here?

I stretched out my arm to see if I could feel anything and it very quickly hit against something solid covered in a fine, rough carpet. I was lying on my side and I rolled onto my back and reached up, hitting a very low ceiling… It wasn't a ceiling.

It was a trunk.

He locked me up inside the trunk of his car.

I bit back the panic that immediately tried to grab hold. Panic wouldn't help me now and hyperventilating would only reduce my oxygen supply. I closed my eyes, forcing myself to take a deep breath, and then I thought of somewhere else, somewhere I would rather be.

A vision of the northern lights flashed through my mind and the memory of lying against the snow so close to Dex calmed me. *That's where I'd rather be.*

I had to be calm and rational about this. I couldn't fall apart. If I died, Frankie would never forgive me.

Feeling more in control I opened my eyes. There had to be a way out of here.

I thought back to the features of the car. It was a newer car and newer cars all had safety latches in the trunks. If I could find it, I could get out and run for help.

I began running my hands along the sides of the trunk, looking for a button or a handle, anything I could use to set myself free. At times, I had to stop and remind myself not to panic. This tiny enclosed space made it really hard to breathe. After a few minutes of futile searching, I let out a frustrated cry and let my head fall to the side.

That's when I saw it.

There was a very faint glowing just past the center (or what I thought was the center) of the side. It was shaped kind of like a handle. *It must be glow-in-the-dark,* I thought as I reached for the handle, hope bubbling up inside me.

Then from outside the car I heard a sound. A slam. Then the engine started and the car began to move. He was driving off, taking me somewhere he could probably kill me and then hide my body.

Chapter Forty-Nine

"Anger - A strong feeling of displeasure or hostility."

Dex

As soon as Piper's building was out of sight, my cell phone rang. It was Storm. "Tell me you know where she is," I said as soon as I answered the call.

"He stuffed her in the trunk of a white car," he said. "He's driving now."

"Is she dead?" I asked, the words sticking in my throat. The vivid image of Charming shutting up her dead body in his trunk flashed before my eyes.

"No. Not yet. But he hit her in the head with his gun and knocked her out."

"So G.R. has this rule about Escorts not fighting," I said. "But does he have a rule about us killing each other?"

Storm made a sound on the other end of the line; it sounded like a laugh. "You want to find out the hard way?"

Maybe.

"Where are they?"

"He just pulled onto the street with the diner."

"I'm on my way," I said, hitting the gas and fishtailing a little on the ice. I didn't slow down until I came to a red light and had to stop.

"Seriously, man, I know you're pissed he would try to take out your Target, but killing Charming will only get him a new body and you recalled."

I heard his words, but I didn't say anything.

"Dex? Are you still there?"

"Yeah, yeah, I'm here." This was the longest red light ever.

"He just parked. He's right by the diner. He's… wait, she's just jumped out of the trunk. She's running… You need to hurry!"

I threw the phone onto the seat next to me and pressed down on the gas, ignoring the red light.

Chapter Fifty

"Escape - To break loose from confinement; get free."

Piper

The car didn't go very far before it came to a complete stop. I lay there for long moments with my heart pounding out of my chest, just listening, wondering if he was coming for me. Wondering where we were and if he was just going to open the trunk and shoot me.

Am I just going to lie here and let him come for me?

No.

I wasn't.

My hand tightened around the trunk release and I pulled it. I didn't know where we were, but I'd rather die trying to escape than doing nothing at all. I kicked the trunk lid up and leapt out of the back, landing on the hard pavement. I hit hard, but I ignored the screaming of my muscles and bones and stood looking wildly around. We were at the diner.

But going inside wouldn't help me because they weren't open. They closed early every Sunday night. I'd always liked that. Until now.

"Hey!" shouted the man who kidnapped me when he climbed out of the car and saw me standing there in the street.

I took off running, my feet slipping a little in the snow and ice. But I kept running, running away from the diner and down the street toward another business.

But he caught me.

He caught my arm and spun me around, laughing and pulling me in for a hug. He was trying to make it look like we'd been playing around. That I really hadn't been running for my life.

I felt the hard metal of the gun ram into my rib cage and I wanted to shake with defeat.

But I wouldn't.

"Let's go. We're going inside," he said into my ear and then pulled me along beside him to the entrance of the diner.

"It's closed. The door's locked," I told him, hoping to fluster him for a brief second to get away again.

It didn't work.

He laughed low. "Do you think I hadn't thought of that?" He reached out and pulled the door handle. It opened with ease. "They don't call me Charming for nothing."

"People think you're charming?" I scoffed.

"The waitress here tonight certainly thought so." He was so smug I wanted to kick him.

So I did. Right in the shin.

He hissed a breath between his teeth. "Careful, you don't want me to knock you out again. Then you'll miss all the fun."

The diner was darkened, with only a few lights on close to the back and one near the cook's line. As we moved farther into the diner, he shoved me away and I ran behind the counter and grabbed a steak knife in one hand and a heavy glass sugar shaker in the other.

He actually set the gun on a nearby table and smiled. "This is going to be fun."

And then he was leaping over the counter at me and I struck out with the knife. It caught his arm but did nothing other than damage the fine wool of his coat. He shouted in outrage and grabbed my arm, twisting so that the knife fell out of my grip and clattered on the floor. I slung the sugar shaker at him, catching him in the temple and snapping his head back. He let go as he stumbled and I stumbled too, stepping on the knife and slipping.

I landed on my butt, my tailbone stinging as I scrambled back up, still clutching my weapon. The man jumped right back up, blood gushing down the side of his face and into his mouth. It outlined all those perfect teeth and made him look like a rabid monster. He began unbuttoning his coat with slow, deliberate movements, but I wasn't transfixed. I grabbed up a glass bottle of ketchup and threw it at the floor by his feet. It burst open, splattering everything with red sauce. Then I rushed to the line and reached through the opening, feeling around for a heavy pan I could knock him out with.

He came forward, slipping in the ketchup and falling over, taking me with him. He landed heavy and hard on top of me and sat up, his legs straddling my middle, and then he smiled that maniacal smile and wrapped his hands around my throat.

He didn't squeeze at first, but applied enough pressure that I had to work a little harder to breathe, and it was just enough to make me start panicking. I tried to kick him off, to shift his weight, but it was no use. He outweighed me by a good eighty pounds.

"Your ability will be mine," he said, tightening his grip a little bit more, and I choked.

Was that what this was about? My ability to have visions?

"Dex was supposed to kill you, but he didn't, and I'm tired of waiting. So I'm going to kill you, collect my prize, and he will be recalled. Forever lost in damned eternity."

Black spots began swimming in front of me and I was pretty sure he was going to crush my windpipe. His words echoed through my head over and over and over.

Dex was supposed to kill you...

With one last burst of energy, I threw my hand out, wrapping it around something beneath the counter, and brought it up between our faces. I placed my finger where I knew the trigger was and pressed. I held that button down with everything inside me as Lysol rushed out of the can and into the eyes of my attacker.

He began screaming and released me to wipe at his face. He was stupid because wiping it only made it worse and pushed it deeper into his eyes.

I hoped it burned like hell.

He rolled off me, squirming and screaming curses at me as I gasped for breath and made it to my hands and knees. I was beyond dizzy. My throat hurt so badly I would've cried if I was able, and it was hard to see.

But none of that mattered. All that mattered was surviving.

I began to crawl away, still clutching the aerosol can in my hand, desperately trying to move quickly when something latched onto my ankle. I shook my leg, trying to get free, but I was towed backward, behind the counter…

Toward my death.

I rolled onto my back and, taking aim with the disinfectant, pressed the button. This time only a small cloud released because in my haste earlier I'd used what was left in the can. I threw it at him in frustration, hitting him square in the face.

I hoped his nose swelled up like the rest of his face.

If I was going to die on the floor of some crappy diner, I was at least going to inflict as much damage as possible to the man who murdered me.

I began looking for something else I could use to fend him off when I felt warm hands come around my back and lift me up away from the floor. I used my feet to push myself up until the person behind me swung me up completely and into his arms.

I blinked. My vision was blurred, but I caught the outline of black-rimmed glasses.

Dex.

Considering that this other guy just told me Dex wanted me dead too, I wasn't sure I was any safer than moments before.

But the way he held me tight made me doubt what I'd heard. I was so relieved to see him that my cheek fell against his chest and my eyes closed.

"Hang on, Piper. Don't pass out on me," he said, low, into my ear then he shifted my weight so he held me even closer against him.

"I thought I told you to stay away from *my* Target," Dex growled in menacing tones. "What the hell do you think you're doing, Charming?"

"I'm doing what you haven't and taking my reward."

Dex stepped closer to the killer and I stiffened. He was supposed to be stepping away…

"I'll do *my* job on *my* own time. If you don't like it, then you take that up with me or G.R."

His words made ice form in my belly, but then he was stepping away, heading toward the door of the diner and out into the cold.

Dex didn't say anything as he walked to his car, parked halfway on the sidewalk, and leaned down to open the passenger-side door. He sat me onto the warm leather and shrugged out of his jacket and draped it over my body, tucking it around me. Tears sprang to my eyes for so many reasons I couldn't even name them all, and I turned my face away from him.

The car door shut softly behind me and then he was climbing into the driver's seat, revving the engine and aiming all the heating vents at me as he pulled away from the curb.

I didn't bother to turn away from him again. I was too stiff and sore and I wanted to watch his expressions when I asked him the question I had to ask.

I opened my lips, but my voice came out as a strained whisper. He glanced at me sharply and reached out to pull the coat closer around me.

"Don't talk. You might make it worse. I'm taking you to the clinic."

When he pulled his hand back, it stopped and hovered beside my face. I watched his jaw clench as I felt his fingers brush over my cheek and stroke downward. My eyes closed at the contact. So rarely did he touch me like this.

God help me, I craved it.

"You're going to kill me, aren't you?" I managed to rasp once he pulled his hand away.

The silence in the car was so absolute I was beginning to think he hadn't heard, but then he glanced at me. His eyes were all the answer I needed.

He was.

I lost it. I freaking lost it right there.

I jerked my body up, throwing aside his coat, pushing it away from me. I didn't want the comfort of it. How could someone comfort me one moment, then kill me the next?

I would rather just have what happened in the diner. At least that was clearer. This was just... This was... It was messed up.

"What are you, an assassin?"

"Calm down, Piper. You're going to hurt your throat," he said in a perfectly reasonable tone.

I laughed. It hurt. "What do you care?"

I shoved at his shoulder and the car jerked, but he quickly righted it. He didn't respond. He just drove, staring out the window with his jaw set.

"So if all you wanted was to kill me, why not just do it? Why bother getting to know me? Why bother with all of... of... *this*?" I motioned between us and he glanced at me and lifted a brow.

Something inside of me shriveled with that kind of mocking look.

It said *This? You're a silly girl with a silly one-sided crush. If you thought there was something between us then it was all in your head.*

I wanted to die right then. I felt like such a fool.

I slapped him across his face, wiping that smug look right off it.

"Piper..." he growled, down shifting the car.

My hand stung, but I didn't care, and then I gasped as another realization hit me.

"All those accidents... all those times... that was you wasn't it? That was you all along, trying to kill me!"

His jaw clenched again and he refused to look me in the eye, and I knew. I knew I was right. All those times I thought we were getting closer, all those times we spent together that I thought meant something really hadn't.

The things I replayed in my head when I lay in bed at night hadn't been romantic. They were attempted murder.

Why had I never seen a vision of this? Of all things, why couldn't I have seen this?

"Kill me now," I said low, the words sounding as raw as my throat felt.

This earned me a glance.

"If you want me dead so bad, kill me now."

I saw his hand flex on the gearshift. I could taste the temptation in the tiny space between us. He really wanted to kill me...

I punched him in the shoulder, taking us both off guard. I didn't stop hitting him. I kept at it, punching, hurling my fists as hard as I could, landing blows wherever allowed.

"Piper, stop it!" he said, turning, grabbing both my wrists and squeezing. He was breathing hard and his chest was rising and falling rapidly. The temperature in the car was intense from my anger and the fact we never turned down the heat. But as soon as he grabbed me and our eyes collided, everything around us kind of slowed down...

In his eyes I saw a flash of regret and a flash of determination. I didn't know which was stronger and I never got the chance to ask.

Because the minute he took his hands off the steering wheel to grab me, he lost control of the car.

It fishtailed, spinning us in circles until we slammed against a dense patch of frozen trees, bouncing off and hurtling farther away from the road, only to crash into another patch of trees. When the car finally came to a halt, a large mass of snow fell from the tree we'd just rammed and fell onto the hood, breaking the already cracked windshield. Glass rained down upon us and then everything fell still.

Chapter Fifty-One

"Realization - The act of realizing or the condition of being realized."

Dex

I blinked open my eyes, aware of stinging pain in my face and hands. Memories of Piper hitting me and of the pain in her eyes came over me. If those weren't hard enough, I was assaulted with even more memories of my car going out of control, the panic of not being able to do anything as we hurtled toward the trees and of the realization we were going to die.

Those memories were like a bucket of cold water to my fog and I was instantly alert, sitting up and turning toward Piper.

I never thought anything would be worse than the feeling of being recalled.

There was.

Seeing Charming over her with blood on his face and a wild look in his eyes had been shattering. I felt horrified and broken apart looking down at Piper—seeing her bruises, hearing her gasp for air.

How had things come to this? How did my basic life on the streets, my daily struggle to survive turn into this?

In the seat next to me, she was bleeding and battered and her still form unleashed a panicked frenzy within me. This was the closest I'd ever come to actually killing her and all I could think about was what I could do to make sure she didn't die.

It was then I realized with absolute clarity that I wasn't going to kill this girl.

I couldn't.

I reached across the seat and grasped her gently. Her head rolled backward revealing deep purple rings around her neck and various shallow, bleeding cuts in her face. No, I wasn't going to kill her, but the idea of killing Charming was very, very appealing.

"Piper," I said, my voice shaky and weak. "Piper, please wake up."

There was no sound, no response, and a desperate sound ripped out of me as I released her and climbed through the destroyed car, cutting myself on jagged pieces of broken glass to get closer to her. I was practically in her seat when I lowered my ear to her chest to listen for her heart beat.

It was there and her chest rose and fell with air.

I let out a shuddering breath and climbed back into my seat. I opened the door, having to kick at it to get it to cooperate, and then I all but fell out into the snow. I reached into the waistband of my jeans and pulled out the gun. It was heavy and lethal in my hand. With a loud, frustrated cry, I launched it into the darkness, out into the snow-covered landscape. I felt sick inside and I knew it wasn't because my body still wanted me to do the job.

The war between this body and my soul was over.

My soul won.

And with that victory, feelings I'd held back, feelings I hadn't understood or wanted to feel flooded me. I was so ashamed of everything I'd done.

I reached into my jeans and pulled out my cell.

"Hobbs," I rasped when my butler answered on the first ring. "I've been in an accident… Piper… she's unconscious. Please help us."

I rattled off our location, then dropped the phone in the snow, completely ignoring his questions and demands. I knew he would come.

I couldn't get Piper out of her side because it was smashed into a tree. So, I climbed back in my side and found my leather jacket to wrap around her. Every muscle in my body quivered and protested as I lifted her out. A couple times I had to stop with her in my arms and take a few breaths. I did what I could to make sure she wasn't injured more, but I knew she got a few more scrapes as I tried to wiggle her out.

Once free of the twisted metal, I carried her to the road where I dropped, still holding her in my arms, to wait.

I looked down at her in the dark and more feelings rushed to the surface. I wouldn't kill her. I was never going to. All of the times I'd "attempted" to do so were never a success because I hadn't really been trying. If I were, she'd be dead.

And I didn't want her to die.

Even if it meant I'd be recalled.

Chapter Fifty-Two

"Safe - Free from danger or injury; unhurt. Secure from danger, harm,

or evil."

Piper

I heard the beeping, I felt the gentle pressure of a blanket over my body, and I knew finally I was somewhere safe. I didn't open my eyes because I wasn't ready yet. When I opened them, I'd have to see. I'd have to see everything I'd been blind to for so long.

All this time I'd been falling. Falling for a man who wanted me dead. I thought of him fondly while he thought of ways to erase me from this earth. Had I let my obsession with the man who died for me get in the way of everything else? Did I yearn for him so badly that I didn't care what I had to do to get answers?

My brain lost these thoughts as a feeling of pain came over me. My body was so tired. I'd fought to stay alive and I was… but for how much longer?

I heard a soft noise beside me and then felt a presence that had probably been there all along. Was it Frankie? No. Frankie would be demanding that I open my eyes. She'd be yelling at me for scaring her this way.

This presence was heavy and silent, laced with regret. Was he here, then? Was he waiting to kill me in my sleep?

Perhaps if I was going to die, doing so peacefully would be best. I tried to die while fighting and that hadn't gotten me anywhere.

Something cold touched my skin and then was drawn away. I lay there without one ounce of energy to open my eyes. As I began to fall asleep, I heard a heavy sigh and something warm wrapped around my fingers.

Dex.

I thought about reaching for the call button. I thought about getting some help. But I never got that far. Because as soon as the thought entered my mind, Dex began to talk.

He began to confess.

Chapter Fifty-Three

"Confess - To disclose (something damaging or inconvenient to oneself);

admit."

Dex

If she dies, it's going to be my fault.

The thought mixed with the sound of beeping monitors—the two blending together into a constant rhythm that hummed through me as I hunched close to the hospital bed.

The doctors said she wasn't going to die. They said she'd be okay, and the beeping of the monitors was proof she was still alive.

It was also a reminder that in a short time I most likely would be dead.

I shivered a bit, wondering why the hospital room was so cold, and I reached over to pull the blankets closer around her.

She was pale. Her cheeks lacked that pink glow that I'd come to associate with her. Because she looked so white, the bruises on her neck stood out even more and so did the many cuts on her face from the shattered windshield. In many ways she looked like a creation of Frankenstein—all pieced together with many different colors.

Even still, she would be Frankenstein's most beautiful creation.

I found the edge of the blanket and pushed my hand under it, my fingers seeking her hand, and when I found it, my skin felt like ice against her warmth so instead of wrapping my fingers around hers I settled for resting mine beside them.

I felt heavy and confused. I knew exactly how we got here, but the reasoning behind my actions no longer made sense. What made me think death was more important than life? What made me think it was okay to kill for money, clothes, and my own preservation? When I died—when I pushed her out of the way of that bus—I hadn't been thinking I would gain from my actions. I hadn't been thinking anything other than this girl couldn't die.

What happened to that thought? It somehow got lost between death and life, and now here I was sitting in a hospital beside someone I'd been trying to kill for over a month when, really, from the second I saw her I only wanted her to live.

It seemed hers was the only life I'd ever valued, but it was to her that I brought the promise of death. Charming wanted her abilities and G.R. wanted her body and soul.

And me… what did I want?

I wanted her heart.

My hand flexed when the thought whispered into my mind… My fingers were no longer cold and of their own accord, they sought and entwined with hers. Somewhere between the plotting and the lying, I'd fallen in love with her.

I'd never known love in my life. I always felt like I had a slow leak in my heart… that eventually everything good would drain away until I was left with nothing but a deflated, useless organ inside my chest. But now… now I felt like the leak was patched and someone was slowly breathing life back into what I thought was a lost cause.

And this was how I repaid her.

"I'm a miserable excuse for a person," I whispered to her, glancing at the closed door. "They let me in here without question when really they should've kept me far away."

The monitors continued their steady beeping as my confession poured right out.

"That man that died for you, the man you mourn for everyday… I'm that man. I know it sounds impossible, I know it sounds like a lie, but it's the truth and it's where our story began."

My fingers curled a little more closely around hers and I took a breath. "I was given a new body and I was promised money and cars and homes… I was promised an eternal life to enjoy and all I had to do was Escort people to death. I never thought death was that big of a deal. But then I was told to kill you. I thought I could do it. I told them I would. I did try… but when it came down to it, I just couldn't. Death feels like a very heavy burden now."

I bowed my head so all I could see was my feet.

"I wanted to tell you that I'm sorry. That from here on out, your life is safe. I won't hurt you and no one else will either. Your life is ten times more valuable to me than anything else. I know you won't forgive me, and I don't think I deserve it, but I had to say it before I walked out this door and never came back."

I gently untangled my fingers from hers and pushed out of the chair. I leaned in close, taking advantage of the fact she was still asleep to brush the hair from her face and press my lips against her forehead. She hadn't heard anything I said and when she opened her eyes, I wouldn't be there. But I figured leaving now was the kindest thing I could do.

I pulled away and looked down one last time before I went.

She was watching me.

There were tears on her face.

Without thought, I brushed them away with my fingers, watching as her eyes briefly closed. When they reopened they were filled with fear. I pulled my hands back, stuffing them in my pockets, and took a small step backward.

"I know you're scared of me. I'm not going to hurt you. I'm leaving,"

I turned away and went to the door, reaching for the handle.

"Wait," she called from the bed. Her voice was still hoarse and scratchy, but it was loud enough that my hand paused.

I looked over my shoulder.

"I heard what you said."

"I know it seems unbelievable," I began, but she shook her head.

"I believe you," she whispered, her voice growing lighter. She held out her hand and motioned for me to come closer.

I released the handle and went back to her bedside.

"I knew you were connected to him," she whispered. "That night he—you—died… when he touched me, I had a vision. A vision of him smiling."

I sat down in the chair, heavily, listening to her words.

"Then that first time in the diner, that time I met you again… when you touched me… I had the exact same vision. I've never been more confused. When I touch someone and get a vision, it's about that person and *only that person*. But here I was, touching a stranger and having a vision about someone else. Someone that died."

"You have visions?" I asked, understanding dawning. I finally knew what Charming was after. And I also finally understood why she'd been so sure I was connected to the man who got hit by the bus.

She nodded. "Ever since I was a little girl."

Her voice cracked on the last word and I reached to grab the pitcher of water and pour her a glass, holding it out so she could sip through the straw. She drank it gratefully and then fell back against her pillow.

"You should rest," I told her. "You've been through a lot."

She reached for my hand, her grip surprisingly strong. "Please don't go."

"You want me to stay?" *After everything I admitted?*

"I feel like I only just found you," she whispered.

"Listen to me, the guy you think I am… the guy that got hit by that bus. That *is* me. The me standing in front of you. I know I look different, but I'm the same. I still tried to kill you."

"Stay," she whispered, her eyes getting heavy, but the grip on my hand remained.

I pulled the chair closer and sat down, knowing I should go but wanting to stay.

* * *

She was sleeping when I slipped out the door. The doctor said she was going to be just fine, would probably sleep all night long and be released tomorrow. My clothes were rumpled and ripped, I had blood all over my shirt, and my face hurt from all the cuts from the shattered windshield. I needed some glasses because I couldn't see and it was giving me a headache.

I told myself those were the reasons I was leaving.

But I couldn't fool myself, no matter how badly I wanted to.

I was leaving because I couldn't sit there and watch her die.

No, she wouldn't die from the car accident. But she was dying. Somewhere right now Charming and G.R. were plotting against us, against her. I couldn't sit by while someone planned the death of the only person I ever loved.

That's the thing about death. It doesn't care about love. It doesn't care if you're not done living. It doesn't stop... It keeps coming until it claims everything a person has, until there's nothing left.

When I walked by the waiting area I saw Hobbs leaning back in a chair with his feet outstretched before him and his ankles crossed. He had his hands lying over his middle and his head leaned back, looking up toward the ceiling. His eyes were closed. I stepped up before him and he opened his eyes and straightened.

"Is she all right?"

I nodded. "She's sleeping and I need to get cleaned up. Can you drive me home?"

The Roadster was totaled. And I really didn't care.

"Of course." He stood. The gray suit he always wore looked fresh and unlined—even though he'd spent most of the night sleeping in a hospital chair.

In the car, Hobbs tried to talk to me. "About the accident, sir, what happened?"

I leaned my head back against the seat. "I don't want to talk about it, Hobbs."

"Of course," he murmured.

There was nothing left to say. I knew what I had to do.

Chapter Fifty-Four

"Love - an intense emotion of affection, warmth, fondness, and regard towards a person or thing."

Piper

When I opened my eyes, they went to the chair pulled up close beside the bed. It was empty. Dex was gone. I wasn't sure how long he stayed, but I know he had for quite a while because the chair cushions still bore the imprint from his body.

As much as I wanted to see him, I was sort of relieved he wasn't here. I needed to sort out everything that happened and I knew that I wouldn't be able to do that with him so close.

I'd always known there was something about him I recognized—something I was missing. It wasn't just the vision. The night Dex walked into the diner, I knew he was there for me. I hadn't understood it at the time; I probably would've brushed those feelings off right then if he hadn't touched me. If I hadn't seen the man that saved me in that vision.

And I was right. All along. He was connected to the man who was hit by the bus and he'd also been there for me.

But he wasn't there with good intentions.

The cold truth was that he tried to kill me. More than once.

But he also saved me. More than once.

What was a girl supposed to do with that?

A smart girl—*me*—would run far away. Would hit the call button beside me and tell the nurse when Dex came back to keep him away, to ban him from the room.

I heard his confession. I felt his hand holding mine and I heard the acceptance and finality in his tone that he would walk away and I would never see him again.

A smart girl would have let him go.

But I loved him.

Did that make me stupid?

Maybe so, but I wasn't going to change my mind. For so long I was torn between a man that I hadn't known, a man who was dead but still felt alive, and a man who was right in front of me, a man I had feelings for but tried not to.

Turns out they were one in the same.

I wasn't entirely sure how that was possible and what it meant for us, but I was sure whatever it was we could figure it out. I saw the way he looked at me when he thought I was still asleep. I felt the gentleness in his touch and heard the longing in his voice. He loved me too, and for now, I was going to hold on to that. I guess time would tell if it was enough.

Chapter Fifty-Five

"Cracked—Broken so that fissures appear on the surface."

Dex

I rushed through my shower and then quickly pulled on a pair of beat up jeans, a white long-sleeved thermal shirt, and a navy blue zip-up hoodie. I rummaged through the bathroom until I found the wire-rimmed glasses that came with my body—the glasses I thought were dorky and stupid looking—and shoved them onto my face. My vision straightened out and I breathed a sigh of relief. It no longer mattered what kind of glasses I wore; there were more important things in life.

Like living.

I pushed my hands through my damp hair a couple times and jammed my feet into the black converse sneakers before rushing downstairs into the kitchen.

"Can I borrow your car, Hobbs?"

Hobbs turned from the stove where he was frying bacon and looked at me with lifted eyebrows. "Going somewhere?"

"I have something I need to take care of."

I thought I saw a flash of respect in his eyes, but then it was gone and he was gesturing toward the keys on the island. I grabbed them up and snagged my coat off the back of a chair.

"Thanks, I don't know when I'll be back." *Or even if I'll come back.*

"Don't you want something to eat?" Hobbs asked in mild surprise.

"No time."

"Here, I made you a coffee to go," he said, sitting a travel mug on the counter.

"Sweet," I said, taking the coffee and then snatching a couple pieces of bacon right from the pan.

It was snowing when I pulled out of the garage and onto the street—big, fat flakes that were the purest shade of white. They seemed to attack the car in a frenzy, clinging to what parts it could and rushing at the windshield as I drove.

I remembered exactly how to get to G.R.'s. The Grim Reaper's address wasn't something I think anyone would forget. True, I hadn't known at the time he was the Grim Reaper, but it had always been obvious he wasn't just an ordinary rich guy in the suburbs. As I drove through the gate of the community where he lived, I wondered what all the residents in the neighborhood would think if they knew they lived next to the ultimate life stealer.

They'd never believe it.

I could hear the news interviews now… "He was always the most cheerful, friendly neighbor. He never caused any trouble and he always brought his trash cans in on time."

I snorted. That was the thing about the Grim Reaper. He didn't have to be scary. He didn't have to walk around in a cloak carrying a scythe because all he had to do to take your life was touch you. His friendly, almost jolly personality was the ultimate weapon because it allowed him to get close enough to touch. Before you even knew what was happening, you were dead and G.R. claimed your body for his closet, your soul (for God only knew what), and then handed out your money or your abilities to his Escorts.

And he did it all in a matter of moments.

But I wasn't going to help him. And I wasn't going to let him have Piper.

His mansion came into view and I turned down the long, curving driveway and stopped haphazardly near the front of the house. I got out of the car and went to the front door and rang the bell. The door was opened by a man in a black coat and tails who bowed as I walked in.

To anyone who might be watching, it appeared I was just a guy visiting a friend and being welcomed by the butler. But I knew better.

This was the beginning of the end.

I followed the butler through a long hallway draped in art until we stopped in front of wide dark wood double doors. The butler motioned for me to stay and he let himself quietly into the room.

I wasn't fool enough to think I could stop the Grim Reaper. I couldn't. But I was hoping I could make some kind of deal to keep Piper alive.

"He will see you now," the butler said when he came out of the door, holding it so I could enter the large office where I came when I was nothing but a ghost. The memory had me looking down at myself, half expecting to see my body was gone and I was nothing but purple mist. But I still had a body and nothing on me was purple.

I stopped in front of the desk and watched the massive black leather chair turn slowly around, revealing the bony frame of the Grim Reaper. Knowing now who he really was, I realized he had the perfect look for the taker of life.

"Ah, Dexter! I had a feeling you would be by today," he said, actually with friendliness in his tone. Then his brow furrowed a bit and he said, "Where is my body?"

He meant Piper. He thought I'd come because I killed her and wanted to deliver her body. I figured Charming would've come running to tattle when I interrupted his plans to murder my Target.

"Were you aware that Charming tried to interfere with my assignment? That he tried to kill *my* Target?"

"Yes." G.R. smiled fondly. "He is a most impatient Escort, but that's what makes him so good at what he does. He doesn't play games."

I ignored the last remark, which was no doubt a barb at me for taking so long in delivering my Target. Charming probably dispatched all his Targets with record speed.

"My Target. My rules," I said with a hint of challenge to my tone.

G.R. steepled his fingers beneath his chin in a pose I was beginning to think of as his signature and he smiled. "Well, he did say you interrupted his attempt. So when I heard you were here I assumed it was because you hurried and finished the job before Charming could try again and take your victory away."

Of course that's what he thought. Dead bodies around here were almost like trophies.

"I came to tell you I won't do it. I'm not going to kill her."

He dropped his hands as his eyes widened. "No? Do you not remember the price for refusing my deal?"

"I remember." My mind shied away from remembering the black void of being recalled.

"So you would give it all up, the money, the cars, the immortality…" He said the last word with deliberate pronunciation. "You would give it all up for a girl?"

I would give it all up for *her*.

But saying that out loud would only put a bigger target on her so, instead, I replied, "I've tried out the lifestyle and decided that immortality doesn't look good on me."

G.R. laughed and stood from his chair. "Perhaps a new body would make immortality more appealing?" He flicked his wrists and all the closet doors behind him opened. My eyes went to the spot where I knew he kept my body.

"It's still there," he said, following my gaze. "Waiting for you to complete your assignment and claim a spot as a permanent Death Escort."

I looked away from my body. "No."

He must've heard something in my voice that he hadn't before. Maybe it was the ring of finality because a great change came over him. The closet door slammed shut and a cold wind blew through the room. His cheekbones seemed to strain against his skin and his lips drew into a fine, hard line.

"So you would take from me, then?" he began in a deep, relentless voice as he came around the desk. His dark, beady eyes speared me with cold fury. "You would spend my money, live in my house, and drive a car I paid for and give me nothing in return?"

The floor beneath my feet shook with a slight tremor that I did my best to pretend I hadn't felt.

"You can have it all back. You can take this body and my soul—do whatever you want to me—if you leave Piper out of it."

He smiled and I knew I'd revealed my weakness to him.

"All in the name of love?" he said gently, almost whimsically. Then he slammed his fist on the edge of his desk and screamed, "Death doesn't care about love!"

"I won't let you take her," I ground out.

"You think your bargain is of any prize to me? I already own your body and your soul. The money and the house will not be lost. We had a deal. No one goes back on a deal with the Grim Reaper."

"I said I would kill someone. So pick someone else. Anyone else. I'll do it."

"It doesn't work that way. The Target has been made. A deal was struck. You are going back on your end of the deal and you will be recalled!"

With that, he held out his hand, palm up, and spread his fingers wide. With a jerk of his arm I felt a tug and a deep pull within. I started to gag as I sank to my knees and purple mist began to lift out of my skin.

I never got to say good-bye.

It was all I could think of. I would be gone and Piper would wonder where I went...

And then Charming would come for her.

I watched helplessly as the purple mist that was my essence began swirling around the body that contained it. I couldn't make a sound to beg. I could do nothing but watch as he claimed what he thought was his.

"Wait!" he cried suddenly, the fingers in his outstretched hand curled in toward his palm. Everything around me stilled. The purple, translucent mist seemed to stop and suspend in the air around me.

Then G.R. made a pushing motion and all the mist—all my essence—went right back into my body.

I scrambled to my feet as he said, "Recalling you now would be too easy. I think a more fitting punishment for your betrayal would be to watch the very Target you wanted to save be taken anyway. Then you shall be recalled. Then you will fully understand that no one refuses the Grim Reaper." His chin was tipped down and he stared up at me, giving his face a hollow, savage look.

Just then the office doors swung wide and Charming burst through. He stopped short when he saw me standing there and then he glanced at G.R. and a sly smile broke over his features. "Ah, so you know," he said.

"Know that this boy is a complete and utter disappointment?" G.R. sighed. "Yes. I was just about to go collect the Target he refuses to kill. You can stay and make sure he doesn't do anything stupid while I am gone."

"With pleasure," Charming said, coming farther into the room.

I watched as G.R. paused beside his coffee table to study the bowl of smooth stones. He debated for long seconds before choosing a very pale-colored one with a crack in the side. He glanced at me.

"It would've been the perfect stone if not for this damned crack. Very fitting, I would say, that it be the representation of the death that should have been yours to claim. You would have been the perfect Escort... but it seems you are also cracked."

He left then. He didn't use the door or even take a step. He was simply gone.

I wasted no time rushing toward the doors. If I could get there fast enough, maybe I could save her. Then Charming was there, shoving me back, sending me sprawling onto the hard floor.

With a roar, I was up and launching myself at him. I slammed into him so hard we both fell backwards with me straddling his chest. I had a flashback of the night before when I entered the diner to see the very same pose, except Piper was on the bottom while he tried to rob her of her life.

I plowed my fist into his jaw so hard I heard my knuckles crack, but I ignored it and did it again. Charming might be a seasoned killer, but I was from the streets and the one thing the streets taught me was how to fight.

He tried to push me off. He kicked and scratched, but I rebuffed his attempts with punches and jabs to the ribs. All I could see in my mind were the mottled purple bruises—the marks from his hands—that covered Piper's throat.

His hits became weaker and I climbed off, pulling him up by the shirt and slamming him into the wall. He made a sound and swung, connecting with my jaw. It was a solid hit and I felt it, but it wasn't enough to get me to release him.

"Would you look at that." I taunted. "Pretty boy isn't so pretty anymore."

He kicked me, and this time I released him to stumble back. But he didn't do what I would've done and take my weak moment to get in a good hit. Instead, he leaned against the wall, dabbing at the blood at the corner of his split lip.

"You can hit me all you want. My bruises will heal. My blood will dry, and in the end I'll go back to killing and you'll be dead."

"I'd rather be dead than be like you," I spat.

The realization hit me like a ton of bricks. It was true. All my life I thought I was some hellion, a product of something bad… I wasn't. But I'd believed it so absolutely that my wake-up call had been death.

I had to die in order to see the way I should've been living.

It was a strong revelation to have, but even so, I knew it was too late for me. But it wasn't for Piper.

I rushed toward the door as Charming caught hold of my sleeve. "You can't stop it," he said, for once the mocking disgust wasn't in his tone.

"I have to."

"Once the Grim Reaper leaves a stone, that person's death is sealed."

The stone.

It was the answer to all of this.

I looked at Charming. "What if I destroy the stone?"

He shook his head. "That's impossible. Those stones are unbreakable. They're perfect in their strength."

A devious smile turned my lips. "But this stone isn't perfect. It's cracked—like me," I said, repeating what we both heard G.R. say.

He digested my words for long seconds, then let go of my sleeve and looked at the door. "It won't work."

But it might and I could see that admission in his eyes.

I rushed to the door. Behind me, Charming called, "One stone. One death. One shot."

Those were the kindest words I ever heard him say.

It was those words that sped my feet and gave me hope.

This wasn't over. Not by a long shot.

Chapter Fifty-Six

"Visitor - a person who pays a visit; caller, guest, tourist, etc."

Piper

The door to my room opened and my heart sped up, anticipating Dex, but it wasn't him. It was a nurse dressed in a white uniform and wearing a cheerful smile.

"You look wide awake and ready to get out of here!" she said, coming to stand at the side of the bed.

"I'm feeling good, thank you. Will I be able to leave today?" I replied.

"I think so. The doctor will be in shortly to examine you one more time, and as long as he thinks you look good, then you'll be able to go."

I nodded. I was so ready to get out of here. "Thank you."

"I will go get your discharge papers ready so when the doc gives his okay, we'll be ready." She motioned to a bag on the floor near the wall and said, "Your friends brought you some clean clothes."

"Great," I said, eyeing the bag.

I assumed she was talking about Dex's butler, Hobbs. Dex hadn't left to get me anything, and Frankie had no clue I was in here. I thought about calling her but figured I'd wait until after I saw the doctor. I wasn't quite ready to deal with all her questions and explain what had been going on all these months. I wondered if she would even believe me.

The nurse bustled around the room a bit more, checking the IV machine, and then let herself out. My eyes wandered over to the bag with the clothes. I couldn't help but be curious about what the butler chose for me.

I threw the covers back and went to the bag, bending to pick it up and bring it to the bed. When I bent down, I felt a gusty draft at the back of my robe. I grabbed it, bunching the material together around me. Why did hospital gowns have to be open at the butt? I mean, people here were already sick. Why make them wave around their bare booty?

Like a kid at Christmas, I delved into the plastic shopping bag to see what was there. I pulled out a pile of brand new clothes… all of them with the tags still attached and all of them in my size. Hobbs was good… and his taste was fantastic. It was also very expensive, I noted when I lifted one of the price tags. I couldn't accept this outfit! It was worth more than an entire week of tips at the diner.

I stared down at the beautiful things… things I never had before. Hobbs probably paid for them with Dex's money… A little smile curved my lips. He kind of owed me… I mean, he *did* try to kill me.

I tossed away the hospital gown and slipped the white silk tank top over my head, pulling it in place. Then I picked up the light-blue cashmere sweater and did the same. I never knew fabric could feel so soft and luxurious all while being warm. Next I pulled on a brand new pair of dark-colored designer jeans, a pair of cashmere socks, and slid my feet into a pair of light-brown Uggs. The sheepskin felt like heaven against my toes. Oh my goodness, I wanted a pair of Uggs since I first saw them… Talk about warm and comfy on a cold Alaskan day.

I went into the bathroom and winced at my face. No amount of cashmere could detract from the cuts and bruises. Frankie was going to flip when I finally called her. I had no idea what I would say. I'd tell her the truth because she was like a freaking walking lie detector machine. But I would need to make something up for the police. I knew it was only a matter of time before they came knocking at my door. I wouldn't really be able to tell them much about the man who kidnapped me because I didn't know anything. Maybe I would tell them that I got away and called Dex, who came to get me, and then on the way to the hospital we hit some black ice and the car crashed.

Just thinking about it all made me tired, and a wave of homesickness came over me. I felt like I was still kind of in shock over everything that happened. And I needed to talk to Dex. I needed more answers.

I rinsed my mouth out and did what I could with my hair—which equated to pulling the tangled mess up onto my head in an even more tangled knot—then left the bathroom.

The homesickness in my belly was still tugging at me and so I went toward the phone by the bed. I knew I said I'd wait to call Frankie, but I couldn't. I just wanted to hear her voice. She was like my sister.

She answered on the first ring. "Hello? Piper, is that you?"

"Hey, Frank. Yeah, it's me," I replied, as that feeling of homesickness ebbed away at just the sound of her voice.

"Oh my God! I've been so worried about you! What happened? Are you okay? Where are you?" Her words tumbled over one another, and when she finally fell silent, I heard her take a shuddering breath.

"I don't have time to explain everything now… but I will. I promise. I just wanted to call and tell you that I'm okay. I'm at the hospital."

"The hospital!" She gasped.

"Yeah, Dex and I got into a car accident."

"You're with Dex? What does he have to do with all this?"

"He's not here right now, but I think he'll be back. I'll explain later. I have to go, but I'll call you as soon as I get out of here."

"Piper—"

"Yeah, I know. It was scary. It's over. I'll talk to you soon."

I hung up the phone and stared down at it for long moments. It was good to hear her voice. After that vision I was so afraid I was going to lose her. When I pushed her out of the way of the gun, her future must've changed. Hopefully, that meant her life was no longer in danger.

I turned from the phone and began gathering up the tags from my new clothes when the door opened behind me.

"I think Hobbs should give up his current line of work to become a personal shopper," I said, smiling as I turned.

My smile faltered when I saw it wasn't Dex. It wasn't the nurse or the doctor, either.

It was a man, a man dressed in black slacks and a steel-grey button-up shirt. He wasn't a big man and although there wasn't a wrinkle on his face (he was kind of bony-looking though), I knew he was old.

At first, I thought he was just here to visit someone else and he came into the wrong room. But that theory was shot down when he said my name.

"Ahh, so wonderful to see you out of that hospital bed, Piper. What a time you have had."

"Do I know you?" I said, glancing at the door, which already closed behind him.

"I'm here as your Escort."

Escort. Isn't that what Dex said he was? A Death Escort.

I took a step backward and reached behind me for the call button to signal the nurse. This wasn't some harmless old man.

"I wouldn't do that if I were you," he said, watching me move. "We wouldn't want anyone else to get hurt."

"What do you want with me?" I asked, even though I already knew. Dex was supposed to kill me. He didn't. This guy still wanted me dead.

I watched as he came forward, smiling. If I didn't suspect what he was here for, I wouldn't even be alarmed. He reached into his pocket and pulled something out and held it in his palm.

"It's nothing personal, really. It's just death." He spoke like he was talking about visiting a friend for dinner, or going out to watch a movie. Did he think death was so trivial?

I watched as he reached out and laid something on the bed. A light-colored stone. A chill ran up my spine. This guy was creeping me out.

"Come along, then," he said, crooking a finger at me like I'd just follow after him.

"I'm not coming anywhere with you."

He sighed, rather dramatically, and spoke like he was speaking only to himself. "This is why I always just touch them. No drama in that." Then he speared me with eyes that seemed to grow very cold. "Death has come for you. I, the Grim Reaper, have laid claim to your life. There is no getting out of it. If you run, I will follow. If you hide, I will hunt you down. Usually, I just touch the people I want to claim, but you, you are lucky."

I was lucky? Really, I didn't feel like I'd won the lotto.

"You can come with me now to where Dex is waiting, and I will give you the chance to say good-bye or I can touch you." He extended his fingers toward me and wiggled them. "Here. Now. And you will die. Instantly."

Those were my choices? Die now or die later? That was hardly fathomable. Yet, when I looked at this man with his bony features and almost jolly presence, how could I not believe it? Only something this bizarre could be true. And besides, hadn't Dex tried to explain something like this to me earlier?

"How do I know Dex is where you say he is?" I asked.

"I am a lot of things, young lady… Grim Reaper, Death dealer, fate sealer… but I am no liar."

"So if I come with you, you'll let me say good-bye to him?"

"Oh yes. It will be quite the show." He actually clapped his hands together.

"Okay, I'll come with you. But don't touch me."

"I wouldn't dream of it. Not yet anyway."

The door to the hospital room opened, but instead of seeing out into the hallway like I should have, all I saw was white. The man who called himself the Grim Reaper motioned for me to go ahead and so I did, very slowly. When I walked past him, I made an effort to stay as far away from his hands as possible. My muscles tensed when I stepped into the white of the doorway, but I felt no pain. I felt nothing really, and then I was stepping completely through and into a whole other place.

* * *

It was an office—a rather large one with the usual furnishings and an entire row of closets. I didn't really take the time to notice my complete surroundings because the man sitting in the room was the same man that tried to kill me the night before.

I gasped, stepping back slightly, the bruises on my neck throbbing.

"Watch it there. You don't want to accidently bump into me and die," The Grim Reaper said jovially. If I hadn't known he was serious, I would've thought he was joking.

I jumped forward like a scared cat and landed on a thick sand-colored rug.

The man in the chair laughed. "I knew we would meet again," he said.

"Your face is bleeding," I said with satisfaction. Clearly, whatever made him bleed wasn't a threat to his life, but I still liked to see him suffer a little.

That seemed to wipe the smug look off his face and he glanced away from me toward the Grim Reaper. I could only assume he was employed by this man to kill. He probably did the same job they wanted Dex to do.

"What happened to your face? And where is Dex?" The Grim Reaper demanded.

"Turns out he didn't want to hang around and wait for you to come back," the guy answered. He was sprawled in his chair, but his eyes weren't as relaxed as his body appeared.

"You let him leave?" There was disapproval in his tone.

"I didn't have much say in the matter."

"Don't give me that," The Reaper retorted. "You and I both know you have advantages over him. You've been quite greedy with the powers you have collected over the years. In fact, isn't that why you are invested here, now, in this girl?" He motioned toward me.

"Me?" I said. "What could I possibly have that you want?"

"Nothing," he said, looking at the floor.

"Don't I have a right to know why I'm going to die?"

"Why, yes, you do," The Grim Reaper said, causing me to look at him. "You have the gift of vision. It's a gift that could be of use to my Escort."

So I was right. The guy who tried to kill me—the guy bleeding, presumably at the hands of Dex—was an Escort for the Grim Reaper. A killer.

"You want to kill me so you can take my ability to have visions? What could you possibly need it for?"

"All my Escorts have particular talents, something that makes them very good at what they do. Charming here has certain specialties in his field."

"How can you have a specialty in death?" I scoffed.

The Grim Reaper threw back his head and laughed. "At last, Charming, someone who seems to be blind to your skills." Then he shook his head. "Such a shame she must die."

I swallowed and glanced around for something I could use as a weapon. I was thinking if I came here I would see Dex and we could fight out of this together.

But he wasn't here.

My stomach was in knots trying to decide what that meant. I had a very bad feeling it meant he really didn't care I was going to die. Maybe everything he said at the hospital had all been part of his plan to get me here… to get me closer to death. I almost preferred death by the Grim Reaper. At least he didn't play with his prey before he disposed of it.

I forced myself back into the conversation, wanting to buy myself some time. "So what is this special skill you have?" I looked at the man in the chair.

"His name says it all," The Reaper said as he made his way over to a little cart with glasses and a decanter of dark liquid. As he poured himself a drink, I turned toward the man called Charming.

"That's your name? Charming? You're kidding."

"That's me. Charming. So good with the ladies they changed my name." He got up from the chair and rose to his full height. He was good-looking... even with all the blood on his face. I watched as he found a tissue to wipe away some of the blood.

"Charming is the best Escort I have at getting lonely heiresses to fall madly in love with him, signing over their riches, and then killing them so the company can seize all their assets."

I looked at Charming. "You seduce women and then kill them for their money?"

"Not just women," Grim said snidely.

Charming made a face like his stomach hurt. But then the sour look smoothed away and he said, "Relax, princess. It's only the really rich, and they usually have more than just money that we want."

That knot in my stomach grew. This was disgusting. These people were horrible and I was sorry to even know there were people out there like this.

"I don't understand how having visions could make you any better at what you do."

"When I mentioned earlier that you were the only one that was resistant to his, ah... charms, that wasn't exactly accurate," Grim said, taking a seat on the couch. "It seems Charming here might be losing his touch. He isn't as charming as he once was."

"Yes," Charming growled. "I am."

Grim made a tsking sound. "You have two failed jobs this year. You used to have *none.*"

"They weren't failed, because I killed them," Charming said, making another sour face.

"True, true," Grim offered. "If you hadn't managed to kill them, I would have recalled you on the spot. But still, we didn't collect the money we should have."

Charming didn't say anything and the Grim Reaper kept talking.

"So, we thought giving him the ability to have visions," Grim began, "might help us know if his certain charms would work before he put in the time and effort."

They wanted to use my visions to pick and choose people to rob and kill. They wanted to *kill* me to make it easier to kill even more people. I felt tears sting the backs of my eyes, but I pushed them back. I wasn't going to show weakness in front of these two men who talked about life and death as if it were something as trivial as which shoes to wear. How could anyone have so little value for life?

Without thinking, I turned toward Charming. "I get why he cares so little about life—he is the Grim Reaper—but why… why don't you?"

He didn't reply right away and Grim stood from his seat and changed the subject. "This has been fun, but duty calls. Where is Dex?"

Charming shrugged. "He went to the hospital. He went to destroy the stone."

A sharp gust of wind swept through the room and the crystal glass in Grim's hand shattered. "What did you just say to me?"

Just like that, the jolly air around him transformed into something sinister and absolute. His eyes glowed with an electric spark and his skin turned paper thin and stretched out over his bones. These things made him look scary and a little crazy, but it was the lightning from his fingers tips that seemed to spark out and rain down onto the carpet that was truly terrifying.

This was the man that claimed death with a single touch. This was how I envisioned someone like the Grim Reaper.

"You allowed this little conversation to go on when you knew what he was up to? You knew he was trying to break my claim!"

When he spoke the wind around the room blew, picking up the papers on his desk and sending them flying. The massive chair behind his desk began to spin rapidly with great whipping circles.

"I knew he'd never be able to do it," Charming said, but there was fear in his voice. He knew his charm wouldn't work on the likes of Grim.

"This betrayal will not go unpunished," he said, taking a shuddering breath as another doorway appeared. This one I could see through, and on the other side was my hospital room. I didn't wait for an invitation or for an order. I ran at the door and jumped through.

Unfortunately, Grim was right behind me.

Chapter Fifty-Seven

"Recall - to cancel, take back, or revoke."

Dex

The nurses tried to talk to me when I burst through the second-floor doors. I ignored them and rushed past the desk and the slowly moving patients to Piper's room. I slammed through the door, the handle banging against the wall when I flung it open wide…

Then I stopped, cold.

The bed was made.

The room was empty.

Not wanting to accept what I saw, I hurried into the bathroom only to find it vacant too. The nurse came in behind me and shifted nervously.

"Where is she?" I demanded, breathing hard.

"We thought you might know. She was all set to be released and then when we brought her papers to sign, she was gone."

"Damn it!" I yelled. The nurse flinched.

I held out my hands and tried to steady my voice. "I'm sorry. Could I have a minute?" I dug my phone out of my pocket and held it up. "I'll try to call her and let you know if I get ahold of her."

The nurse nodded and quickly left the room, shutting the door behind her. I think she just wanted away from me. I figured I had about four minutes until security showed up.

I paced the room, gripping the phone, trying to think about what my next move would be. G.R. had her. He was going to kill her. Then I stopped mid-pace. He wouldn't kill her until I was there to watch.

I pivoted around and looked at the table beside the bed. Empty. I looked at the traveling tray. Empty. I looked at the chair I sat in all night long. Empty.

Then I looked at the bed.

Bingo.

It would be easy to overlook because the pale color of the stone blended with the white of the sheets, but I saw it. That crack called to me like a kindred spirit.

I dropped my phone, ignoring when it broke into pieces at my feet, and hastily scooped up the stone. It was ice cold, smooth, and heavier than one might think. But the weight made sense because it was carrying someone's life.

With all the force I had, I threw the stone at the white tile of the floor. It made a sharp cracking sound and I looked down, expecting to see it in pieces.

It was still whole. But the tiles in the floor were busted. I picked it up and threw it at the wall. It bounced off, landing on the bed, still frustratingly unbroken.

I knocked it onto the floor where it skidded to a stop in the middle of the room. I looked around for something, anything that would have the strength to break the stone—to break the claim that the Grim Reaper had on Piper's life.

Nothing seemed strong enough.

I let out a frustrated wail.

You alone possess far more strength than even you realize. Hobbs's words whispered in the back of my head, and I understood their meaning. At the time I thought he meant I had the strength to turn away from the deal I'd made. And in a way, that's what he meant, but this—*this*—was the only true way to get out of that deal.

I went around the bed and toward the stone. I stood over it, looking down at how it landed: cracked side up.

I smiled and lifted my foot.

On the other side of the room, movement caught my eye. Piper stumbled into the room through some open doorway and she was closely followed by G.R.

"Dex," she called, tears on her face.

"It's going to be all right, Piper," I said and looked back at the stone.

"No!" G.R. roared and rushed past Piper, but it was already too late. I brought my heel down as hard and fast as I could to land on the stone. Then I ground it into the surface of the floor for good measure.

G.R. had stopped in front of me and was staring down at my shoe and what could possibly lie beneath it. I could see the doubt creep into his features, and I knew then if this stone really was broken, then his claim on Piper's life would be too.

I looked at her and then looked down at my foot and slowly… slowly… lifted it away.

G.R. and I stood staring down.

The stone was broken. Cracked into four pieces and lying amongst some fine white dust.

I gave a shout of joy and rushed across the room to scoop Piper up into my arms. I don't know if she completely understood what that broken stone meant, but she laughed anyway and wrapped her arms around my neck.

I spun her around in circles. The knowledge that she was free made me want to dance. Then I stopped and she pulled back, just slightly, to stare into my eyes.

"You're safe now," I told her, reaching up to touch her cheek.

"I love you," she whispered.

If I thought I knew happiness moments before, it was nothing compared to this. If my heart had been deflated before, it was overfull now—to the point it was about to burst with joy.

I dipped her backward, holding her tight, and leaned close.

"I love you."

Then I kissed her.

My lips brushed over hers, meeting what was the most satisfying taste I'd ever known. She kissed me back, her lips claiming what was left of my heart and tucking it safely within her. I would've kissed her for hours. I would've kissed her for a lifetime… but as my lips covered hers, something reminded me that this single moment would have to do.

That our first kiss would also be our last.

As my lips melted with hers, the very dark voice of the Grim Reaper filled the room.

"I release you, Piper McCall, from the claim I made on your life. You are free. You will no longer have to fear death by the hand of the Grim Reaper. But you, Dexter Allen Roth, my claim to you holds strong,"

Beneath my kiss, Piper's lips trembled. "Dex?" she asked against me.

I kissed her harder. I kissed her for the first time, the last time, and all the times in between. I devoured her lips and tightened my arms around her until there was no space between us, knowing if I had to die, this would be the way to go.

I felt that familiar tug inside me and I knew G.R. was making his claim right now. Down the hall I heard the nurses exclaiming and security coming toward the room, but I pushed it all away.

I held on to Piper while I could, and I kissed her with a passion that would have to last the rest of her life. She kissed me back just as fiercely, gripping my face like she knew it was going to be gone in a matter of seconds, and mingling with our desperation was the taste of her tears.

When there was almost nothing left inside my body, I had to pull back. I looked in her eyes for the final time, blocking out the purple mist that curtained us from the rest of the room, and I whispered two words.

"Be happy."

She squeezed her eyes shut as more tears fell over her cheeks and shook her head quickly.

And then I was a ghost. I no longer had a body and the purple mist that made up my essence was being pulled away—toward G.R. and wherever he would take me.

I held on to the sight of her as long as I could, and my final words seemed to drift around us like they, too, had become mist.

Be happy.

And then there was nothing.

Chapter Fifty-Eight

"Grief - keen mental suffering or distress over affliction or loss;

sharp sorrow; painful regret."

Piper

I stared down at the body lying at my feet. He was nothing now but a heap of skin and bones. What was once animated was now lifeless. What used to be so full was now empty.

I dashed away the tears that wouldn't stop flowing and looked up at the man who caused all of this.

"What have you done to him?"

The man looked at me with pleasure on his face. "I have merely held him up to his end of the bargain. He didn't do what he agreed to do so he paid. With his life."

"You're sick and cold!" I yelled.

"No. I'm a business man." He glanced at the door where the security guards were gathering and then he stepped toward me.

I took a step back as the door opened and Frankie pushed her way through the guards, shutting them out.

"Leave her alone!" she yelled at the Grim Reaper.

"Frankie, don't touch him," I warned, the vision of her death still haunting me. I couldn't bear to lose her too.

The old man smiled. "For the first time ever, my claim on a human life has been broken. Dex might not have been able to save himself, but he saved you."

He reached down and grabbed the body, lifting it like it was a doll, and then the doorway that we came through earlier opened and he stepped through without looking back.

Just as it closed, the door to my room opened and the security guards entered. All I could do was stand there. I stood there in a room full of people and I felt entirely lost and alone. Dex was gone. He sacrificed his life for me... again.

I felt a hand on my shoulder and I blinked, looking up. It was Frankie. Somehow she'd managed to clear the room of people and it was just she and I standing there.

"I thought I told you not to come," I said, my voice watery.

"You didn't actually say that. Besides, I thought you might need me. I was right."

I leaned into her side. She was right. I did need her.

"You have a lot of explaining to do," she said.

"I don't even know where to start," I whispered, staring at the space where Dex's body had been.

"At the beginning, but not until you're ready."

She ushered me toward the door and I felt a moment of panic. I wasn't ready to leave. I dug my feet into the floor and turned back to where Dex had been.

But he wasn't there.

I would never see him again.

Being in this room wouldn't make me any closer to him. It wouldn't bring him back. As more tears spilled over my cheeks I looked back at Frankie.

"I'm ready now," I whispered.

We walked out of the room, past the prying eyes and whispering mouths, but I scarcely paid attention to them. I was too busy wondering how I was going to say good-bye to a man that had impossibly found his way into my heart.

Chapter Fifty-Nine

"Heaven - the abode of God, the angels, and the spirits of the righteous after death; the place or state of existence of the blessed after the mortal life."

Dex

This time around, dying didn't hurt. I wasn't lying on a frozen street, my body wasn't crushed, and I didn't struggle to breathe. It didn't hurt to lose my body—it was never really mine anyway. It was almost a relief to be out of it, to not have to live in a place that I didn't really belong.

I was back to the purple mist—the translucent body that really had no form. I looked but didn't see the body anywhere. I didn't see G.R. either. I thought for sure he'd want a front row seat to watch me go into hell—to watch the beginning of my eternal torment.

But I was in a place that was completely quiet, completely devoid of anything.

And then a yellow glow seemed to open and spread before me. It started out small but expanded until it was all I could see. It was beautiful and it was warm. From out of the yellow glow stepped a man in a charcoal-gray suit with a white flower in his lapel. I blinked against the light as he came forward, almost as if he were floating.

When he stopped in front of me, I realized he wasn't a stranger.

"Hobbs, what are you doing here? Did you die too?"

Hobbs smiled with a joy I'd never seen from him before and something behind him unfolded. Wings. Huge white wings unfurled from his back, covered in downy, snow-colored feathers.

"I didn't know butlers had wings," I said, still staring at them.

"Butler's do not, but angels do."

Why would I be with an angel? Was the bright, welcoming light he came from heaven?

"There was no butler job really, was there?" I asked, thinking of the night he showed up at my house for a job I hadn't been hiring for.

He smiled. "No, but being your butler was highly amusing."

"Then why?" I asked, wanting to understand. I stepped closer because the warmth around him was so inviting.

"Because you were lost and you needed a guide. You were really never meant for hell, and it was my duty to make sure you stayed that way."

"But I've done horrible things."

"Most of earth's population does horrible things. God is very forgiving and he forgives you."

His words washed over me and something inside me that I hadn't known was broken and began to heal. It felt wonderful and I felt something I never felt in all my life … peace.

"I don't know if I deserve it," I whispered, desperately wanting it anyway.

"That's exactly why you have it. You have been tempted—tempted with promises and riches and infinite lives to live. Yet you resisted. And you loved."

He held out his hand.

"Come. Your eternity will not be of torment. It will be of light and peace."

I looked at his hand and once more at the yellow glow around him. I reached out slowly, afraid what little form I had would evaporate and hold me back. But that didn't happen. An outline of electric purple formed around me and held me together.

My hand slid into his and instead of going right through him, our hands caught and held.

"Welcome, my friend," Hobbs whispered and then together we stepped into the brightest part of the light, and it wrapped itself around me. For once, I didn't feel cold and I didn't look back, not once. I didn't think about what I was leaving behind. I only thought about where I was going.

Finally, there was somewhere I truly belonged. Finally, I was home.

Yes, I always *thought* I was going to hell…

I was wrong.

Epilogue

"Impossible - Incapable of having existence or of occurring."

Piper

I wrapped my hands around a steaming cup of coffee and shivered against the cold. It was the coldest morning yet this year. Dex hated the cold. I hoped he was warm wherever he was.

I felt the rush of tears to my eyes and I didn't bother to blink them back. It had been a week since he was recalled. A week since I watched his spirit pulled from his body. I kept hoping he would come back, that he would find a way back to me.

I looked for him everywhere I went—in faces of everyone on the street, in the clinic, and in the diner. I searched stranger's eyes for just a glimpse of someone I knew. I would take him in any body, but the more days that passed, the more I realized he really was gone.

He died so I could live. He did so more than once. And I was so very afraid that death would not be his only punishment. I didn't want him to suffer.

I loved him.

I probably always would.

I knew being with him wasn't our destiny, but I would've at least liked to know wherever he was, he was happy.

I walked to the window to look out at the snow-covered street, but my eyes never made it that far. They zeroed in on the frozen flower box that decorated my windowsill. It was iced over and mounded with a white cap of snow. Yet, in the center something grew…

It grew impossibly—wonderfully—right out of the snow and ice.

Its green stem was sturdy and it stretched up toward the morning rays of sun. Its petals, wide and smooth, were completely open and welcoming. It was the most perfect daisy I'd ever seen and it was growing in the middle of winter.

It wasn't lost on me that this was mine and Dex's flower. It represented so much.

And it was an answer.

I sat my coffee aside and opened the window, laughing when snow fell onto my slippers. I ignored the harsh biting wind to reach out and tug the perfect flower from the ice. It wasn't cold like it should be.

It was warm.

It radiated heat in the center of my palm.

I knew then without a doubt that Dex was okay. He was better than okay. He wasn't being punished for the things he did.

A single tear fell from my eye and landed on one of the perfectly formed petals. When the moisture touched, it shimmered purple and then soaked in.

Dex was in heaven. He was safe and warm… He was at peace.

I knew someday I would meet him again and whenever that was, it wouldn't matter what form either of us took because…

We would be together.

The End

Acknowledgements

The definition of success is *"The achievement of something desired, planned, or attempted."* (Note: all definitions in this book are courtesy of http://www.thefreedictionary.com). One could say finishing this book is a success. To be frank, sometimes I wondered if there was other life during/after the *Heven and Hell* series (my first fabulous publications). I wondered if that series would suck all my writing mojo right out of me and leave me empty and soulless. Okay, I never worried about being soulless… That's just creepy and weird. But I did wonder if I would ever write again. Yes, I am dramatic.

Anyway, so when Dex started talking to me about bodies in the closet and how he hated wearing glasses (apparently, I am not the only dramatic one around here) I decided to keep *Recalled* a super secret project in case I couldn't hack it. That brings me to the reason I gave you the definition of success. I not only finished *Recalled*, but I rocked it out. Ha ha ha. Note: that's my personal opinion. But it IS a success.

But don't let the fact that this was a super secret project fool you into thinking I did this all on my own. I had help—as every author does. That's what this section is really for, to acknowledge those people (and not for my longwinded monologues—I'll save those for my husband!).

As always, I would like to acknowledge my family. To my husband, Shawn, who read the first twenty pages of this book (when that was all that was written), declared it was going to be a good read, and then I never looked back. Thanks for never doubting my writing mojo. To my children, Kaydence and Nathan, for never complaining too much when I sit at the computer for too long. To my mommom, Aurora, for always buying copies of my books and then sharing them with all your friends. To my mom, Elizabeth, for babysitting my "angelic" children and my very hairy, sporadically peeing dog.

And to my other family who aren't relatives, but still family all the same. These are the people I go to for writing support, for advice, and to talk about the business of being a writer (Yes, people, it's more than sitting around a computer, looking fabulous). To Jennifer Pringle, for being the first to read *Recalled* in its finished, uncut draft. For always telling me that I can do it even when I think I can't. To Cassie McCown, a true book doctor, who sees my writing naked and still doesn't laugh (my writing wears polka dot undies). Thanks for using your shovel to get rid of my favorite word: that. Thank you to Regina Wamba for designing me a cover that makes my heart race and for being patient through the process of working with me.

I want to mention my fellow writing buddies—Airicka Phoenix, Cameo Renae, Amber Garza, Melissa Andrea, Alexia Purdy, Ella James, Alivia Anders, Tara Brown and Ambear Shellea. When I first started in this business, I didn't know any other writers and now I have a list... a list of women who inspire me every day. It's awesome to be in your company.

Also, I want to acknowledge Gladys Gonzales Atwell for your enthusiastic support. Someday you will wear a color besides black... one as vibrant as the rest of you. To the maker's of Puff's Plus tissues, I like that lotion you put in your tissues. I did a lot of crying when I wrote this book but my nose never got red. And finally, to the maker's of Lipton tea. I practically lived off Ginger Twist tea while I wrote this book... and now I can't find it anywhere. I'm going through withdrawals.... Please, someone find me some of that tea!!!!!

P.S. If I forget to mention anyone, we can just blame it on my withdrawals. Ha ha ha ha.

Cambria Hebert is the author of the young adult *Heven and Hell* series and the *Death Escorts* series. She loves a caramel latte, hates math and is afraid of chickens (yes, chickens). She went to college for a bachelor's degree, couldn't pick a major and ended up with a degree in cosmetology. So rest assured, her characters will always have good hair. She currently lives in Pennsylvania with her husband and children (both human and furry), where she is plotting her next book. You can find out more about Cambria and her work by visiting her fan page on Facebook or her website http://www.cambriahebert.com.

Please turn the page and enjoy an excerpt from Airicka Phoenix's novel, Games of Fire.

Chapter One

Grandma Valdez had a saying, *beware surprises that come with gloomy weather.* Sophia had never put much stock in the prediction. Grandma was a ninety year old woman who thought tux wearing mice were giving her winning lottery ticket numbers. But during that rainy January, Sophia Valdez became a believer and it all started with the enormous white truck parked next door.

"We've got new neighbors." Dishtowel wringing between slender fingers, her mother joined her at the living room window. They peered out over the quaint, cookie-cutter suburban neighborhood with its neatly trimmed lawns, soft, pastel tones and nosy housewives.

Sophie folded her arms and propped a hip against the frame. Rain splattered against glass, running like teardrops down the smooth sheet. It was just a drizzle, but the movers didn't seem to mind getting wet. They trudged down the metal ramp, making a world of noise while balancing a cream-colored sofa between them. Her gaze dropped to their scuffed, mud encrusted boots and she nearly smirked. If the lady of the house was anything like her mother, she was no doubt having a heart attack at all the filth being dragged across her polished floors.

"We should go over," her mother said decidedly. "I have a casserole in the freezer we can take. It'll be nice."

What her mother really meant was, *let's make sure our new neighbors aren't serial killers or worse, salesmen.*

"I'm good," Sophie replied.

Her mother smacked her lightly on the arm. "Don't be silly. Go get dressed."

Sophie frowned down at her faded jeans and Green Day t-shirt. "I am dressed! Overdressed if you take half the girls in my school into account."

But her mother was already walking away, back to the kitchen and the many casserole dishes stacked in the freezer.

No one pulled Suzy Homemaker off the way her mother did. Standing at the same height as Sophie in all her five foot five inch glory, with dirty blonde hair and green eyes, her mother was every Stepford Wife's role model. The only thing missing was the 60s hairdo and the fondness for words such as gee and golly. The woman did her own upholstery for crying out loud. Sophie couldn't imagine the number of valiums her mother had to take daily to maintain that level of perkiness, but it was certainly working.

"Sophia!" Casserole dish in hand, her mother appeared in the kitchen doorway, dishtowel tossed neatly over one shoulder. "You're not dressed."

Sophie arched a brow. "I'm not naked, either."

Her mother's lips pursed, disapproval defining every line in her heart-shaped face. "I'm not taking you over there dressed like that. What will the new neighbors think?"

"That you have an average teenage daughter whose best friend went to a Green Day concert and brought her back a t-shirt?"

Eyes the green of polished emeralds narrowed. "Please put something pretty on."

Sophie pushed away from the frame and turned to face her mother fully. "But I don't want to go."

"Of course you do!" her mother insisted, stalking across the room to stand over the coffee table. She nimbly whipped the towel off her shoulder, draped it over the gleaming sheet of glass and set the casserole down on top. She straightened, dusting her blouse for invisible particles. "They may have children your age and it might be nice if you could become friends. I'm sure moving isn't easy for them and they might appreciate knowing at least one person when they go to school Monday."

"I can just meet them Monday," Sophie pointed out. "I even promise to wave to them in the hall, just please don't make me go over there with a tuna fish casserole! That's so humiliating!"

"Sophia Marie Valdez, I have not raised you to be so impolite!" her mother huffed, outraged. "Now march upstairs and put on a nice dress."

Sophie did as she was told if for no other reason than to save herself a very long, very repetitive lecture. She let her feet drag with her ascent up the stairs, falling like bowling balls on each step all the way to her room. The door slamming behind her wasn't intentional, but it was satisfying all the same.

It wasn't as if she had so many friends she couldn't use anymore. Had her mother been normal, she probably would have gone over to introduce herself. But her mother wasn't normal. There was nothing normal about defrosted tuna fish casserole. Wasn't it kind of bad manners to offer a dish that followed you around like one of Mary's lambs for days?

Kissing goodbye to any potential friendships she may have built with the kid next door, Sophie threw on one of the two dresses she owned, a crocheted number in soft, navy-blue that had forearm-length sleeves and a modest U-shaped collar. She added a pair of black leggings and flat black pumps to complete it and twisted her long blonde curls into a messy French braid over her left shoulder. In the gilded mirror above the vanity, she checked her reflection. Her heart-shaped face with its pale complexion and speckle of freckles across the nose and cheeks looked as ordinary as ever. She thought about adding some color to her lips and cheeks, but decided against it. It was the most she was going to do under protest. Considering it a success, she joined her mother downstairs.

Her mother beamed. "You look lovely!"

Sophie grunted.

She was passed the casserole dish of doom while her mother grabbed an umbrella and together, they started out the door and down the sidewalk. The umbrella protected them from the light mist spraying from the heavens, but it did nothing to guard from the chilling blanket of air whipping around them. Sophie wished she'd thought to grab a jacket. Fingers of ice crept through the loosely knitted dress and nipped at the bare skin underneath.

"This is a bad idea," Sophie muttered through clenched teeth.

"Don't be silly!" her mother scolded, bright, toothpaste-commercial smile already plastered into place.

She smiled and greeted the movers and ignored their bewildered gawking as she turned into the neighbor's walkway, past the picket fence and neatly trimmed lawn. They ascended the two steps onto a white porch and stopped facing the open doorway.

"Hello?" her mother called into the opening.

Sophie shifted anxiously from foot to foot. She turned her head to the side and peered longingly at her house, at the warmth and security of it. It was separated from her by a single white fence, but it could have been across the world. She exhaled wistfully.

"Yes?" A small, blonde woman with big blue eyes and skin as white as milk appeared in the doorway. She smiled at them prettily, wringing her hands on a dishrag that was remarkably the same cream color as her slacks. She wore a white, silk blouse and gold around her throat and wrists. When she politely tilted her head to the side in question, gold glinted from her ears. "Can I help you?"

Sophie's mother beamed, thrusting out a hand. "Hello! I'm Mary Valdez. This is my daughter, Sophia—"

"Sophie," Sophie corrected quickly, and was ignored by both as her mother went on seamlessly.

"We live next door and thought we'd stop by and introduce ourselves."

The woman flashed straight white teeth in a blinding smile. "That was so thoughtful of you! I'm Jackie Rowth." She extended her hand which Sophie's mother accepted. "Won't you come inside? The place is an absolute disaster, but I would love the company."

Smiling as widely as the woman, her mother snapped the umbrella closed and hurried after her, saying, "We would love to!"

Sophie loitered a moment longer on the porch, weighing her choices. She could turn and run. Now would be her chance. Her mother may not even notice. Or she could stay and suffer through boring grownup bonding.

"Hey, girl, we gots to get through!"

Sophie jumped, whirling around. A hulking figure glowered at her from over a stack of boxes.

"Oh!" She leapt aside. "Sorry!"

The man grunted, ambling past her into the house. His two partners stomped after him, carting two lamps and an end table. They moved quickly, massive, hulking figures choking the narrow hall with their wide shoulders. Bits of dirt dropped in clumps from their boots, marking their progress to the opening at the far end where the smooth laminate washed into soft carpet. The leader grunted what she assumed was orders, caveman style, but it seemed to work, because the two men at the end grumbled, pivoted with impressive finesse that Sophie couldn't help marvel at and marched back towards her. She started to dodge out of the doorway, but they twisted at the last second and ascended the stairs instead.

"Sophia!" Her mother appeared in the doorway. "What are you doing? Get in here!"

She should have made her escape, she realized, skulking into the small foyer. It branched off, she noticed, following her mother right. On the other side of the stairs, divided by a wall, was the kitchen, overwhelmed by a boggling number of boxes all stacked nearly shoulder-high. There was a tight path from the doorway to the adjacent door on the other side, leaving no room for maneuvering left or right. It was every claustrophobic's worst nightmare, Sophie decided, eyeing the cardboard walls.

"Sophia!"

Sophie blinked and turned to her mother to find the other woman already looking at her, hands outstretched. "What?"

"The casserole!" her mother said, opening and closing her hands in a *give me* motion.

"Oh!" Hurriedly, she thrust the dish into her mother's waiting hands. "Sorry."

Giving her an odd look, her mother turned to their hostess. "This is for you!" she said, taking the dish over to Jackie, who had maneuvered her way quite effortlessly to the other side of the kitchen and the doorway leading into the dining room. "I know how hard it is to be in the middle of a move and find time to cook something."

No you don't! Sophie thought, barely repressing her eye-roll. Her parents hadn't moved since before Sophie was born, seventeen years ago. Any memories of that surely should have faded by now, right?

Jackie gasped, clutching a hand over her heart. "You are just so sweet!" She took the casserole. "Thank you so much!

It's just me and my son here and you saved me from having to order pizza for the fourth time this week."

"How many children do you have?" her mother asked.

"Three!" Jackie said. "But my oldest and youngest live with my husband. The youngest, my daughter Suzy, only stays with me on the weekends. My other son is upstairs, fixing his room."

Whatever her mother was about to say was interrupted by the thundering of feet on the stairs and a very deep, husky, very male voice echoing from the hall.

"Mom? Have you seen my duffle bag?" The guy that rounded the corner and appeared in the doorway behind Sophie was clad in nothing but a pair of black jeans slung low over tapered hips. Black leather bands clasped his wrists, just under the scrawling black, gray and white sleeves inked into his toned arms, twisting up to narrow shoulders in a winding design. There were four jagged gashes tattooed into each of his pecs as though he'd had his chest clawed by a large animal. A silver chain with dog tags on the end dangled down the center of his chest, drawing attention to washboard abs and the carved V disappearing into the waistband of his unfastened jeans. It took all of her willpower to coax her gaze away from that general vicinity and look past his shoulders to a chiseled chin, firm lips, high cheekbones and a hard nose. Hair a shade shy of platinum hung in shaggy wisps over a single arched eyebrow and curled at the nape of his neck.

He definitely won major hottie of the decade in her book. Sophie had never been so mesmerized by another person before and never to the point of openly gawking, but this guy was wrong in all the right ways. He practically had a *your mother did warn you* stamp on his forehead right next to the *yes, I do taste as good as I look* and it made her want to touch all the more.

Long arms lifted and folded over his pale chest. "Who are they?" The accusation didn't stop in his tone, but seemed to burn behind his dove gray eyes as he studied her.

"Spencer!" Jackie set the casserole dish down on the counter, nudging aside a stack of magazines to make room. She forced a smile. "This is Mary and Sophia. Our neighbors." Sophie didn't bother trying to correct her. Somehow she doubted he cared if there was an *e* or an *a* in her name. He already looked bored, if not just a tad bit annoyed. "They brought over a casserole for tonight. Isn't that thoughtful?"

Spencer cocked his head to the side. "Sophia," he repeated slowly, tasting each syllable. "Interesting." His gaze swept over her, leaving a hot trail in its wake that nearly made her want to whimper. "You're like what? Twelve?"

That was a bucket of ice cold glacial water being dumped straight on her head.

Sophie stiffened. "Excuse me?" Surely she'd heard wrong.

Okay so she looked younger than she was, but twelve? Who taught this guy to count? Or speak, for that matter?

Only the left corner of his mouth tweaked upwards, but ice crystals seemed to drip from that single gesture. "No offense." Oh there was total offense meant to be had! She could see it in his smirk. "You just look very… young."

He was probably the only guy on the planet that could say *young* and make it sound inappropriate.

"At least I don't look like… like…" Words failed her when there really was nothing wrong with him. "I am not young!"

His eyebrow lifted in a very, very dirty gesture of interest and she realized he was silently mocking her. There was literally a red haze now curtaining her vision, shimmering with the hot temptation to beat him over the head with something blunt and metal, possibly encrusted with spikes. The desire to commit murder must have shown on her face, because, he snickered. "Easy, Blondie. You might pop an artery."

"Blondie?" she seethed, forcing the word through her teeth. "Look who's talking? You're blonder than I am and—"

Her razor sharp retort was cut off by Jackie's giggle, a nervous tittering sound that amplified the unease swirling around the woman. "Spencer is such a kidder," she said to Sophie's mother, who looked stunned into silence by the argument unfolding like a sitcom before her. "He doesn't mean anything by it."

"Kidder is not the word I would use," Sophie bit out, matching Spencer's gaze unflinchingly. "Jackass comes to mind. Asshat. Pr—"

"Sophia!" Her mother seemed to come out of her shock instantly at the flow of cuss words pouring from her daughter's mouth.

Spencer rolled his tongue over his teeth in a manner that suggested he was laughing at her on the inside. His thick, dark lashes lowered so he was peering very dangerously at her through them, as he tapped a finger thoughtfully over his bottom lip—a very firm, sexy lip, too. Then, in a tone that probably should have been illegal, he purred, "Down kitty."

"What were you looking for, Spence?" Jackie quickly interjected before Sophie could open her mouth again.

Spencer, with a flick of his lashes, turned his gaze to his mother. "The black duffle with my clothes."

Jackie's hands fluttered up into the air. "Oh! Yes! Yes!" She turned towards the dining room, hands still fluttering, beckoning. "Over here. The movers left it on the table. I was going to ask you to come get it, but…" she trailed off and did that tittering thing again. "You beat me to it."

Spencer stole another glance at Sophie. The left corner of his lips twisted upwards again in that arrogant smirk of his, as he pushed into the cramped kitchen. It took Sophie all of two seconds to realize she was trapped in a narrow path with no way to dodge his approach, short of throwing herself over the mountain of boxes or crawling up on the table—both of which were looking extremely tempting just then. She scrambled back three steps and nearly tumbled backwards over a box. She might have made an embarrassing sound like a mouse being trodden on as her arms pin wheeled, her body fighting against gravity. She would have gone down had it not been for the blunt fingers that clamped down on her hips, making her wobble and latch on to the only solid object available, which turned out to be his shoulders. Sharp slivers of electricity spiked up through each fingertip upon contact, shooting up her arm and imploding somewhere deep inside her, showering her skin with goose bumps. It was a struggle not to succumb to the shiver working its way up her spine. She bit her lip to repress the gasp bouncing on the tip of her tongue, preparing to do a swan dive off her lips.

The heat beneath her fingers flexed, pale, taut and smooth and oh so distracting. Her near tumble was momentarily forgotten as she battled with the urge to follow the hard slope of his shoulders down to the ridged muscles of his arms. She bit back a dreamy sigh as her body was pulled forward, closer into his and steadied. It was so not fair that a body like that belonged to such a jerk. There should have been laws preventing such tragedy.

"Careful, Blondie." There was no amusement in his words this time, no arrogance or mockery. It vibrated with something deep and primal. Sophie shivered before she could stop herself.

The ten fingers gripping her sides tightened, driving pressure into her already muddled thoughts as all her attention melted down to where he was touching her. His fingers. His thighs. His heat. His eyes.

Damn it! Damn it! Damn it!

"I can show you more if you like what you see," he said in a whisper just for her ears.

Sophie blinked, walloped upside the head by reality. She bristled, smacking his hands away. "Hands off, pal."

Straight, white teeth flashed in a knee-dissolving smirk. He dropped his head an inch so she was forced to hold her breath or suffer breathing in his delicious scent of spices, smoke and shampoo. "You only say that because you've never had my hands on you."

Heat swept into her cheeks, propelling her to speak. "Which is perfectly fine! I'd rather swim in shark infested waters with a bloody leg."

He snickered. "You already are."

Amused by her stunned expression, he nimbly squeezed past her, somehow brushing every inch of her in the process. He sidestepped her mother and ducked into the dining room.

Sophie hissed through her teeth, her gaze swinging wildly around for that blunt instrument. But all that was lying around were boxes and crumpled pieces of newspaper and magazines. Nothing remotely violent enough. She caught her mother's gaze and growled low in her throat when she was given a subtle shake of the head and a very clear, *Be nice!* warning. She glared at her mother before turning her attention back to the object of her distaste. She watched as he hooked his hand through the straps of a hockey bag, hoisted it over his shoulder and stalked back in her direction. It took all of her resolve not to crawl on top of the boxes in escape.

He paused midway between her and her mother and glanced back. "It was nice to meet you," he told her mother with all the innocence and manners of a choirboy. Then he turned to Sophie and his face instantly morphed into one she wanted to either smack or... no, no *or*, she definitely wanted to smack. His dark eyes took her in from head to toe, somehow sending off all the warning bells throughout her body, before giving her that arrogant grin of his. "Later, Blondie."

"It's Sophie!" But he was gone and Sophie was left glowering at the empty air in the doorway, wishing she'd thought to trip him in passing.

"I am so sorry!" Jackie said in a rush, dainty hands wringing together in front of her. "I promise he's not normally like that. This move and the divorce have been so hard on him."

Her mother went into instant sympathy mode. She slung her arm around the other woman's tiny shoulders and led her into the dining room. Sophie watched, slightly annoyed, slightly amused, as Jackie was guided into a chair. Her mother made quiet cooing sounds, like a mother trying to soothe a small, hurt child.

"Sophie, why don't you bring us over some coffee?"

Jackie leapt to her feet. "Oh my, where are my manners? I am so sorry. Please, let me just get the pot together. I'm afraid I don't have anything to go with it, but…"

"Oh it's perfectly fine! I made some double chocolate cake this morning. Sophie can run and grab it while we have a nice chat!" Her mother turned her green eyes on Sophie and smiled.

Having been given her orders, Sophie left the kitchen. In passing, she darted a quick glance up the stairs and started to find Mr. Gorgeous-Jerkface looming at the top, propped up against the wall with his shoulder. He had his arms folded, still bare chested, his duffle at his feet. He caught Sophie's gaze.

She scowled. "Shouldn't you be torturing kittens or kicking puppies?" she asked. "And why aren't you dressed yet?" The last question really shouldn't have been said out loud and she mentally kicked herself the moment the question spilled free.

The smile was slow, creeping across his face with such intensity that she had an unexpected understanding of how natural disasters took people by surprise.

"Am I distracting you?"

Concealing her flush by folding her arms, Sophie raised her chin defiantly. "I just don't want to see that."

"Is that why you've been undressing me with your eyes since we met?"

The heat was sweltering, practically coming off her in waves. "I was not! In fact, you're not even my type. I don't go for egotistical jerks." *Even if they are super hot.*

He snickered. "Careful, witch, I might mistakenly think you like me."

"Ha!" The barking laugh escaped before she could control it. "I'd rather pet a cobra!"

He looked like he was about to laugh. "I have something you're more than welcome to come pet." With a smirk that dared her to follow, he hoisted up his bag and sauntered out of sight.

"I will not commit murder! I will not commit murder!" she muttered, stalking out the door into the steady downpour.

Protected by distance, shielded by stealth, a camera shutter snapped in rapid succession, immortalizing every motion of Sophie's body, every flicker of her eyes as they swept over the neighborhood. It caught her in the act of pushing a curl behind her ear, of her lips moving in cuss words. Every moment, trapped, plucked up with greedy hunger. The hand wielding the camera remained firm, while inside he quivered with glee. His entire body ached, a thrum of anticipation for the day she would finally be where she belonged. Lips bowed into a satisfied smile.

She was so absolutely perfect.

ALSO CHECK OUT THESE
EXTRAORDINARY AUTHORS & BOOKS:

Alivia Anders ~ Illumine
Cambria Hebert ~ Recalled
Angela Orlowski Peart ~ Forged by Greed
Julia Crane ~ Freak of Nature
J. A. Huss ~ Clutch
Cameo Renae ~ Hidden Wings
Alexia Purdy ~ Reign of Blood
Tabatha Vargo ~ On the Plus Side
Tiffany King ~ Meant to Be
Beth Balmanno ~ Set in Stone
Lizzy Ford ~ Dark Summer (Witchling Saga #1)
Ella James ~ Stained
Tara West ~ Visions of the Witch
Heidi McLaughlin ~ Forever Your Girl
Melissa Andrea ~ Flutter
Komal Lewis ~ Falling for Hadie
Melissa Pearl ~ Golden Blood
L.P. Dover ~ Forever Fae
Sarah M. Ross ~ Awaken
Brina Courtney ~ Reveal